Sister Witches

Book 1 of the Sister Witches

FELICIA JEDLICKA

For the righteous and the rest of us.

More titles by **FELICIA JEDLICKA**

DESTINY REJECTED
DESTINY RECLAIMED
DESTINY RAZED
DESTINY RESTORED

DÉJÀ VU

SAVE THE HUMANS

THE NECROMANCER'S CHILD

SISTER WITCHES
THE DEVIL'S SHADOW
THE DEVIL'S SOUL

THE NEBRASKA APOCALYPSE NOVELS
CORN COWS AND THE APOCALYPSE
COW TIPPING AFTER THE APOCALYPSE
CORN HUSKING AFTER THE APOCALYPSE

THE WARDEN SERIES
SUCCESSORS
RIVALS
LOVERS AND LIARS
BAD BLOOD
TENANTS AND TYRANTS
THE RING BEARER
GODS AND MONSTERS
BEASTS AND BURDENS
MAGIC AND MAYHEM
FORK IN THE ROAD
DETAILS AND DEADLINES

Sister Witches

Book 1 of the Sister Witches

FELICIA JEDLICKA

PROLOGUE

S HADOWS.

That's all they used to be to me.

A flicker of movement against the wall where my body blocked the light.

I know better now. I know that's where they hide. I know that's where they wait, whispering in your mind. Trying to convince you that your hatred is justified.

You can't run from them. You can't hide. You can only turn the lights on bright and pretend you don't hear them.

If you're strong enough, you can keep them silent, and if you aren't, the whispers turn to screams. You can't fight your own mind, but you can fight to keep it sane.

For most, the battle remains cerebral, from birth to death. A constant battle to maintain control and not let the gift of free will crush them. I wish mine had stayed that way. I wish my shadow would have stayed in the shadows.

But he didn't.

He walked right out of my nightmares and stood beside me. He watched me writhe and debate with a gun in my hand. Lips curled in a cruel smile, he laughed at my pain as I tried to right too many wrongs with a bullet and a prayer.

The prayer never stood much of a chance, but the bullet worked just fine.

CHAPTER 1

I LEANED OVER MY knees and stared at the blurred figures through the glass door of Sister Agatha's office. I couldn't believe my father was consulting a nun about my behavior. It was beyond mortifying.

I was nearly 18 years old. It was a little late to be putting the fear of God into me. At best, Sister Aggie could smack me with a ruler a few times. Corporal punishment was always a good motivator. Unless it involved bruises, in which case the only motivation was to call the local news station to sell my story of Catholic abuse.

My father opened the door to the office and motioned for me to come in. He was a tall, slender man with prematurely gray hair and a far too shaggy goatee he refused to shave. I frowned at him, once more trying to impress upon him my aversion to this strategy of parenting. He wavered slightly, but only because he hated being the bad guy, not because he thought he was wrong.

He motioned again, but this time his eyes were begging me. If I misbehaved now, then I would humiliate him.

I stood up and pulled down my black tank top to cover the pink belt buckle that read "Got Pussy." It was a fashion statement I found particularly amusing, but I imagined my former grade school teacher would not agree.

My father gestured to his shoulders, and I noticed my bra straps were also showing. I tucked them under my shirt straps, but they would eventually find their way out again.

There was nothing I could do about my ripped skinny jeans or the black eye. Those would just have to fall under the category of fashion statements.

I slipped past my father into the office. He touched my back, somehow offering me reassurance, but it only made me feel pressured. I was once again being put under a microscope to be examined and dissected. As if the answer to all teenage rebellion was just to make you feel more rejected.

"Sit down, Hennie," Sister Aggie said in her flinty, almost masculine tone. She wasn't the gentle, loving picture of servitude that nuns should have been. She was stern, borderline crass, and loud. Her age had done nothing to improve her mood, either. "Cliff, get out." She motioned to the door.

My father looked at me as if to ask permission, but Aggie shot him a scolding look and he scurried out, closing the door behind him. I sat down in the chair in front of her desk, propping my heel on the edge. I was certain it made me look like a typical slouchy teenager, but I really just wanted to have something more than air between me and the stoic nun.

Sister Aggie leaned against her desk, examining me. Her habit covered most of her features, but I could see the last eight years had put a little more weight on her, and the creases around her eyes and mouth were no longer due to laughter. Her nose was still much too big for her face. Add that to her oversized orthopedic loafers, and it was easy to see why she had the reputation at the school as a witch. She never seemed to mind the jokes, and had even dressed up in green makeup one year for Halloween.

Her eyes shifted away from my face, judging my appearance with a condescension that could only be achieved by an old woman. I wasn't sure what offended her more: the isolated streak of black running through my long blond hair, or the nose ring. I was fairly certain it was all the above and then some.

I defended my style with an eye roll and looked around the messy office. She had papers piled everywhere. Several coffee mugs were scattered around the room, as if she was constantly forgetting where she had left it and simply got a new one. There were various heavy metal safes in the room. I wondered why a nun would need one safe, let alone several.

The room was once the principal's office for my grade school, but the student population had long since outgrown the quaint brick building, so they built a new one across town. Rather than demolish the old one, the church used it to create a learning annex. Besides language classes and diet groups, there were various drug rehab programs available to the public. After a fire at the old convent, the church converted the upper level into living space for the nuns.

"How did you get that black eye?" Sister asked. She didn't seem to have any sympathy for it.

"Margo Gentre." I tossed back my hair so she could get a better view of it.

"Why did Margo hit you?"

"Because I spit in her face." I perked my brow and waited for the lecture to begin. It wasn't the first time my aggression had earned me a reprimand. My reputation for being a bitch had outgrown my actual behavior long ago, but nobody ever distinguished the two.

"Why did you spit in her face?" Aggie asked, unfazed by the admission.

"Because I'm named after a chicken, and sometimes girls find that funny." I leaned forward, getting in her face as much as I could without standing.

"You don't like your name?" Aggie asked, glancing at the door. My father was practically leaning against it outside, no doubt trying to listen in on the conversation.

"That's not what I said, but no, I don't."

"Why don't you change it?" Aggie moved to the door and opened it, surprising Cliff on the other side. "Mr. James, this may take a while. Why don't you go have a coffee in the lounge? It's just down the hall." She motioned to the hall perpendicular to the office. She didn't bother listening to his blubbered demurral before she shut the door again. "I said why don't you change it?" she asked again and moved behind her desk.

"What do you mean?"

"I mean, legally change your name." She pulled open the center drawer and reached into the very back, cramming her hand under the rim of the desk to reach what she wanted. "It's a simple process, especially at your age. Paperwork and signatures." She pulled her hand back, revealing a pack of cigarettes. I crinkled my brow as she slipped one between her lips and lit it with a quick, proficient movement. "Huh?" She beckoned curtly, still wanting an answer as she exhaled the smoke.

She flipped a switch on the miniature air purifier on her desk. The contraption groaned more than hummed, as if years of sucking down secondhand smoke had given it the mechanical equivalent of emphysema.

Aggie moved to the window and cranked it open. She continued to puff her smoke out the window. She glanced back at me. "Well, have I solved your problem?"

"My father would never let me change my name."

"Bullshit," she mumbled over her cigarette. My mouth dropped slightly. I had never thought of Sister Aggie as a soft woman, but she was now crossing the border into surly truck driver territory. "That man loves the dickens out of you. He'll do anything for you. Especially now that your mother is gone."

My back stiffened at even the mention of my mother. It shouldn't have surprised that me she knew. Her death was very public. A car crash—and not the type that required paramedics. She was unfortunately too... *mangled* to have a traditional open casket. I wasn't sure if it would have been easier, seeing her one last time, but I knew that three years later I was still looking for her face in crowds. That little part of me that still believed in magic and miracles couldn't let her go.

"So, how about it? Do you hate your name?" Aggie puffed on her cigarette. "Or do you hate Margo?"

"I hate Margo," I admitted. "Isn't that wrong or something?" I asked.

"To hate someone?"

"Yeah."

"Of course not. People can be cruel, annoying, and self-serving. And teenagers are worse. You hate her all you want, just don't hate yourself. You can always get over your hatred for another, but getting past your own hatred is tricky."

"Is that your way of telling me to love myself?"

Aggie snorted and put out her cigarette. She placed it in a special box and suffocated us with a stash of aerosol spray before closing the window. "Do you really hate yourself?"

"Sometimes." I went with honesty, since she was trusting me with her secrets.

"Well crap, I guess that makes you normal." She clucked her tongue and sat down behind her desk. "Your father wants me to give you a pep talk. He wants me to inspire you to change your attitude. He misses the innocent little girl you used to be."

"Innocent? What exactly am I guilty of now?"

"Hormones. Survivor's guilt. In essence, you are guilty of feeling too much."

"And how do I stop that?"

Aggie's face blanked, and for a moment, she stared into nothingness. Though slightly creepy, I waited for her senior moment to pass. "Nothing." She sighed and shook her head somberly. Before I could answer, she slammed her hand on her desk, making me jump. When she looked back at me, her expression was a mixture of sadness and anger.

"What's wrong with you?" I shrank back into the chair.

"You were always such a bright girl," she said. "I know I can't judge the woman you would become by your ten-year-old self, but you were. You were eager to help and always so generous. I liked you."

"Okay." I shifted uncomfortably. "Do you need me to call someone?"

"Sometimes life is hard. I imagine you're blaming yourself for everything that happened, but you're wrong in doing that." She pinched her lips tightly for a moment. "I would love to tell you it's going to get easier for you, but I can't."

"Is this the pep talk? Cause it kind of sucks." I glanced at the door. This conversation needed to be over.

"Your father wants his little girl back. Though I imagine you aren't ever going to be her again. However, I would strongly advise that you make an effort to include him in your life from now on, because you don't have much time left with him."

"What?" I whispered and gaped at her. "That's not funny."

"No, it's not. It's downright sadistic if you ask me, but I don't make the rules."

I shook my head. "Are you seriously trying to scare me into behaving? Because that's messed up." I stood up. Therapy was definitely over.

"You always know when someone is lying, don't you?" she asked. I paused and looked back at her. She tipped her head, probing me for the answer, but I wouldn't give it to her. She glanced at the door before she spoke again. "After the cancer has taken him—"

"This is a sick joke!" I yelled, trying to shut her up.

"—come back to me and I will help you." She rose from her seat. "Don't try to do it alone, Hennie." I backpedaled to the door. "It will be too much for you. It's either the convent or the grave for you."

"Go to hell!" I yelled and scrambled to the door. My father was on the other side, racing to interject something.

"Hennie, you can't speak to her like that!" he scolded me until he saw the fear in my eyes, quickly followed by tears. He glanced at Sister Aggie, but she said nothing to defend the words that had caused my reaction.

"Take me home!" I bawled.

"Hennie... what...?" he stuttered.

"Daddy, please, just take me home," I sniffled and his face melted into concern. He wrapped his arm around me and pulled me along. He dropped his coffee in a trashcan on the way, so he didn't have to release me to pick up his briefcase.

"Remember what I said, Hennie," Sister Aggie called down the hall after us.

"Thank you, Sister," my father hollered back to her, but he was no longer slobbering with respect for the woman.

"I'll be waiting for you," she said more quietly.

CHAPTER 2

I stood outside the school, staring at the single lit window on the second floor. It was raining, but I was too drunk to care how cold I was. The pain in my wrists was minimal but aggravating. The blood wouldn't drain fast enough, even with the rain drawing it down to the puddles at my feet.

I wasn't sure when the voices had started, but I couldn't tell the difference between them and the vicious remarks my own mind threw at me on a daily basis. They had wanted blood. I gave it to them, but two split wrists weren't enough. They wanted vengeance, and the longer they had demanded it, the more it made sense to me.

I sprinted across the street and reached the double doors with paned glass. I found them locked, but I already knew a brick would be nearby. They used it to hold the doors open at the start of school. It hadn't moved more than six inches in the last decade.

I rammed the red brick through the window, shattering it with ease. I reached past the broken glass to release the door, adding more cuts to my arms. Pushing past another set of unlocked doors, I arrived in the hall of my former grade school.

I knew the school well. Like everything else from my childhood, I had deeply ingrained memories of it. It always looked a little smaller than I remembered, but it was still the same.

I stalked down the dimly lit hallway past the principal's office and the intersection that would have taken me down to the classrooms. I kept going straight and marched up the wide stairs toward the second level.

On the upper floor, I walked along the windowed library, which still contained the breadth of reading material it had when I was a child. I turned down the long hallway, which mirrored the downstairs. However, the convent had now divided most of these classrooms into living quarters.

I passed by several tall, slender doors that looked like they belonged to closets. I could only imagine the narrow confinement the members of the convent endured.

I found the only light in the hall, streaming from a windowed door. I recognized it as my fifth-grade room. The door was exactly the same: pebbled glass, glossy yellow wood, and a brassy knob. It even had Mrs. Blake's name plate still on it. I paused outside the door. A wave of nostalgia temporarily blocked out my anger, but soon enough, the memories of my mother's death caught up to me.

I was in this very room the day my father came to school to pick me up. The day he came to tell me about the accident. The look on his face and the tremble in his voice burned themselves into my memory. It was a scar too deep to heal. The only option was to let it change me. And change me, it did.

I overcame adversity much easier after that. I faced it with a sour grapes mindset. Anything I couldn't do, I decided I didn't want to do, anyway. Anyone who didn't like me became my enemy. I used violence to solve any situation I couldn't overcome with indifference. That was how I intended to come to terms with my anger for Sister Aggie.

Violence.

I yanked open the classroom door and drew out the very knife I had used to slash my wrists. I raised it high, prepared to stab Sister Aggie with it. To make her feel the pain I felt. To make her understand how she had unraveled my life.

From the moment I knew my father was going to die, my world changed. Death was no longer in my past; it was in my future and looming over my present. It didn't matter that cancer was the diagnosis; in my mind, Aggie was the disease. She brought it on us with her premonitory speech. I suppose somewhere in the back of my mind, I really believed she was a witch. That she had somehow cursed my father and caused the cancer that robbed him of his vitality and eventually his life.

The time we had together had been good, but I had no expectation would survive. I had nothing left to hope for or wish for. All my dreams vanished, and I was empty. Following his burial, my loneliness overwhelmed me, and I wanted to die. When my body didn't do as I commanded, I took things into my own hands.

Somewhere in the midst of my despair, I could feel someone watching me, guiding my hand. I was in control of my actions, but yet I was also being directed. The strangeness of it was that the presence felt almost affectionate, as if I was making the right choice by ending my life.

That was when the voices I had been ignoring screamed. This life wasn't done with me. I still had one last thing to accomplish before my life drained away with my blood.

I ran into the room, teeth bared, knife drawn. I expected to find Sister Aggie praying alone as she usually did until all hours of the night, but to my surprise, I found the entire convent.

The circle of women in plain clothes, sitting on the floor amongst stacks of old desks and chairs, didn't even look up as I entered. They held hands, with rosaries dangling between their clasped palms. They were praying, but their unified monotone sounded more like a chant. The dim flames of candles flickered in front of each one of them, casting eerie shadows all over the room.

In the bevy of random identities, I found Sister Aggie and ran forward. I didn't think twice about the insanity it took to murder a nun right in front of her entire convent. I just wanted it to be over. To satisfy the voices and silence my aching anger.

The women chanted louder as I jumped over a set of linked hands and landed inside the circle. I turned to Sister Aggie and looked at her. She stared back at me, unfazed by my performance, despite my lethal intent.

Her indifference infuriated me even more, and the voices compelling my actions demanded retribution. I dove at her, blade and all. I aimed at her heart. To bury it inside the cold stone organ. I expected to hear it shatter like glass, but it didn't. The blade never reached her.

Nor did I.

I had thrown myself at her, but my body hadn't fallen. I hung frozen in thin air over her. My extended knife threatened death, but I couldn't complete the task. I couldn't move beyond blinking and turning my head.

Sister Aggie stared up at me. She hadn't flinched at my vicious actions and, with only inches between us, she was looking at me like an errant child rather than her would-be murderer.

The women recited their prayer relentlessly. Their eyes rolled back in their heads, revealing the unnatural whites. I looked around, examining the casual state of the women. They didn't look like nuns. Most of them didn't even look like austere Christians. Some looked more like... me. Long hair, tattoos, and piercings. None of them were wearing their robes and habits, including Aggie. For the first time, I could see her wavy gray hair. It was humanizing.

I looked over my unnatural state as I hovered above the wood floor. There were no wires holding me up, nor a mirrored box responsible for my elevation. The only thing I could see beneath me was my blood plopping onto the shiny golden planks. If I could have moved, I would have reached down to wipe it up. I almost spilled liters of blood, but I was still concerned about those few drops sullying the hardwood.

I looked back at Aggie and she made the sign of the cross at me. She gripped her rosary and spoke a quick prayer before opening her eyes on me again. "Do you want to kill me, Hennie?" she asked bluntly.

"Yes," I seethed.

"Why?"

"You killed my father," I whispered, as if it were a secret the others shouldn't hear.

"Did I?"

"YES!" I yelled and cried. "This is all your fault! You ruined my life!"

"Nothing I have done has changed the outcome of your life," she scolded. "Your mother was meant to die. Your father was meant to die. You were meant to feel this pain."

"Why?" I moaned and gripped my knife tighter. "WHY?" I screamed when she didn't answer.

"So you would empty yourself of expectation," Aggie said mournfully. "I'm sorry this has happened to you. I'm sorry the woman you were designed to be is not the woman you are destined to be. I'm sorry that life *sucks* sometimes. And most of all, I'm sorry I have to be the one to remind you of that."

"What are you talking about?" I tried to fight the air, but the power levitating me kept my movements restricted. "How are you doing this?"

"This isn't you, Hennie. You've let them get into your head."

I stopped struggling and stared at her. "Who's in my head?"

"I can help you," she said—for once sounding sympathetic. "But you have to put down the knife and give up this anger."

I shook my head. It was all I had left. "I don't want to be helped. I want to die."

"That's your choice to make," she said. Her lack of lecturing on the sin of suicide surprised me. "Die if you want. Kill if you want. Or release yourself from the life you know... and join us."

"What are you talking about?"

"You are at an impasse. You cannot go on as you have before. You have to make a choice. Either kill me and suffer the fires of hell. Kill yourself and suffer the fires of hell. Or you can take a third option and become one of us."

"I'm not joining a convent!" I screeched, baffled by her odd timing for recruitment.

"You'll only be joining a convent on the surface. You will actually be joining a coven."

Visions of witches' brews and broomsticks fluttered through my mind. After that, though, I looked over the concentrated faces around me, and the two feet between me and my gravitational obligation. This wasn't a knitting group or a Tupperware party. These were real women wielding genuine power.

"How is this even possible?" I looked at Aggie. "Are you devil worshipers?"

"Not at all." She opened her hands, proudly displaying her rosary.

"Are you saying God is doing this?"

"Not exactly. We are in control of the magic, but the actual power is drawn from God." I frowned and she gave me the tiniest of smiles. "Don't worry, we have permission."

I looked over the room again. Searching, once again, for the trick, but I knew it was true. I could sense lies, and Aggie had never lied to me.

She touched my hand, pressing me to release the knife. I stared at the weapon, listening for the voices in my mind, but they were gone. I wasn't sure if Aggie had made them disappear with magic, or if I had willed them away myself.

Only moments before, I had wanted to plunge my knife into her heart, but I no longer desired to hurt her. The idea of it seemed so far from my mind, I almost wondered if any part of the potential homicide had been my idea. I wasn't a murderer. I was just a puppet in someone's game. The question of *whose* game sent chills down my spine.

I dropped the knife and my body slowly lowered to the floor. I sat up, kneeling within the circle of women. Each of them woke from their partial trance and looked at me. Despite my almost killing one of their own, they were giving me odd welcoming smiles. I barely belonged outside of a straitjacket, but somehow I already knew I belonged here.

I put all thoughts of suicide to the back of my mind and embraced what I had to look forward to. I was about to be a part of something awesome. Something magical.

Something powerful.

CHAPTER 3

"**H**URRY," AGGIE SNARLED FROM my bedroom door. "You can't take that."

I looked down at the teddy bear in my hand. "Why not? It was my mother's," I explained.

Aggie stepped through the mess that camouflaged the location of my floor. She ripped the stuffed toy from my hand. "Don't get sentimental on me now, Hennie. That is too big to hide. You may not actually be a nun, but you will need to maintain the appearance of it. I can't have stuffed animals, jukeboxes, and roller skates littering the nunnery."

"I can't give up *everything*," I protested, taking back the bear.

"Then you can't join." Aggie flipped the suitcase off my bed, adding its contents to the floor. "There is nothing in this room that will make this transition easier. If you are not ready to give up this shit, then you are not ready. Period."

"Why are you being such a bitch? It's just a bear."

"Yes, it is *just* a bear. It does nothing except signify the memories you possess, with or without the bear."

"Fine!" I threw down the bear and stared at it. "Why did you bring me here if you didn't want me to bring anything back with me?" Aggie looked around the room, searching for something. Her eyes stopped on my dresser. She moved to it and opened my jewelry box to dig through it. "Help yourself," I mumbled.

"This." She pulled out a necklace with a tiny silver cross pendant on it. "Your mother gave you this at your first communion, right?"

"Yes."

"Take this as your memorabilia." She waved the necklace in front of me. I couldn't have found an object with less meaning to me. My parents gave it to me as a communion gift, but I hadn't worn it since that day.

"Look, Sister." I rubbed my face. "I think we should talk about this nun thing a little more."

"There is no distinction between the coven and the convent anymore. Sisters of God, sisters of blood, sisters of the circle. There is no difference to us anymore."

"Yes, and I am all for being part of that family. I've never had siblings, so it will be a nice change, but..." I stared at Sister Aggie's face, hoping she might already sense where my apprehension was stemming from. "There are aspects of this deception that are easy to hide. That necklace will be easy to hide. My clothes can be changed, and I can stop swearing—I think. But there are things I'm not sure I can give up... at least not forever."

"Sex," Aggie said candidly, as if she had already had this conversation before.

I sighed. "Yes, Sister Aggie, I would still like to have... a boyfriend."

"Are you currently dating anyone?"

"No, but—"

"Then what's the problem? We can deal with that when it comes time."

I chuckled. "The problem is, if I join your convent and pretend to be a nun, then I will have no chance of having... a boyfriend ever again. I think the habit will scare away my prospects."

"I think you're wrong about that, but rest assured, many of my girls are not sisters of the cloth. As long as your socializing is done outside of town and under an assumed name, I don't think you'll have trouble achieving a dating life."

"What about marriage and kids?"

"I think you may find that when marriage and children enter the picture, being a part of our group may no longer appeal to you."

"Are you saying I have to choose between sisterhood and motherhood?"

"No, I am saying a good mother would not continue to do the work we do, for the sake of her children."

"What does that mean?"

"It means we are doing God's work, and that work is not always pleasant."

"Pleasant?"

"Hennie, I do not have the patience to explain everything now, and frankly, if I did, you wouldn't believe me. Too much of your world is grounded in earthly knowledge. When you come to understand the similarities between magic and miracles, you will also understand the connection between dark magic and demons." I furrowed my brow at the word *demons*. "So, yes, motherhood and sisterhood may not be a path you can walk simultaneously. At least while you are still obligated to protect your children from the things that go bump in the night."

"You said before that this is who I am destined to be, but not who I was designed to be. What did you mean by that?"

"Think of yourself as a late-in-the-game pitcher. Something has changed in the outlook of the game, and God is calling you to the mound."

"What exactly is the game?

"The game is protecting the human race from the fires of hell."

Chapter 4

I SAT OUTSIDE OF Aggie's office, leaning over my knees as I waited for her to conclude her business with Father Mitchell. I touched the scars on my wrists left over from my attempted suicide. My sisters had offered to heal them, but I preferred to keep them as a reminder of how easy it was to let my anger and grief destroy me.

Joining the coven was an easy decision. The power they possessed was far more alluring than anything my life had offered me. Saying no to the chance of becoming a real live witch was like saying no to the lottery. Never gonna happen.

Even the decision to join the convent was fairly simple. I didn't have a job. I had already dropped out of college to care for my dad. No boyfriend, of course. Except for my friend Jessica, there was really no one on the outside to miss me. It was rather pathetic how easy my decision was.

While the choice to join was easy, the daily reality of it was not. In order to portray a nun, I had to behave like one. Besides the obvious drawbacks—no social life, extended time on my knees, and no money—I essentially had to pretend to be someone else. My days started with a polyester penguin outfit and ended with prayers, prayers, and more prayers. The worldly possessions part sounded easy, but when you took into consideration the lack of stimulation in the convent, stir crazy became an inevitability.

Despite my involvement with the coven, I had barely interacted with them between my duties. I was in the cafeteria nearly every day, feeding the underprivileged that came in for free lunch. Then I got to sort through the clothing donations. If I was really lucky, I would get to clean the bathrooms.

I hadn't left the school in weeks and I was starting to think I was being used.

To supplement my desire for more cerebral activities, Aggie suggested I take part in a support group that met on Sundays. We discussed the difficulties of living life without the ones we loved. I was meant to be the director of the group and help engage everyone, but I presumed Aggie also wanted me to see that other people struggled with loss. Even alone, we were never alone. We just needed to find the right company for our stage in life.

The door to the office opened, and I bolted upright. Father Mitchell stepped out of the office and turned back to Aggie. He was a good deal shorter than her, and even me. His blond frizz bordered on being an Afro, but he was so white, he bordered on albino. He was a nice enough man, but he had a few irritating social qualities. He was the type of man to criticize dust on the underside of a table. He took a few too many liberties with his influence over the convent, and Aggie didn't appreciate that.

"You understand my position," he said, cupping his hands together in front of him. "It just doesn't make sense that a woman of your distinction could succumb to such an earthly vice while she has the Lord to give her strength."

"Yes, I understand, Father. Thank you for reminding me of that," Aggie responded sweetly. Completely fake, of course.

"Pray for His assistance. I know He can help you get past this." He touched her arm and turned to leave. He caught sight of me and looked me over. "Sister Hennie," he greeted me.

"Father." I nodded back to him politely. As he neared the exit, I watch Sister Aggie's face smolder.

"Idiot," she said and turned into her office.

I chuckled and followed her. "Did he catch you smoking again?"

"Yes. I swear that man has feathered feet." She slumped down in her desk chair and pulled her cigarettes from her robe and placed them in her desk drawer.

"There is a solution, you know," I offered with some merriment as I sat down across from her. She perked an eyebrow, waiting for my enlightenment. "Quit smoking."

She snorted. "The good Lord has seen fit to put me in charge of eight insufferable women. If He wishes me to remain sane, then He will forgive this minor vice."

"Insufferable, really?"

"Hmm, how about unique?"

"Unique sounds a little better."

"Aren't you supposed to be cleaning the kitchen?" Aggie asked.

"Yeah, about that," I drawled.

"Hennie, everyone has to help."

"I know, but I wanted to talk to you about expanding my duties..." I glanced at the door in case Father Mitchell might be lurking. "...within the circle."

Aggie sighed and stood back up. She checked the hall and shut the door before sitting.

"I've been here for six months," I negotiated before she could placate me. "I've spent more time developing my ruse than practicing magic. I'd like to start learning the good stuff."

"The ruse is important. With very few of you committing to God, it is important at least that you understand who we are representing. This witchcraft doesn't draw power from some mythical goddess of crops. We are here to serve Him, just in a less provincial capacity."

"I'm not a heathen," I objected.

"I know, but the *good stuff* can be overwhelming. I don't want you to start thinking of yourself as a witch. You are a member of a coven. That isn't as simple as hanging out with your girlfriends on a Friday night playing the Ouija board."

"I know."

"No, you don't." Aggie spoke sternly, but she wasn't outright saying no, so I restrained my arguments. "We aren't playing games, or meditating, or performing rituals of vanity. We are protecting people from demonic influence. We balance the spirit with the mind." She looked down before continuing. "We see the future. We walk through the veil of darkness and retrieve souls before they can be corrupted. And when we can't save them, we make sure they are punished for their crimes in this life and the next."

"What about the exorcisms?" I asked. "When will I get to see one?"

"Exorcisms are dangerous for an amateur, even if you aren't participating. I would rather not bring you in on that until—"

"Until I've proven myself a good mopper?" I snapped.

"Attitude does not equate maturity," she snapped back.

"Could have fooled me." I nodded to her. "A smoking, swearing, spell-casting nun. I think you've cultivated a good amount of attitude over your years."

Sister Aggie glared at me and sat back in her chair to examine me. "You really think you're ready, don't you?"

"I think I'm ready to see what the hell we do, yes." I glanced at the door. "Is this about what I did? Are you concerned I'm not... good enough or pure enough?"

Aggie's expression didn't change, but her eyes wavered momentarily. "Purity isn't found in a habit, Hennie. When I was your age, I was hearing the voice of God. I didn't feel pure or chosen or gifted. I felt like I was going insane." She pulled out her drawer and grabbed her cigarettes. She threw them down again and shut the drawer. "I became a nun because being a diviner sounded better than schizophrenia. For a while, things were normal. I became a teacher, which I loved. I helped people, in little benign ways. My intuition was simply convenient timing and good luck. Then you came along." Aggie gave me an accusatory look.

"Me?" I furrowed my brow. I had come to Aggie's school in the second grade, but I didn't see what this had to do with me. "What did I have to do with anything?"

"That's when I started listening to my intuition."

"And what was it telling you?"

"Are you sure you want to know?"

"No, but tell me anyway."

"It was telling me I needed to start paving a path for you. I was forewarned about your arrival into this little group even before the group had been formed."

"I thought I was a late-in-the-game pitcher or something. Now you're making it sound like I'm the chosen one."

Aggie looked out the window. "Not everything is clear to me. I only harbor the knowledge I've earned, but as you might imagine, the world didn't suddenly develop a demonic problem over the last few years. This problem has been going on since the very beginning. This duty to God has been fulfilled by a thousand women before you. There is no chosen *one*. We are all a part of this. One may lead, but that doesn't make her more important than those who follow." She paused a moment and frowned. "It just makes her the first target."

Aggie turned back to me and leaned forward. "There is no protection for us, Hennie. The work we do comes at the risk of your life and your sanity and your soul. We are mortal man fighting shadows, ghosts, and demons. Once you see, you can't be blind again. Once you know, you can't simply forget and hide under your covers. If you stumble, you will have to catch yourself. If you fall—"

"I know you're trying to test me, scaring me to weaken my resolve, but it won't work. I want to do this. I want to be part of this. I want to help."

Aggie nodded. "Well then, I guess there is only one thing to do. It's time for you to see what we do here."

CHAPTER 5

WE DROVE EIGHTY MILES into the country to find the house that Halloween forgot. I stepped out of the van with Aggie, Rachel, and Paula. I had cleverly disguised myself as my alter ego, Sister Hennie, but their costumes were legitimate. Unless the Catholics could start making celibacy and poverty sound ultra-cool and fun, these women would probably be the last of the real nuns for this convent.

"What in hell threw up on this house?" I asked, observing the endless vines that were likely the only thing holding the house up. The chipped paint and faded wood siding left the house an unwholesome gray. The boarded-up windows further detracted from the fading country charm.

"Come on, Hennie. It's not the outside of the house I'm concerned with," Aggie said as she walked toward the broad porch.

"Who lives here?" I asked as I followed her.

"Mr. and Mrs. Eady," Aggie said as she rang the bell. "They are hard of hearing, so don't be afraid to yell."

The door whipped open, and a shotgun came to rest on Aggie's temple.

"Holy crap!" I nearly stumbled off the porch in my retreat.

"Who are you?" the old man, presumably Mr. Eady, croaked behind the weapon.

"I'm Sister Aggie! These are my fellow sisters, Paula, Rachel, and Hennie."

"Henry?" he questioned. "You brought a priest?"

"Not Henry! *Hennie*!" Aggie yelled a little louder.

"Hennie? Is that short for Henrietta?"

I rolled my eyes. "No, that would have at least made sense," I mumbled well under the old man's hearing aid capacity.

"May we come in!" Aggie asked, tapping the muzzle of the man's shotgun. I wondered if she was used to having weapons in her face or if the thrill of demon casting had taken the threat out of man-made hazards.

"Oh, yes, come in." Mr. Eady lowered the gun and waved us all inside. "Mom made a pie. I hope you all like rhubarb."

I heard a groan from behind me, but wasn't sure who it had come from, Rachel or Paula.

A few minutes later, we were all seated in the kitchen with Mrs. Eady, enjoying the bounty of her rhubarb plant. I looked up at Aggie to see if this was a normal pre-exorcism ritual. She was politely eating her pie and complimenting Mrs. Eady on her china pattern. When she caught my gaze, she winked at me. The playfulness of it made me smile.

I looked at Paula for her take on this event. She looked at the skinny elderly woman leaning over Aggie's shoulder, pointing at her china pattern. She leaned forward and scraped her pie onto my plate with decisive speed. When I gave her a questioning look, she frowned and stuck out her tongue. Apparently, she was not a fan of rhubarb. Burdened by another slice, I gobbled it down, lest I look impolite.

"What are we doing?" I whispered to Paula.

"We are socializing," she answered without moving her lips.

Under her veil was a beautiful dark umber bob that, despite the mounting odds of hat-head probably looked bouncy and shiny. Not that she needed her hair to look beautiful. Her face alone radiated a natural tan that belonged on the cover of a magazine. Had she been even the slightest bit mean to me, I would have been obligated to hate her, but to top off her outer beauty, she was a damn fine human being too.

"Aren't we supposed to be freeing the world of evil?" I asked her.

"We aren't freeing the world of anything tonight," Rachel mumbled from the end of the table where she perched on a footstool that was much too low for the table. She was a few inches shorter than us already, making her current position a reason for hilarity, but I wouldn't dare laugh at her. Her personality was acerbic, almost mean. She reminded me of Aggie, but without the authority to make it a respectable trait.

"Quiet, Rachel," Paula whispered.

I looked at Rachel, searching for more information. I could see a hint of her orange-red hair peeking past her wimple, which, contrary to Paula's, was most likely a frazzled mess. It was her most notable feature, aside from her eyes. Her bright baby blues could beat my muddy blue orbs every day of the week and twice on Sunday. When she smiled—which was rare—she was a match for Paula, but with her best traits hidden by a veil and a glare, she would not make it to the magazine cover anytime soon.

"What does that mean?" I asked.

"You'll see," Rachel sang.

"Seriously, what's up?" I whispered.

"Not every ritual is successful," Paula explained. "That's why you are here. Mr. and Mrs. Eady have a mentally challenged son. He's been the victim of demonic possession for over thirty years."

"Thirty years!" I hissed.

Aggie cleared her throat and widened her eyes at me behind her coffee mug. Luckily, Mrs. Eady was too busy telling her about the origin of her expensive china to hear our conversation.

"How is that possible?" I shielded my lips with praying hands.

"People can live with demons for their entire lives," Paula continued.

"Haven't you ever met an asshole you thought belonged in hell?" Rachel perked her brow.

"Rachel," Paula admonished her again, "that isn't helping."

"She's gotta learn." Rachel shrugged and took her coffee for a stroll through the house.

"Don't mind her." Paula stroked my arm. "She's not good with... people in general."

"I heard that," Rachel called in from the hallway.

"Good." Paula smiled at me.

"Would you girls like some more pie?" Mrs. Eady leaned over my shoulder and plopped another piece on my plate before I had consented.

"No, thank you." Paula jumped from her seat and left the table before the woman could burden her—and consequently me—with another slice.

CHAPTER 6

"**L**ORD BLESS US ON this evening, bless this house and all who live here, now and in the future." Aggie squeezed her rosary as she spoke her prayer at the bedroom door. "Protect us, oh Lord, as we try once again to free Gregory of this parasitic invasion. May the evil that resides behind this door find solace in the depths of hell where he can rot like the sick, twisted son of a bitch he is."

My solemn observation of the prayer diminished, and I glanced at Paula and Rachel to see if this was a typical prayer. They were both staring hard at the door, like Aggie.

"Amen," they all said in unison.

Aggie opened the bedroom door, and with the mental focus of soldiers—or at least, very committed boxers—they filed in to fight off the aforementioned son of a bitch. I glanced down the narrow hallway as I moved to follow them and I saw Mr. and Mrs. Eady. They were at the top of the stairs, huddled together in prayer. Mrs. Eady was crying, and Mr. Eady looked tired.

Thirty years.

How long had they even had with their son before he became someone or something else? How many times had Aggie and the sisters been to this house? This was a new level of grief I was unfamiliar with. I had lost my mother in a car wreck, but she had died quickly. She was not in a coma on the brink of death. My father endured the trials of chemo and radiation, but his pain was over now. He was free, and as much as I hated to be without them both, I was free, too. Mr. and Mrs. Eady were, however, were prisoners to the same possession as their son.

I gave the couple a sympathetic smile and stepped into the bedroom. Paula closed the door behind me and locked it. I glanced between her and the door, but she didn't explain the need for it. I assumed she didn't want the elderly couple to burst in on the ritual.

I looked around the lamp-lit room, taking in the strange mix of child's toys, movie posters, and family photos. On closer inspection, I noticed that all the framed photos had broken glass. Gouges and scrapes marred the plaster walls between the posters. Several areas, including the ceiling, looked to have scratches, as if an animal had lived inside the room at some point.

The underlying smell didn't match the rest of the house. It didn't smell of old wood, home cooking, and aged linens. It smelled like burned matches.

The hospital bed against the back wall contained a man. Not a boy, but an adult man. He was portly. His sallow face was evidence of his extra chromosome. He was asleep despite four new bodies in his room.

Aggie, Rachel, and Paula moved around the room, dousing it with holy water, lighting candles, and quietly murmuring prayers. "What should I do?" I asked.

Three heads turned to look at me with wide eyes. Then they looked at the man sleeping in the bed. I looked at him as well. He was still asleep. Apparently, they wanted it to stay that way—a conversation that probably should have happened prior to entering the room.

Aggie pressed her finger to her lips, then directed two fingers at her eyes. Tonight was about observation, not participation, I guess. I nodded and moved away from the man. I sat down in a chair by the window.

The singular window under the slanted roof had a view of the gravel driveway and the cornfields that lined it. The sun was setting off to the right, putting an orange tint on the sky. It made the earthen greens look almost lime-colored.

Despite the warm evening outside, I felt a chill come over the room. I shivered and rubbed my arms. I glanced at the others, but they were too busy with their routine. I looked back out the window and noticed my reflection was becoming more visible with the shift of light.

I stared back at the woman in the black habit before me. That wasn't me. I wasn't a chaste, Catholic girl with ideals of godly duties. Truthfully, I never had much respect for the profession. It seemed like a cop-out on life. Given what Sister Aggie had said about the voices in her head, she had no choice but to devote herself to God. But what about Rachel and Paula? Why had they chosen this servitude?

I touched my smock, trying to make sense of the abnormal shape of my reflection. My shoulder ended, but the darkness of the fabric continued. I noted that the outline followed my whole body. It was as if my shadow was reflecting on the window. A few years of art classes came back to me, and I tried to remember shading and perspective. I focused on the darkness, trying to decide the reason for the abnormality. Then it moved.

My shadow, the fringe around my body, tipped to the side—peeking out from behind me. As if it was just as curious about me as I was about it. I whipped around, thoroughly creeped out by the prospect of my shadow looking back at me.

As I suspected, there was nothing there. No one was behind me. No one except the man in his bed. His dark blue eyes stared back at me, awake and attentive to the unfamiliar presence in his room. I felt a tangible shift in the air in the room. In another time, I might have dismissed the change as my imagination, but Aggie and the others paused in their movements, no doubt noting the same change.

The air *was* cooler. The room was darker, despite the lamp and candles being perfectly functional. It was even quieter. The cicadas and crickets outside had stopped droning and chirping.

The only sound was a slight groan in the house, and a cracking of the floorboards.

The women turned to face the man in the bed. His stare never left my face, and mine never left his. If everything I knew about exorcisms was true, it was not a good stalemate to be in. And yet I couldn't peel my gaze away.

"You've brought me another plaything," Gregory croaked through damaged vocal cords.

Aggie shook her head and opened her Bible. Rachel moved to me and shoved my shoulder. "Move." I broke my trance and stood. She took the chair from behind me and positioned it at the foot of the bed.

"Back and forth. Back and forth." The man's head tipped from side to side as he spoke.

Aggie sat down in the chair and impatiently flipped to her page.

"Such a pretty face." Gregory directed the comment at me. "I could just eat you up." He chortled and tapped his teeth together. "Or perhaps you would prefer I eat you out." He lapped his tongue at me. "Come to me, and I will make you howl, girl."

I looked away before my cheeks could redden. I was prepared for vomiting, backbends, and cussing. Somehow, I didn't think we would get to the propositioning part so quickly.

Rachel and Paula kneeled down beside Aggie and embraced her around the waist. I waited for them to retract, but they didn't. They began to chant. The nonsensical words didn't sound Hebrew or Latin. They didn't even sound like a language.

"Such a waste," Gregory continued. "Let's skip this bullshit and have an orgy." He chuckled. "Come on! You know you want it. Every last one of you is in desperate need of a hard fuck. Especially you." He looked back at me.

As serious as the moment was, I opened my mouth to object to the statement. I may have been on a dry spell for dates, but I certainly had more luck than three nuns.

"Ignore him," Paula interrupted me before I could speak. She continued her chant.

Gregory threw his head back and laughed. "Almost." He looked back at me. "You have no idea what you are doing, do you?" he asked. "An amateur! You brought me an amateur, Sister!" he yelled at Aggie. "Disgraceful and a little insulting. I thought we had more respect for each other than that." He looked back at me. "I'm not afraid of you, girl."

I frowned at him and narrowed my eyes. He was lying. I was about to say as much, but Aggie began the ritual. She read the biblical words fast, nearly incomprehensibly. She must have spoken the passages a hundred times before this.

The rambling monologue was inconsequential to me, but to Gregory it was acid in his ears. He bared his teeth and growled as he struggled against the invisible assault. "You bitch!" he spat the insult out. "Why must you waste my time?"

Gregory flung his arms out, and the impact hit me like a punch in the stomach. I coughed and dropped to my knees. Rachel and Paula glanced at me but remained in position to protect Aggie.

"Kneel before a real power, you whore of God!" he ranted. I rose to my feet again, but Gregory had other plans. He swiped the air, and my cheek burned. I touched the hot pain and found it wet with blood.

"What the hell do I do?" I asked Paula.

She turned to me, barely missing a beat in her chant to respond. "Fight him."

"How?" I asked.

Gregory chuckled. "She can't answer that question, little one. You should have read the manual." His eyes sparkled red, and I looked away.

My wrists ached. I already knew why. The fresh blood looked so familiar. It pooled at my feet, dripping into the fresh rain. When I looked back up, I was outside the school again, just like the night I tried to kill Aggie.

"Aggie!" I spun around, looking for evidence that this was a hallucination. "Rachel! Paula! Where are you?"

"They can't hear you." A man spoke behind me.

I turned around, but no one was there.

"Who are you?" I asked.

"Do you really want to know?" he asked in a deep dulcet tone.

I took a breath and turned slightly. I could see him in the periphery of my vision. I couldn't distinguish his features. All I could be sure of was that he was taller than me. "What's happening?"

"It's time to go, Hennie."

"How do you know my name?"

"I've always known your name. I've been with you a long time." He shifted behind me and whispered into my ear. "She did this to you."

My wrists announced their pain again. I looked down at the puddle beneath me, turning red from my blood. I looked up at Aggie's window. Even before I thought to move, I was at the door of the school, breaking in and tromping up the stairs in wet sneakers.

I was down the hall before I had even reached the turn. The door opened, and I ran in, except this time the circle wasn't there. Sister Aggie was praying alone. Just as I had imagined she would be.

She jumped to her feet, surprised and baffled by my appearance. I raised the knife, and she screamed. I vaulted onto her, stabbing her neck and chest, intermittently hitting her hands as she tried to fend me off. She cried and wailed in pain.

I tried to stop myself, but I couldn't even look away.

Aggie dropped to the ground, huddled in a ball as she continued to bleed onto the floor. I dropped with her and rolled her over to give the final death blow. I raised the knife high, but as I plunged it down, I realized I was no longer stabbing Aggie, but my mother.

"No!" I screamed, and the imagery melted away.

I was back in the bedroom, on the floor, staring at nothing. My wrists weren't even bleeding. I looked up at Gregory, and his smirk turned to a scowl. He closed his eyes and hummed. The deep bass vibration from his throat tickled my eardrums and pressed against my skin.

I steeled myself for an attack. The air around me thickened with humidity. The smell of sulfur permeated the room. I was only beginning to feel the heat when the explosion threw me into the wall.

The flames swirled away from Gregory, engulfing the room and trapping the sisters in a vortex of heat. I screamed as flames lashed out in front of me. The sisters winced and huddled tighter together. Rachel and Paula chanted louder; Aggie yelled her verses over the inferno.

"You are nothing to me!" Gregory opened his mouth and exhaled a swarm of wasps.

The yellow jackets and hornets attacked the sisters, stinging them everywhere. They yelped and squirmed, unable to hold their focus on the words through the pain. Welts and blisters instantly appeared on their faces and hands.

Gregory raised his hands and Aggie's chair lifted from the floor. Rachel and Paula struggled to pull her back down, but they rose right along with her. Dangling beneath the chair, they held on as best they could, but their grips eventually failed and they fell to the floor below her.

They jumped back to their feet, still chanting, and grabbed the legs of the chair. Even with both their bodies weighing on the chair, Aggie continued to hover above them.

"I am the lion." Gregory's voice echoed through the room. "You are the lamb." He twirled his finger and Aggie spun. The force of it sent Rachel and Paula sprawling onto the floor.

Aggie continued to speak the words to dispel the hateful demon, but as the speed of her spin increased, she faltered. If this continued, it would either be vomit or unconsciousness that would prevent her from continuing the ceremony.

I rose from my quarantined space, ignoring the flames that hissed in my ears and stung my skin as I passed through them. I stepped toward Aggie's spinning chair. I had no idea what I was doing, but I had to do something. I had to help her.

Gregory laughed. "Your anger is petulance to me, girl. Swallow your pride and bow to me. If you are lucky, I will let you keep your scars."

My wrists ignited in pain. Open once again, they bled onto the center rug beneath me. I pushed aside the pain and took another step forward.

A wave of heat hit my body as I reached out for the spinning chair. It was moving so fast I wasn't sure I could even grab it without losing a finger or two.

"You are no match for me!" Gregory wailed ahead of me.

My hand retracted slightly, and I stared at him. I never quite knew what it was: the tip of the brow, the nearly imperceptible widening of the eyes—then again, I didn't need to see his face to know.

He was lying to me.

I looked to my left and saw Rachel screaming at me. The flames had surrounded me, blocking the sisters' access to Aggie and me. I couldn't make out the words, but I knew she didn't approve of what I was about to do.

I looked to my right and saw Paula. She was on her knees, rocking and bashing her clenched hands into her forehead. The rosary clenched in her hands was making her forehead bleed, but she continued to pray.

I disregarded their concerns and reached blindly into the blur of legs spinning above my head.

I caught a leg, and the chair stopped.

I looked at Gregory to see what he thought of this, but he was no longer in his bed. He was coming right at me.

Gregory passed through the fire shield without singeing a hair on his head. He marched toward me, his red-eyed gaze targeting me. "You want to join the party? You should have waited for an invitation."

I didn't know what to do. My mind frantically searched for an answer. What could I do to defend myself against a possessed man? I had no idea, so I kicked him in the nuts. Not my proudest moment, but then again, I had so few.

Gregory leaned over and held himself. He looked up at me as if I were the stupidest creature that had ever walked the earth. "Is that the best you can do?" He reached out and grabbed my chin. "You are like a pebble, aren't you?" He twisted my face back and forth, examining me. "So small, yet such a pain in the ass. I should dispose of you right now." I whimpered in his pinching grip. "No, no, Hennie. It's not time for that. Not yet."

"What do you want?"

"It's not what *I* want." He moved his lips closer to my ear. "It's what *he* wants."

Before I could ask who "he" was, Gregory screamed. He released me, backpedaling away from Sister Aggie as she vomited all over him. The noxious mixture of rhubarb and stomach juices was burning him.

The ring of fire surrounding us diminished, and Rachel launched to Aggie's side. She shoved me out of the way and yanked the chair back to the floor. Paula joined her and they returned to their previous positions.

The prayers came loud, fast, and forceful. Gregory yelled and snarled at the verbal barrage. His body bucked, his mouth frothed, and his eyes bled. I watched from my new sideline position. I heard his bones crack, and I covered my mouth. This creature would kill the real Gregory before he left him.

I looked away, not wanting to see the unnatural positions he would attain before it was all through. On the wall behind me was a framed picture of Gregory's childhood photos. He looked so happy. I wondered how many good years he had before everything started going bad.

My eyes watered as I considered something I thought would never cross my mind ever again. Gregory deserved to be free of this torment. He needed to be saved. Someone had to put him out of his misery. Someone had to kill him.

I felt a wisp of air touch my cheek. In the glass's reflection, I could see a shadowy hand caressing my cheek. I turned around, trying to see him, but he wasn't there. I touched my cheek and found that the burning laceration Gregory had given me was gone.

"I cast you back to hell!" Aggie's biblical prose came to a climactic ending, and Gregory's body flopped to the floor. After a moment, his mouth dropped open, and a tarantula crawled from it.

I gasped and clamped a hand over my mouth. Why did it always have to be spiders? I watched the tarantula crawl away without discourse.

Rachel and Paula rushed to Gregory and helped the waking man back to his bed. I came up next to Aggie and pointed at the dark corner the mammoth spider was hiding in.

"Get Mr. and Mrs. Eady," she instructed.

"Okay," I murmured. I unlocked the door and stepped out into the hall, but before I could say anything, they pushed past me and rushed to Gregory's side. Rachel and Paula cleared the path for them.

Mrs. Eady showered her son with kisses, while Mr. Eady pressed his face into Gregory's hand. No one was without tears, including me.

Rachel turned away from the scene, wiping her eyes forcefully. She stormed out of the room, refusing to make eye contact with me. "Is she mad at me?" I asked Aggie.

Sister Aggie looked up at me from her chair. She hadn't moved an inch since the ceremony ended and I could see why. Her eyes were bloodshot and sallow, her skin pale and clammy. She almost seemed thinner, or at the very least, dehydrated. "Are you okay?" I changed topics.

"We should go." She nodded to the happy couple. "They need as much time as they can get."

"Yeah," I agreed and helped her up. She leaned on me more than I expected and we both nearly toppled. Paula came to our rescue and shared her weight. "What about him?" I asked when we reached the door.

"Who?" Paula asked.

"The spider." I nodded to the dark corner of the floor. I could still see the shimmer of shiny black eyes peering out at us. "Should we get a jar or something?"

Paula glanced at Aggie before turning her concerned gaze back on me. "Is that what you see?"

"Yeah, it's right there in the corner. We can't just leave it."

"That's not a spider, Hennie," Aggie whispered.

"Of course it is. I know what spiders look like." I looked at Paula for confirmation of Aggie's early-onset senility.

Paula shook her head and gave me a sympathetic smile. "You're not really seeing a spider. And no, we shouldn't try to catch it."

I glanced back at the corner, trying to see what I was supposed to. Then again, maybe that was what I was supposed to be seeing. A tiny little monster, hiding in the shadows, waiting for prey.

CHAPTER 7

I CHUCKLED AS SISTER Aggie scarfed down two big burgers, a handful of fries, and three bottles of water. Paula and Rachel were doing the same, but in more conservative portions.

"What are you laughing at?" Rachel asked.

"You. Us. It's an interesting image." I smiled and looked around at them. No one seemed to get the humor. "Four nuns at a burger joint; it sounds like the beginning of a joke."

"You aren't a nun," Rachel corrected.

"I know, but I'm wearing the outfit. I'm just saying it's an amusing scene. We're like regular folk."

"Are you saying we aren't regular folk?" Rachel asked. She stared me down, so I backed off the topic entirely.

"Cut her some slack, Rachel," Paula said, taking a sip of her soda.

"Why? She..." Rachel dropped her burger and wiped off her hands. "Oh, never mind. Excuse me, Sister Aggie." Aggie slid out of the bench seat and released Rachel to run away and disappear into the bathroom.

"Don't mind her," Paula said. "She still has trouble with her vows sometimes."

"What does that have to do with me?"

"Being a devoted servant of God is a lot easier when you are around others who feel the same way," Paula explained.

"Are you saying I'm a bad influence?" I asked.

"Yes," Aggie answered curtly.

"What?" I frowned at her insulting honesty.

"I think what Sister Aggie means is that we are a very unusual group of women. All of us are different, but the three of us are more different from the rest, because we are the same."

"So, it's like being on a diet around chocolate cake."

"No, it's like you guys are on the diet and we are the chocolate cake."

I looked at Sister Aggie for a less delicate explanation. "You drain our faith."

"I drain your faith?" I motioned to myself. "I wasn't aware faith was a finite thing."

"It isn't," Paula corrected, "but the tasks we undertake are designated by the Lord. We are all his representatives." She conferred silently with Aggie before continuing. "It's just... you didn't have to make any sacrifices to be included in this group."

I stared over at her, unable to speak or blink for a moment. "I didn't make any sacrifices? You mean other than walking away from what remained of my life after my father died? I think I'm sitting here in the same robe as you are. I'm living with the same arduous schedule of prayer, work, prayer, work, sleep. I don't see how I haven't given up anything to be a part of this group."

Paula gave me a forced smile and nodded at me. She turned back to her fries and continued to eat without further argument. I looked at Aggie to see if I had won my case with her, but she was frowning at me. "What?"

"Why did you step into that circle?"

"I wanted to help."

"You put yourself in danger. This is nothing to play around with."

"You brought me to an exorcism!"

"Lower your voice," Aggie scolded.

I looked around, but no one was in the eating area. "He was lying to me. He said I couldn't help you, but he was lying. I took a chance."

"You weren't afraid."

"Yeah, a little, but I didn't want you to get hurt."

Aggie's frown softened. "I know you want to help, but you need to pace yourself. You have a lot of good instincts, and in time, you will be as powerful as the rest of us, but you need to know we have no protections. We aren't bulletproof."

I nodded. "At least we saved him."

I heard a snort behind me. "Yeah, right." Rachel pushed in beside Aggie, taking the outside position. They rearranged their food and continued eating.

"What?" I shrugged. "We did good tonight, right? I thought he was going to die."

"That guy died years ago. The only thing left of his life is the two or three days we give him every month."

"What?" I bounced my gaze around, looking for answers.

"Rachel," Paula admonished her softly.

"What?" Rachel stared over at her. "Why do you always want to baby everyone?"

"Why do you always want to shock them?"

"Because nobody ever learns anything by being coddled. Throw her in the deep end and let her swim."

"Will you two stop bickering and explain?" I complained. "What are you talking about two or three days? The demon is out. Possession over. Exorcism successful."

Rachel nodded. "Yeah, and it was all thanks to you." She smirked at my confusion. "Oh, that's sweet. Did you think you saved the day? Did you think he was going to live happily ever after?"

"What I think is that you're a little too bitchy to be calling yourself a nun."

Rachel shrugged and shook her head before returning to her meal. Aggie eyed me with a frown but didn't rebuke me for the statement.

After a moment, I asked my question again. "What happens in two or three days?"

"The demon will return," Paula answered before Rachel could clear her mouth. "Gregory is his vessel. He won't give him up. He keeps returning. No matter how many times we displace him."

"You've displaced him before?"

Rachel nearly choked on her beverage.

"Yes, many times," Paula continued.

"We have been doing exorcisms since you were in high school," Rachel flaunted.

"And I have been doing them since you were in diapers, Rachel." Aggie stared her down with a parental glare. "Speaking of diapers, I suggest you trade yours in for big girl pants. I've had enough of your lip for one night. You have been chosen by God to be a leader and a teacher. You are meant to be an example to Hennie, not an instigator. If condescension and mockery is your interpretation of our duties, then I would prefer you shut your mouth."

Rachel dipped her head and nodded. "I'm sorry, Sister Aggie. I will try harder to overcome my ego." She took a deep breath and looked at me. "I'm sorry, Hennie. I'm treating you unkindly and you haven't done anything to deserve it. My anger didn't start with you. I shouldn't end it with you."

I wasn't sure how to respond to the impromptu apology, so I just nodded and leaned back on the bench. "Why do you even bother to save him?" I asked. "I mean, I know you have to try, but... every month you go there?"

Aggie chuckled. "Yes, every month we go there. We go there to sit in Mrs. Eady's kitchen, eating pie and listening to her talk about her china patterns, her figurines, and how proud she was of her son. Every month we step into the path of hell to remind them that God is still with them, even when the devil has taken residence in their son."

"You do it for them?" I asked.

"Yes, we do it for them. We do it for us. We do it for God. We do it, because the few times we have successfully removed the demon, they are eternally grateful."

"But..." I looked away from Aggie. "Isn't the hope crueler than the reality?"

Aggie took in a deep breath. "It's true. Hope can destroy you. Especially when you only have that to live for. But hope is what guides us, allows us to dream beyond the reality of life. Without hope we would be dead on the inside, too."

I frowned, thinking that I was in my current predicament for that very reason. My hope for a happy life had died, so I sought to reap pain on Aggie. It was a strange conundrum, though. Hope was the creator *and* destroyer of life.

CHAPTER 8

I WAS THE LAST in line for the showers the next morning. I
hadn't bothered to wrap my hair, as was customary when
traveling back and forth to the bathroom. It wasn't likely that
Father Mitchell would wander upstairs into our personal space,
but we had to keep up appearances at all times, so we didn't get
lax when it really counted.

I huddled against the wall between the hand dryers and closed
my eyes. I was tired, sore, and bruised head to toe. Apparently,
not everything that happened to me was a hallucination.

When I heard the curtain of one of the shower stalls slide to
one side, I opened my eyes. Rachel was on the other side of it,
covered head to toe in her bathrobe, shower cap, and slippers.
She frowned at my appearance and stomped toward the exit.

"You want to say something?" I asked her.

She stopped and turned back to me. She glanced to where
Meredith was singing behind her shower curtain. "Did you
forget something this morning?" she finally asked.

"Are you serious?" I asked, touching my hair. "This pisses
you off?"

Her jaw clenched, as if she were biting back a few choice
words. "I can see that black crap in your hair and that stupid
little double heart tattoo behind your ear."

I narrowed my eyes at her. She acted like we were living as
nuns through the turn of the century. I couldn't have been the
first nun to have a visible tattoo or an extra piercing. Modern

nuns didn't even have to cut their hair short. Hell, she hadn't cut her hair because she knew it would make her look like a walking, used Q-tip. Where was she getting off judging me for lifestyle choices that were made long before I was ever involved with them? "Is this personal for you, or do you just hate anyone who doesn't live up to your expectations?"

Her face blanked, and she took a step back. "Try to remember your head towel in the future. The routine will help you stay in character," she said and left.

I turned toward the showers as Meredith slid her curtain open. She had carefully twisted her long, wavy auburn hair in her towel. A second towel, wrapped tightly around her slender waist, left her upper body exposed. Despite my desire to remain immune to her audacity, I dragged my eyes over her creamy skin and her enviously perfect breasts.

Somewhere along the line, I had missed out on the old crones typically associated with a pious lifestyle and gotten dumped in with models and a runner-up for the Playboy mansion. If vanity was ever an issue for me, it was soon going to be raised to a full-on complex.

"She is such a stick in the butt," Meredith said as her bare feet slapped over to the sink.

"She's a pain in one, too." I gave up on my body comparisons and headed into an open shower. Meredith hissed, and I looked back to see what the problem was. I could see her reflection in the mirror, grimacing as she adjusted her nipple ring for its daily cleaning.

Speaking of piercings.

I frowned at her. "How can you stand that thing?"

"It only hurts when I move it," she rationalized.

"No shit, you have a steel ring stabbed through your tit." I winced as she tugged on the tender tissue again. I shivered and closed the curtain to stop myself from watching the train wreck of fashion.

"Oh, you're just jealous because I got to keep my piercing, and you didn't," Meredith teased.

I chuckled as I got situated for my shower. "Yeah, well, apparently a nun with a nose ring is a little too much for Sister Aggie." I touched the spot on my nose that had already healed closed. "I can always do it again." I turned on the water, thankful it was already warmed up.

"I heard Sister Aggie is ready to anoint you into our little group soon." Meredith's voice nearly disappeared under the waterfall.

"What?" I shut the water off again and popped my head out.

Meredith smiled back at me through the mirror. "You impressed her last night."

"Really? I thought she was mad."

"Eh, Aggie's always mad. What did you do last night, anyway?"

"I just helped gravity out a little."

"You actually joined in?" she asked.

"Yeah, I guess."

"Wow. My first exorcism, I got feces thrown at me and ended up in the corner of the room vomiting." Meredith giggled. "As you might imagine, Aggie wasn't too impressed with my fortitude." She giggled again, and I laughed with her.

"Can I ask you something?"

"Sure." She grinned as if she had just agreed to play truth or dare with me.

"How long did it take for you to feel comfortable here? Feel like you belong?"

"You belong already, but after the ceremony, you'll feel like one of us. You'll feel like one of *His*." She poked her finger upward and clicked her tongue.

"Is that a good thing?" I frowned.

"Oh, yeah," Meredith chuckled and rearranged her towel to cover her breasts. "He's the one supplying all the juice, so yeah, you definitely want to be on the receiving end of that. Happy showering." She grabbed her plastic bag of products and headed out, leaving me with the rare joy of an empty bathroom.

I moved back into the shower stall and started the water again. I twisted the knobs, adjusting the temperature to ease my aching muscles, and dove in. I let the water pound against my head, draping my eyes and ears in the deluge.

The fluorescent lights above flickered and shut off. The room went dark, except for the meager light from the painted-over window by the sink.

"Hey! I'm still in here!" I peeked out to see if one of the girls was playing a trick on me, but there was no one in the bathroom with me. "Hello! Can someone turn on the light?"

I sighed and grabbed my robe off the hook. I wrapped it around me and tiptoed to the light switch. I flicked it on and jetted back into the warmth of my shower.

I managed to wash my hair before the light switched off again. I huffed. "Very funny, you guys! Ha, ha, new girl has to shower in the dark. What is this, grade school?"

I finished my shower in the dark and ignored the creepy feeling of eyes on me.

It was just my imagination. The shiver of threat running down my spine was only my animal instincts in overdrive.

Why can't humans see in the dark?

All the other mammals can see in the dark.

What would we see, if we could see into the shadows? Are we afraid of the dark because we don't know what's there? Or because we do?

I slipped out of the shower and put my robe on as fast as I could. My wet arms snagged on the material, but I yanked it on and wrapped the belt tight. Unable to resist my fear, I left my supplies behind and jogged toward the door.

I pulled open the door and heard the creaking hinges overlapped by a growl. My eyes blurred with tears as I stared out at the light flooding in from the hallway. Just to my right, behind the door, at the edge of my peripheral vision, was... something. A movement.

The little hairs on my body were being summoned by my fear. My legs froze, awaiting the result of my mental debate. I had to see it. To disprove my fear. It wasn't real.

But what if it was?

I forced a breath into my lungs and took a step forward. It growled again. I nearly squealed and bolted out the door, but I eased my steps forward slowly, refusing to look at it, and denying it control of my fear. It was the hardest three steps of my life, especially since by the last step I could feel hot breath on my neck.

The door to the bathroom clanked shut behind me and I walked down the hall to my room. My controlled walk ended with me behind my locked door, hugging the crucifix from my wall and praying prayers I hadn't spoken aloud since I was in Sunday school.

CHAPTER 9

F OR SEVERAL DAYS, I pretended the bathroom incident was all in my head. It didn't happen again, so I assumed it was only my imagination. It was all the things that everyone says it is: the wind; the floor cracking; an electrical short. It was all of those things. It wasn't a beastly creature visiting me from the depths of hell.

"He's come to you, hasn't he?" Aggie asked from across the lunch table. The wooden table looked like something out of an Amish furniture showroom. All nine of us fit at it with still room for more. Mealtimes were more devotional than I expected, but I had learned to appreciate the silent revelry they offered.

I looked down the table at Sister Aggie. She was several chairs down from me on the other side. It was the first time anyone had opened their mouth during a mealtime in weeks—outside of "pass the salt"—but I was even more surprised she was directing the question at me.

"What?" I whispered, still not wanting to disturb the others. However, they were joining Aggie in her observation of me.

"You've been too quiet. You don't have questions for me. You haven't spoken to anyone in days." I shrugged at her. "And you have been wearing your necklace."

I lifted the rosary that hung around my neck. "I thought I was supposed to."

"Not the rosary. The communion necklace."

I glanced around at the other women. I suspected they might have told her about the recent addition to my wardrobe. Although well hidden beneath my habit, I kept the tiny cross necklace on, even while showering.

I caught Katherine's eye, and she looked down at her plate. She always reminded me of a scared child, no matter what she was doing, but this time might have actually been in response to guilt. I had suspected from her timid nature that she was a proper nun, like Paula and Rachel, but as it turned out, she was the last to join before me.

Although she never talked to me, I knew from the others she had a nervous disorder. Her compulsions, though manageable, seemed to pop up now and then, in the oddest ways. Mainly as outbursts of conversation that rarely, if ever, had meaning to me.

"Has he come to you?" Aggie asked again.

"Has who come to me?" I asked.

"The devil," she said.

I frowned and looked around at everyone before shaking my head. I didn't want to acknowledge the lunacy of a scary creature in the dark, let alone that. "I don't know what you mean."

"Yes, you do. You can deny it. You can pretend it's your imagination, but we have all been in your situation. It's different for everyone, but I need to know what he told you."

"Told me?" I looked around the table and saw several faces duck away from me. "Nothing was said. I just thought I saw something. And maybe heard something.

"What did you hear?"

"It sounded like a growl."

Aggie frowned. "You're sure?"

"No, I mean, like you said. I thought it was my imagination."

Rachel huffed and threw her napkin on the table. Sister Aggie watched her leave the table.

"What does that mean?" I asked.

"Did you see it?"

"No, I couldn't look at it. I was too scared. What does that mean?"

"It doesn't mean anything." Aggie went back to eating and so did everyone else.

"That's bullshit," I griped.

"Hennie!" Aggie glared down the table at me. "Mind your language at this table."

"What aren't you telling me?" I asked.

"This isn't the time to discuss it."

"You started this conversation. I want to finish it."

Aggie dropped her fork and stood. "Fine, come with me."

I pushed away from my meal and followed her out, ignoring the surreptitious glances from my fellow coven. I followed Aggie into her sparse room and found her sitting on her cot with a Bible in one hand and a pair of reading glasses in the other.

"Sit," she directed, and I sat beside her. She placed her glasses on and cleared her throat before opening her Bible to read a passage to me. "Be sober, be vigilant; because your adversary the devil, as a roaring lion, walks about, seeking whom he may devour." She slapped the book shut and looked at me. "Do you remember the serpent, from the bible? The one that tempted Eve?"

"Of course. The *Applegate Scandal*," I joked. She offered me a small smile for the effort, but it soon disappeared behind her teacher's facade.

"We teach that the devil is serpentine. He is beguiling. He plays on our addictions and predilections to steer us towards evil." I nodded. "However, that isn't the only form or tactic takes. For many of us devoted to God, he presents himself as angelic, or as a person of definitive faith—like a priest, nun, or someone familiar to us."

"Familiar?"

"Sometimes, but only when the subject is extremely clever."

"Familiar... like you?"

Aggie smirked, but didn't answer. "In this state, he won't trick you so much as manipulate you. He will use your own beliefs against you. He twists the truth, just enough to cause doubt and discontent."

"What about the lion?"

Aggie stood up abruptly, as if she was uncomfortable. "The third way the devil may approach you is by way of the lion—the beast."

"Okay, so how does the lion trick me, or manipulate me?"

"The lion is the form he takes when he knows tricks and manipulation won't work. The lion is the form he takes when he wishes to destroy you with violent opposition, persecution, and death."

I shook my head and barked a laugh. "What? Are you saying the devil wants me dead?"

"It's an interpretation, Hennie."

"Yeah, but I didn't get a hissing snake. I got a growling freaking beast! That can't be good." I stood and paced the short length between her bed and the wall. "Why would he target me? I just got here. I don't even participate in the rituals yet."

"It's possible is trying to scare you away."

"Well, he's doing a bang-up job."

Aggie pressed her hand across my stomach, stopping my forward movement. "I know this is frightening, but you can't let him control you. In truth, if he is coming after you this hard, this fast, then he must already know how little control of you he has. Your fear is his last-ditch effort to lead you away from us."

I hugged my arms around myself. "You said that everyone went through this."

"Yes. Before the initiation, we are each met with our own version of a devil. We each have to fight him off mentally and spiritually."

"Did anyone else have a lion to fight?"

Aggie looked at the floor. "No. I have never heard of anyone facing a lion."

"Then how do you even know if I can fight him off?"

"Because Hennie, generals don't go to the front lines for just anyone. If he is angry enough to want you dead, then he must see something that scares him. And if you can frighten the devil, then you are going to be an important asset to our team."

CHAPTER 10

"**W**HY NOT THIRTEEN?**" I asked as Ruby anointed me with lemon oil. I already smelled like a bush fire from the burning sage, so smelling like a freshly polished floor was an improvement.

We were kneeling together in my fifth-grade school room—what I had come to know as the altar room. It was where the coven came to do their rituals. Rituals I had only watched. However, Ruby was preparing me for the initiation ceremony, a very intense ritual that would not only make me a part of the coven but connect me with the power provided by the Big Cheese himself.

To say I was giddy was an understatement.

"What do you mean?" Ruby enunciated slowly, as she usually did. The scar that tugged at her top lip made for the occasional lisp. I had assumed the malformation resulted from a cleft lip. Her permanent Elvis Presley impression was probably the best her surgeons could achieve.

The scar wasn't large or grotesque and hardly detracted from her beauty. Her short black hair and pale skin made her a ringer for the part of Snow White. Unfortunately, no one ever got to see it since her head never rose to eye level more than once a day.

She usually kept to herself, but I had recently discovered she wasn't against conversation, she just didn't pursue it.

"I mean, there are only nine of us. Aren't covens supposed to be thirteen?"

Ruby shook her head and dipped her finger in the oil again. She lifted her hand to my face, dabbing it carefully in little crosses. "Covens can practice in any number greater than two. It takes three to call on God. No less."

"Why not one or two?"

"I don't know. Not loud enough, I guess." Ruby gave me a small smile.

I chuckled at her joke and touched her hand as she anointed me again. "Sister Aggie told me that tonight was going to be very intense. What did she mean by that?"

Ruby's brilliant green eyes landed on me, and for a moment, she stared at me. "I have been through the ritual twice. The first time, I didn't finish."

"Why, was it painful or something?"

Her eyes flickered over mine, and she looked down again. "Some leave after they try the ritual. It can be too much. The power. The burden. The consequence. Being a part of something this great doesn't come without sacrifice. If you can't let go of your doubt, your judgment, and your anger, you can't join this coven."

"How do I do that?"

"You just do. You either accept each offering and submit your own, or the ritual will end."

"Offering? I don't understand."

"You will." Ruby smiled and continued to anoint me.

CHAPTER 11

I STOOD AT ATTENTION in the center of the circle. I was ready to take on the nefarious hazing. I watched Sister Aggie as she prepared the circle, blessing the surrounding floor with holy water followed by a symbolic sprinkling of salt, and then finally the smoky incense that reminded me of the inside of a church.

Right around the time I got thoroughly bored, Sister Aggie took her place in the circle. Everyone joined hands around me and said a quiet Our Father with an added addendum about giving us his sword for mercy and justice.

Following the prayer, they all disrobed. My head twisted around, seeing shoes, socks, pants, and panties flying about, until every last brassiere was on the floor. Mortified by the excess of nudity, I tried to keep my eyes down. I might have succeeded in my prudishness, but then I caught sight of something I couldn't look away from.

Scars.

My gaze gravitated to Rachel's right leg. It was a mixture of scaly and puckered tissue. The result of burns. Horrible burns. The breath I took was almost a gasp. Rachel eyed me, an endless river of bitterness bolstering her, protecting her from my pity.

"Remove your clothes, Hennie," Sister Aggie ordered. I saw her left breast was gone. Without her prosthetic bra on, I would have never guessed she had been a victim of breast cancer.

"Is it really necessary?" I asked.

"It is mostly symbolic, but we find it speeds up the ritual," she answered.

I swallowed my prudish pride and undressed. Once I was naked, I felt less apprehensive about standing amongst the women. We were all the same. Some perhaps a little more damaged than others, but still women. A coven.

"Who will begin?" Aggie asked.

Erin separated from the circle. Everyone linked behind her, filling the gap she had created.

Erin stepped up to face me, her slender body and cropped blond hair reminding me of a ballerina, but she was much too tall for that. "It'll be okay." She smiled timidly. "You will truly be a part of us when it's all over."

The chanting began, and a tangible pressure filled the room. Erin took my shoulders in her hands, and I mimicked her so we were in an arm's-length embrace. I looked into her eyes, prepared for whatever I needed to do, but I had received no instruction.

As I looked at her, I could feel something coming through our connection. At first it was just physical, but then it was mental. My mind fluttered through a thousand memories at once. A child with no one to read to her. Children laughing at her. Wrists bleeding, much as mine had done when I deemed my life pathetic enough to warrant it.

Her memories of depression, drug addiction, and abusive boyfriends flashed through my mind. Cruelties I had not endured. Trauma I had never experienced, and yet each memory became a part of me. The pain of a lifetime's worth of burdens pounded down on me, pushing me to my knees and bringing me to tears.

Erin fell with me, keeping the connection until every childhood taunt and adolescent rejection had me bawling emphatically against her shoulder. When it was over, I clasped onto her and hugged her. I wanted to take her pain away, erase her past, and make her understand they were wrong. She was beautiful, and smart, and funny, and no one had the right to tell her otherwise.

I leaned back and brushed her bangs from her face. She let me fawn over her a moment longer. She seemed to understand what I had just been through, and that I needed to keep contact with her. There was no other way to make her understand the beauty that had blossomed from such an awful childhood.

"Next," Aggie instructed, and I realized I had to go through that process seven more times.

CHAPTER 12

I FELT A WAVE of emotion come at me, and I didn't even know what it was until I was staring at the predator in front of me. Fear. So much fear and the pain. I cried out, unable to contain it. I was bent over on the floor, in the memory and in reality. I held my lip, staunching the blood that poured from it. I watched the perfect red drizzle into the sink and I sobbed, begging for my life.

I pleaded for the ritual to stop, but I could barely see the real world through the vision. I looked up and saw my husband laughing at me. His maniacal condescension that made me feel like an ant under his shoe. I wanted it over. I didn't care how. His death or mine, I just wanted it over.

He yanked me around to face him so he could tower over me while he threatened me. His fingers tangled in my hair, forcing me to crane my head back. The abominable expression on his face made me question his capacity for humanity, let alone the love he supposedly held for me. I grappled at his back to hold myself upright. My other hand searched for the knife block. I pulled a steak knife from the matching set. It wasn't as menacing as his chef's knife, but it didn't need to be. I just needed it to go deep enough, and it did.

His face lit with shock as he stumbled back. He stupidly pulled the blade out of his side, letting the blood into his lungs. He cursed at me and stumbled forward, but he fell before he could reach me.

The vision cleared, and I stared down at the golden wood planks. I couldn't even stay on my knees through the ordeal. The sheer power of the vision was enough to break my emotional restraint, but it was Ruby's turmoil that brought me to such an abject display.

My head was resting on her leg as she stroked my hair back, consoling me for the trauma she had experienced. It should have been me holding her. They were her memories. Her past. Her pain.

This was what she had meant about passing no judgment. Ruby was a murderer. She was hiding from the law. Her identity was being shadowed by the convent. Revealing herself to me was dangerous. I could just as easily condemn her for the death of her husband and turn her in for the crime.

But I wouldn't.

Not because I was almost guilty of the same crime, but because hers was justified. She made a choice. She fought back. It was the only way she could survive. Be safe. Be happy again.

It was a sin by the church's definition, but when the time came, she could debate the morality of self-preservation with God. As far as I was concerned, she made the right choice. Given the same circumstances, I would have chosen the same irreverent path.

CHAPTER 13

"**N**o more, please," I implored as I finished feeling Meredith's wavering emotions. The guilt and disappointment of extramarital affairs. The depredation of a life consumed with sex. The fear, shame, and anger for what followed.

Her prostitution, albeit at the higher end of society, took a toll on her. She eventually found herself in the wrong crowd. Drugged, beaten, and gang-raped, the hotel's maids found her the next morning. Neither they nor the police looked at her with any sympathy. The line between whore and rape victim was too thin to bother with anything as grandiose as human compassion.

I had always considered my life to be on the downside of pitiable, but I realized then that I had no idea what hardship really was. I had lost my parents. I hadn't lost myself.

I huddled in a ball in the center of the circle and cried. It took me a long time to settle from the vision, but eventually the intensity of it faded and I moved onto the next one, and the next.

CHAPTER 14

I WAS FACE TO face with Rachel. I had seen it all. Every manner of sin. I had cried for each of my sisters in sympathy and empathy. I had seen their sins and cast no judgment. I had felt their anger and desire without condescension. Yet it was Rachel's mind that concerned me.

She moved her hands to my shoulders, and I to hers. We stared at each other while the chanting blended our thoughts, converging our minds. Unveiling a child.

Rachel was probably the cutest little girl that ever lived. In an effort to be a grownup, she had gotten curlers tangled in her frizzy red hair and smeared her slightly freckled cheeks with too much blush. The lipstick she was endeavoring to put on was well outside of her lip line and even onto her teeth.

I felt my lips tug into a smile. There would never be a more perfect image of a little girl than her vainly and inadequately trying to be a woman. Boys would always be boys well into manhood, but girls were born to be women. From first steps to first words, they would try to fit into their mother's all too big shoes.

Rachel's free-spirited play was interrupted by a slap that sent her off the vanity stool. My heart raced as I stared out through her eyes. My face burned, and I looked up at my assaulter. Mother was screaming at me. I had never learned this lesson, but I was already being punished for it. Wasteful and disrespectful, I was a horrible child. How could I be so naughty? I didn't have the answers, but none of them would have saved me, anyway. Another slap for my apology.

My father was much the same, only more methodical. It wasn't enough to spank or hit. The key was to add the evidence of my misbehavior into the punishment. Caught smoking his cigarettes in the garage earned me three round scars on my back. Shoplifting earned me a few lashes to the face with my own stolen necklace. When I tried to steal his car and run away from his brutality, he nearly broke my leg with a tire iron.

I lay on the garage floor, wailing in anguish as he casually lit his cigarette. He didn't even have the decency to leave me alone to cry. My tears were the best part of his day, right along with that damned cigarette.

Consumed by the anger had beaten into me since birth, I fought back. I grabbed the gas can behind me and threw it at him. The liquid splattered his clothes, and the fumes ignited in a poof, incited by the glowing ember on the end of his cigarette.

He scrambled to get his clothes off, but I threw more on him, adding to the flames that were blistering his skin. The liquid spilled on my leg, and I screamed from the same pain I was giving him.

I threw the can at him and crawled to safety. I patted out my leg and watched him scramble out of the garage and writhe in the dirt drive outside. I was not horrified. I was not sorry. I was pleased.

Juvenile detention followed, then foster care, and finally Rachel surrendered to God. She wanted to be forgiven, but she still wasn't sorry. She tried to be sorry. She tried to forgive her parents, but she couldn't. Although devoted and pious, her anger persisted, and years of prayer had not healed her inner or outer wounds.

I broke from Rachel without tears or sympathy. I felt angry. I felt the bitterness twisted in a knot in her stomach. She wanted to untie it and break her tether to her past, but she couldn't. It was there to stay. All I could do was accept her for the person she was. I couldn't hold her to the same expectations as I did others.

In truth, society's standards did not apply to any of them. They were good, but a little damaged. I wondered if that was the qualification for becoming part of this group. Was it destiny because I was broken? Or was I broken because I was destined?

CHAPTER 15

I HADN'T EXPECTED TO see much from Sister Aggie. Her vices were commonplace to me now. She had always been a strange duck, but I didn't understand how strange until I saw into her mind.

Premonitions and visions were part of her daily life. The power that resided inside of her was a sitting throne to God. When He happened to be in the neighborhood, He would take a seat and offer a dose of insight that often came with its own burden.

"Mrs. James, what are you doing here?" Aggie asked as my mother's clacking high heels approached her office door.

My mother smiled at her. "Ugh, I've been put in charge of the church bake sale this year. What fool decided I was organized enough for that, I don't know. Anyway, I was told you would have a list of names to call for donations."

"Of course." Aggie smiled and led the way into her office. She looked through her file cabinet for the list and handed it to my mother. As she extended the papers, she faltered and clutched her face.

I felt the vision come into my mind with as much power as I knew it had Aggie's. The squealing tires, the crunching metal, shattered glass, and the smell of gasoline. I saw my mother lying against the steering wheel and I gasped. I tried to pull away from Aggie in real life, but she held me to her.

I had never seen my mother dead. Bleeding from her forehead, into her glazed over eyes, her neck snapped in an awful way. I didn't want to see it, but I couldn't control the vision any more than Aggie could control her premonitions.

"Sister Aggie, are you alright?" My mother pinched her wrist, checking her heart rate.

Aggie shook her head. "Just bent over that filing cabinet too long. I'll be fine."

"Are you sure? Do you want me to call someone?" My mother's face was so endearing and concerned, but it was Aggie who needed to be worried about her.

"Mrs. James..." Aggie swallowed hard, biting back tears.

"Sister Aggie, what is it? Are you in pain?"

Aggie looked at the crucifix on the wall. A burden indeed. She cleared her throat and bypassed her own thoughts and feelings in lieu of the Lord's. "I just wanted you to know that Hennie was one of my favorite students. I think you and your husband did a wonderful job raising her."

My mother looked taken aback, but she recovered with a solid smile. "Thank you, Sister. That's wonderful to hear." She laughed. "I guess the bake sale doesn't feel like too much of a burden anymore. You're good." She waved a finger at her.

Sister Aggie smiled and nodded. She led my mother out and remained in her office to cry for my loss, only a short time before I would.

I felt the realization hit me like a rock, weighing me down into the depths of the sea. I felt the cool darkness sink into my mind and heart. The veil of magic slipped away and reality hit as hard as my gaze did.

I stared at Aggie, frowning at her. The chanting stopped. Everyone could feel the shift. The ritual was over. I couldn't let go of this. I couldn't forgive this.

"You knew."

"Yes."

"You saw her."

"Yes."

"That fucking day!" I screamed into her face.

"I couldn't stop what was to happen."

"That's not the point! You didn't even try. You have a vision of her broken neck and you don't even say 'drive safe!'"

"The accident was meant to happen."

"Then why did He show you? What was the point of the vision if not to stop it? What is the point of all of this, if not to help people?"

"I do not predict the future. I see the future. I see the events that will happen. I cannot change them."

I shook my head and stood up. "Then this is all bullshit." I looked around the room at the misfit toys, pretending to be holier than thou. "The power of God!" I raised my hands. "We can levitate, but we can't even exorcise a demon. We can see the future, but we can't fucking change it! What is the point? If I wanted to be completely useless, I would have stayed in the real world and got a job as a bean counter."

"Is that really what you want?" Aggie asked.

I glared at her. "What I want is to not be a slave like you." I picked up my clothes and left the circle. I could feel the cold air cut into me as I stepped over the barrier of linked hands. I wasn't going to get into the club anymore, and I didn't care.

CHAPTER 16

I PUSHED THE DOOR open, shut off the alarm, and stepped through the mounting junk mail on the floor of the front foyer. It had been months since I had seen my house. Legally, it was still mine, but only as long as my father's insurance policy could cover the debt. My lawyer and just about every person I knew had told me to sell it, but I wasn't ready to start building a new home.

I knew that was yet another reason I was so eager to accept the burden of a new life inside of a convent. I wanted the magic, of course. I also wanted to belong somewhere, but more than anything, it put the rest of my life on hold. I didn't have to make any decisions if Aggie was making them all for me. I was a coward to my own pain.

I picked up the mountain of bills at my feet and thumbed through them. The estate was handling all that as well. My father made sure I had nothing to worry about after he had passed. Unfortunately, that had also given me the freedom to wallow in my pain, and assert blame where it didn't belong.

Or did it?

Sister Aggie was not responsible for my father's death. My mother's life, however, was another story.

She knew what her premonitions meant. The future was as good as written, but she didn't even try. How could she stare into the face of a woman about to die and not say a single word?

I shoved the bills into the letter holder on the wall by the front door and went into the living room. I flipped the switch for the light, but nothing came on. I had forgotten that I had shut off the breaker to save some pennies while I was away.

I flopped down on the couch and picked up the phone on the end table. I had neglected to shut the service off, but I was happy about the mistake. I dialed the first and most pressing number I could think of.

"Thank you for calling Tony's Pizzeria. What can I get you?" a half-hearted teenager said on the other end.

I gave him my order and credit card number before hanging up and dialing the second most pressing number I could think of.

"Jesus, Hennie!" My friend Jessica scolded in my ear. "What the fuck? You send me a message about joining a convent and then you just disappear."

"I'm sorry—"

"Seriously, I thought you killed yourself. I had to go see Sister Aggie from grade school to see if this was bullshit or not."

"You did? What did she say?"

"She said you were there on a trial basis to see if you wanted to join. And in the meantime, she was going to help you deal with your father's loss."

"Huh, I guess that about sums—"

"Are you okay?" Jess shifted the phone and started speaking quieter. "Look, I know I haven't exactly been there for you, but... crap... a convent?"

"It's complicated."

"No, it's not. Either you are okay or you are not."

I sighed and stood up. "I think I'm searching for something to do."

"What do you mean?" Jess asked.

I left the living room and meandered down the hallway toward the breaker box. "It's just the last few years I've been so focused on my dad that I didn't plan anything for myself. College, a job—hell, I don't even have a hobby."

"You can still go back to community college."

"I know, but to do what? I mean, let's face it, I'm not really good at anything."

"That's why you go to college, stupid. To get good at something."

I chuckled and removed the mirror on the wall that was cleverly placed to cover the ugly power box. "I don't even know where to begin." I opened the metal door and switched on the circuits.

"What do you mean, where to begin? Does this mean you are done being a nun?"

I sighed again and shut the door. "I think so."

"What do you mean, you think so? Are you back home?"

"Yeah."

"Bitch, why didn't you say so?"

I laughed. "I just got here. You were the first call I made—aside from the pizza place, of course."

"Of course. I'll be over in ten." Jess clicked off without my consent for her invitation.

I lifted the mirror back into place. As I blindly searched for the screw to hook onto, a shadow amongst the shadows caught my eye. I froze, staring at the slightly darker form behind me in my reflection. I wasn't sure if I could cast a shadow when the hallway was barely lit enough to see my reflection.

I stared at the black blob, willing my mind to find the rationale for its existence. It wasn't real. It was the shadow created by light reflecting off the mirror.

Why was it taller than me?

The angle of the mirror was elongating it.

Why was it moving?

The darkness stirred and moved forward. As a man's face appeared, a shadowy hand reached out. I screamed and dropped the mirror. I whipped around to see the intruder in my home, but no one was there. The face was gone. The shadows were once again blanketing the hallway evenly.

I panted and slid along the wall, refusing to allow anyone to sneak up on me. I flipped on the hall light as I passed it. I flew through the house, flipping on every light I could. I grabbed a knife from the kitchen and did another round to search for potential burglars. When it was clear I was overreacting, I turned on the television in the living room to clutter my mind with infomercials and sitcom dialogue.

The doorbell made me jump, but I ran to answer it, thankful that my sane friend would talk me out of my paranoia. I flung open the door. The young delivery boy on the other side stared at me wide-eyed as he backed away from the door. He dropped the pizza on the porch and ran down the steps, nearly tripping on his own feet.

"Hey, what the...?" I moved to retrieve the pizza, setting the chef's knife on top as I lifted it. I stared at the shiny metal blade and then after the poor frightened boy. "Oh, crap. Sorry!" I yelled after him as he climbed into his way-too-nice-for-a-delivery-boy's-salary car. "I guess I won't be getting any deliveries anymore."

I shook my head and closed the front door. I tossed the knife on the table in the foyer and opened the box of Italian heaven. I took a whiff and debated the courtesy of waiting for Jess to eat. Since she was technically crashing my pizza party, I dove in.

I dug out a slice and took a bite as I made my way back to the living room. I dumped the box on the coffee table and moaned as I relished the cheesy, saucy, calorically challenged invention. The convent had rationed me to the four food groups for too long. It was beneficial to my waistline, but not my sanity.

I chuckled, thinking that if Jess walked up to the door right then, she might have thought I had invited the pizza guy in for a quickie. I polished off the slice in less than a minute and cursed myself for not ordering a soda to go with it.

Licking my fingers, I went in search of a beverage. I navigated the fridge for all of three seconds before I realized I should have cleaned it out properly before I left. There were warm sodas in the back of the pantry, so I poured a couple over ice and brought them back to the living room. As I set them down, I noticed the chef's knife sitting on the coffee table.

I frowned and looked back to the foyer. I remembered placing it on the table by the door. I picked it up and looked around. "Jess! Are you here?" Renewed by concerns of an intruder, I wandered to the stairs. I flipped the switch for the upstairs light, but nothing came on. I must have missed a breaker.

Since I didn't want to risk anyone getting past me, I headed up. The hall was as dim and shadowed as the downstairs had been, but there was enough light coming into the bedrooms to identify a person—or preferably, the lack thereof.

Annoyed by my mounting fear, I clambered through the first bedroom, opening the closet and stomping back out to check the next. Four bedrooms, four closets and two bathrooms later, I was back in the hall with nothing but a knife and sweaty palms to show for my efforts.

"Nobody is here," I stated definitively for my mind to hear aloud. "I am alone."

The door to the bedroom nearest me shut. Not slammed, but slowly closed. I saw movement to my left, and the other one shut. Successively, I heard each latch bolt down the hall behind me click into place. It wasn't until the last door closed that I noticed the significant change in lighting.

The front of the hall was still lit by the light in the downstairs foyer, but farther back it was darker. Impossibly dark. I turned slightly to see as much of the dark as my screaming defenses would allow. I shook my head as unprompted tears sprang to my eyes.

A low growl reverberated from the darkness. It wasn't loud, but the bass behind it promised that something big created it. It was the difference between a dog and a lion.

I gripped the hilt of the knife. It was more of a security blanket for me now than a weapon. I wasn't going to fight the power pressing on me with bluster or blade. I wasn't going to fight it at all.

"You don't have to hurt me," I whispered. "I'm not joining them."

I heard what sounded like a snort and I took it for an acknowledgment. I turned slowly and walked to the stairs. I moved toward the light, and away from the darkness. On the second step, I felt a hand grasp my foot, yanking it out from under me.

For a moment, I was airborne. I hit the stairs face down. My hand twisted under me and my body fell onto the blade. I screamed as the metal skewered my side. I slid and rolled until I hit the floor of the front foyer.

I cried and looked down at the knife impaling my stomach. The pain was still setting in, but the blood was already dribbling out like a leaky faucet.

I looked up to the top of the stairs and I saw the blackness of the hall expanding. It was descending the stairs one step at a time. With each step, the blob of blackness formed into a shadow—a body with legs, arms, and head.

I could hear whispers as it made its way closer, but I couldn't understand them. I panted and gripped the hilt of the knife. "Stay away from me."

"...Hennie..." I heard my name within the nonsense. "...belong with us..." The shadow stopped at the base of the stairs. The incorporeal blob transformed from the feet up. The darkness became a black suit and burgundy silk tie, with tousled charcoal hair and olive skin. Pale green eyes peered at me past a set of thick eyebrows. His jaw clenched behind the scruff of his beard. "Come with me. It's time, Hennie." He reached out his hand, requesting mine.

I stared up at the man and shook my head. "Who the fuck are you, asshole?"

"Now, Hennie," he demanded.

"The only place I am going is to the hospital."

"For that?" He motioned to the ten-inch blade sticking out of my abdomen. "That is nothing. Take my hand and it will be gone."

The knife in my side made every breath burn. I wanted the pain to be gone. I stared at his hand, considering the offer. He was being truthful about helping me, but I still felt like a child being offered candy from a stranger. "Why would you help me? You're the one who pushed me down the stairs, you bastard!"

"Do not try my patience. You will find it lacking. Take my hand. Now!" His demand reminded me of my father, only he had never been so forceful. He had always been gentle; even at his most angry, he would only squeeze my shoulders and beg that I abide by his wishes, so he didn't have to raise his voice.

"You will come to me eventually, Hennie. There is no reason to fight the inevitable."

Something about the smugness in his tone incited my residual teenage defiance. Disregarding the pain it caused, I ripped the knife from my belly and reached up to slash the bloody knife at his outstretched hand. He hissed and yanked his hand away. He examined the slash I had put in his palm and smiled.

It was the opposite reaction I had expected. He kneeled down next to me, his beautiful features bearing down on me with sinister intent. "I enjoy seeing you angry." He licked the blood off his hand, then turned the palm to face me. The injury was gone.

My enthusiasm waned, and I felt a little light-headed. "Who are you?"

His eyes glittered with delight. "Who do you want me to be?" He leaned in closer and I fell back against the floor again to keep the distance between us.

"Are you...?" The words fell apart as I stared up at him.

"Am I who, Hennie?" He came closer, pressing his hands on either side of me to control his slow descent. "Say it. Say my name and I will make all the pain go away."

I stared at him, lips open to say the word, but unable to concentrate on anything but his green eyes. I thought I could see speckles of red within his pupils. "No," I finally murmured. "This can't be real. You can't be real. He can't be real."

He smirked down at me. "Oh, but I am. I am so real you could touch me. Would you like to feel me, Hennie? Would you like to feel the power *I* can give you?"

The seduction was meant to entice me, but it only reminded me that there was another power out there. One that I had just turned my back on.

"No." The word fell out of my mouth before I realized the impact it would have.

The smirk reversed into a frown and he drew away from me, his eyes once again alight with disapproval and reproof. "You will soon learn I am not so easily dissuaded from my goals. You are mine, Hennie, and you will return to me, or die."

The door behind us clicked open. "Sorry I'm late, is the pizza—oh shit, Hennie!" Jess dove to my side. "What the hell happened to you?"

I looked back at my uninvited guest, but he was gone. It was only me on the floor, in a puddle of blood. "I tripped."

CHAPTER 17

S ISTER AGGIE MARCHED INTO the hospital room with her incumbent nuns, Rachel and Paula, right behind her. She stopped at the foot of my bed and looked at Jess. "Leave," she demanded succinctly.

Jess froze, a bite of her confiscated green Jello halfway to her mouth. "Excuse me?"

"Leave, Jessica," Aggie insisted.

"Look, Sister." Jess stood up and tossed the Jello back onto my tray. "I'm not in grade school anymore. You can't just give me detention if I don't do what you say."

Sister Aggie continued to stare at her, breaking down her resolve with little more than determination and forty-plus years of practiced maternal glares.

"Fine," Jess conceded. "I will go get some coffee. You need anything, Hennie? Coffee? Security?"

I smiled at my friend and shook my head. "Thanks, Jess."

Paula smiled at Jess as she shifted between the nuns to vacate the room. Rachel followed and closed the door behind her. I chuckled, which made Aggie's brow dip with a question.

"You guys kind of have a Mafia vibe going on." My voice croaked a little from the tube that had spent several hours down my throat for surgery. The doctors had patched me up, and I was out of pain—as long as I remained medicated. "If you throw in a Brooklyn accent, we might have the makings of a bad screenplay."

"What happened last night?"

I turned to look out the window. "Who called you?"

"No one called me," she answered. "What happened?"

"I don't want to say."

"Why not?"

I looked back at Aggie. "Because I don't believe any of this. I don't want to be a part of this anymore."

"You don't have a choice anymore, Hennie." Aggie moved to the side of the bed. "I told you, once you open your eyes, you can't close them again."

"Did I ever have a choice?"

Aggie looked back at her fellow nuns. "As much of a choice as any of us had."

"So what's the deal, then? We all have shit lives, so the alternatives to devoting ourselves to witchcraft look less enticing."

"We all made a choice to be a part of this," Paula said. "The alternatives don't matter if this is what you really want to do. Do you still want to be a part of this?"

"I don't think I can be anymore." I grabbed my fork and slid my turkey around in its puddle of beige gravy.

"Why do you say that?" Paula asked.

I glanced at the door and paused, my gaze on Rachel. I felt differently about her now, and yet the same. She was never going to be my friend, but she was now my sister. Even if I never finished the ceremony, I would feel that way about all the women I had shared memories with. "He came to me again."

Rachel frowned and exchanged a look with Paula.

"The lion?" Paula clarified.

I nodded. "I thought, once I left, it would be over." I looked at Sister Aggie. She was wearing the same concerned and questioning look as the others. "Why would he still come after me if I wasn't pursuing the power anymore?"

"Did it do this to you?" Sister Aggie leaned down and shifted the covers to view my bandages. There was a little blood seeping through the gauze pad.

"Not exactly." I shook my head. "It tripped me down the stairs and I got impaled by the knife I was carrying."

"Did you talk to it this time?" Paula asked.

I frowned and nodded. "I told it I wasn't going to join you. I said it didn't have to kill me."

"And in response, it tried to kill you?" Aggie grumbled.

"No—I mean yes, but I don't think it intended to kill me. I think it just wanted to hurt me. Get my attention, so he could lure me to give in to him."

"What makes you think that?" Sister Aggie asked.

"Because he said he could heal—"

"The lion spoke to you?" Rachel took a step forward.

"Not the lion... him," I stammered, looking between them. "After I was on the floor, there was a man, a real man—or real to me, at least. He demanded I come with him." Sister Aggie abruptly moved to the window. Paula shook her head slowly. "What does this mean? Why is he coming after me? I thought he just didn't want me to join the group. Why would he come after me even after I had left?"

"Was your mind uncertain?" Paula asked. "Were you thinking about returning to us when he came to you?"

"No. I was ordering pizza. Jess was coming over. I was gonna talk about college and real life shit with her. I was on my way back to feeling normal."

Sister Aggie turned back and nodded to the door. Rachel and Paula turned and left the room without another word.

"Shit, this can't be good," I mumbled.

"You curse much too often for someone of your upbringing."

"What does that have to do with this?"

"Hennie, as you know, I have premonitions." Sister Aggie moved to my food tray and placed everything in a pile before moving it out of my path. "I see things before they happen."

"Is this about my mother?"

"It's about me." She looked at the windows. "Do those open?"

I looked at the large paned glass and frowned. "You can't smoke in here. It's a hospital."

"Your mother's death was a tragedy." She pursed her lips and looked at me. "You want me to apologize, or feel some responsibility for her? I can't and I won't. I am not the drunk driver that hit her. I am not the car that mangled her."

I shut my eyes and fought back the vision I had seen inside of Aggie's mind. The closed casket funeral had spared me the memory of her lifeless body, but now I had the grotesque image of her ruined body stuck in my mind. I wouldn't be looking for her in crowds anymore.

"Yes, that image is the one that resides inside of my mind. In time, it will fade for you, but it won't for me. I am forever linked to that moment. I even know what her final thoughts were at the moment she knew she was going to die." Sister Aggie took a breath to control her rising emotions. "She thought of you." She stabbed her finger at me. "That's why I said what I said to her instead of warnings and cautions. I wanted her to know you were going to be okay with or without her because she had raised you well. Her last thoughts were peaceful, because she knew you were going to be okay."

I wiped away a cluster of tears that had sprung from my eyes without warning. "Why are you telling me this now?"

"Because I want you to understand that your mother's death was written in stone. I only see things that are going to happen. I don't get the could've, would've, should've version of the events. I get the definitive outcome. I couldn't have saved your mother from death if I had blockaded the interstate, or siphoned the gas from her car, or tied her to a damn chair. The event that happened was what had already come to pass. I just got to see it before anyone else."

I nodded my head. "I was angry when I left. I was angry about... her dying, but I was also angry you never told me that you saw her."

"What difference would that have made?"

"None, except that seeing it in your mind play out that way wouldn't have been such a shock. I don't like surprises, Sister. All my surprises have been about dead and dying parents."

"I understand, and you're right. I should have revealed that detail prior to trying to fuse our memories. I underestimated how strong your reaction would be."

I nodded, and for a moment we let the silence ease the tension in the room. "Now what?" I asked. "What do I do about this?" I motioned to my wound. "Do I call a priest to bless my house? Keep him on retainer? Or do I join you again? Can you protect me from him?"

Sister Aggie took in a deep breath. "When I saw the premonition about your father, I knew you would be distraught. I knew your grief would overtake you. I didn't know your anger would morph it into a revenge plot against me, but that wasn't part of the premonition." She moved closer to the bed and took my hand. "In fact, Hennie, in all of my visions, I have never once seen you being a part of this coven."

I dipped my brow. "But you told me to return to you. You said you knew I was special."

"Yes, and that is still true, but those were my instincts. God has never told me specifically that you are meant to be a part of this group, and he has never showed me proof it will come to pass."

"Are you saying I can't come back?"

"No, not at all." She squeezed my hand. "I want you to return. I want you to be a part of something greater than yourself. All I am saying is that your future is uncertain to me.

You have to make this choice for yourself. I can't make it for you. I can't even guide you."

"He said I would eventually come to him. What if he's right?"

Sister Aggie frowned and shrugged. "I'm sorry, Hennie. I don't have the answer. All I can do is open the door. You have to walk through it yourself."

CHAPTER 18

AFTER A WEEK IN the hospital, they released me home with strict orders for home care. I wasn't sure how long it took to heal from a stab wound, but I was certain it was longer than a week. However, I was more than happy to get myself back to a normal bed, without beeps and bleeps waking me up all night.

I had hoped to bunk with Jess, but since she was living in the dorm now, it was a little too awkward to ask her mother to take me in. Not that she could really refuse. Orphaned stab victim wasn't exactly a tough sympathy sell.

I had considered going back to the convent as well, but Aggie suggested in not so many words that I heal a little more before I come back. I was certain Aggie didn't want to answer any more questions about my absence than necessary. A sabbatical was easy enough to explain, but not if I was going to be limping and hissing when I returned.

"Okay, are you sure you don't need anything before I go?" Jess asked as she grabbed her purse from my corner chair. She had propped me up in bed, with the remote in one hand and a sippy-cup of juice in the other, plus an emergency bedpan off to one side. I had initially thought she was crazy, but the more I calculated the steps to the bathroom, the more it sounded reasonable. "I will be in class until 2:00. I'll come back and check on you. I'll get you some lunch and then I can stop in on my break around 6:30. Okay?"

I smiled. "I owe you big time, Jess."

"Yeah, you do. Don't think I won't cash it in some day?" She shut the door behind her and I heard the front door shut a few seconds later. Despite a week of rest in the hospital, I fell right to sleep.

Before I knew it, lunch was being shoved at me. "Hey," I grumbled. "That was fast."

"Did you sleep the whole time?" Jess asked, touching my forehead. "You feel a little warm. Let's take your temperature." She whisked away again, right past the corner chair where my would-be killer was sitting.

I gasped and opened my mouth to warn Jess, but he pulled his finger up to his lips and shook his head. I stared at him, astounded by his blase attitude.

When Jess came back, she walked right past him without a second glance. She shoved the thermometer in my ear and pressed a button. "Hmm, a little high. Are you still taking antibiotics?"

"Yes."

"Okay, let's just monitor it. This might be part of the healing process. I'll take it again tonight." She stood up and grabbed her purse from the bed.

"Jess, wait."

"What?" She turned back, still unaware of the man sitting a few feet away from her, shaking his head at me. "Hennie, I gotta get to work. Do you need anything else?"

"Say no," he ordered.

I glanced at him and shook my head. "Thanks for lunch."

"Okay, 6:30. Take your pills and eat." Jess disappeared and a few seconds later, the front door shut.

I stared at the man in my room. He looked so real to me. How could Jess not even see him?

"Are you afraid of me, Hennie?" He stood slowly.

"Afraid of the man who stabbed me? You think?"

"I didn't stab you. You stabbed yourself."

"You handed me a knife and pushed me down the stairs."

He perked a brow and came closer to the bed. "I did move the knife, but I didn't put it in your hand and I didn't push you. That was the beast."

"What's the difference? You're all the same, right? The devil in one form or another."

He smiled and sat down on the bed next to me. "You're getting braver." He reached out to touch my face, but I moved away.

"Don't touch me."

"Let me help you."

"I don't want your help. I don't want to owe you anything. I want nothing to do with you."

"A little late for that now, don't you think? I will help you without debt." He bowed his head.

"Nothing from hell comes for free."

"That's true, but I will offer it from myself. Not as a bargain, but as a gift."

"And what gift do I have to give in return?"

He raised his eyes in thought before returning them to me. "How about a kiss?"

"Forget it. I'd rather be in pain."

He reached across me, bracing his arm so he could lean over me, his striking features close enough for that kiss I had just refused. "I could take that kiss anytime I wanted."

"Why are you even here? What do you want with me? I told you I wouldn't join the coven. If I'm not your enemy, then why try to kill me?"

"Oh, I see. That little stab wound is distracting you. Let me fix that." He waved his hand over my body and the pain stopped. I touched my side in search of the wound, but I didn't feel it. I ripped the bandage off and found the skin perfectly healed.

"How did you do that?"

"Let's not fuss over dreams and reality. Let's call it... magic." He looked me over. "Is that what you want, Hennie? Do you want the magic? The fantasy of witches and wizards? Unicorns and vampires?"

"I want... something."

He laughed. "You see? You don't even know what you want. You can feel it, but you can't quite understand it. You just keep grabbing on to whatever emotion makes you feel powerful. The anger drives you to fight. The sorrow drives you to take revenge. The hunger drives you to witchcraft. You want to feel in control."

"Everyone wants that."

"No, not like you. You're a cord without a plug. You crave the rawest of energy."

"I don't even know what you're talking about. I only wanted to levitate and do cool séance shit. I didn't want you knocking at my door, threatening me."

"When have I threatened you?" I opened my mouth to recite the endless list of threats, but technically, he hadn't ever threatened me. He made demands, but he had never once highlighted the consequences of denying his demands. "The only thing I have threatened to do is kiss you, and I hardly think you could consider that dangerous." He leaned forward. "Especially if it is merely a thank you for my gift."

I looked over his enticing eyes, chiseled cheekbones, and soft coiffed beard. I grabbed half my sandwich off the tray beside us and stuffed part of it in my mouth. I chewed it and watched him frown at my smacking lips. "Then why haven't you kissed me yet?" I said over a mouthful of bread and cheese. "I mean shit, you're hot." I took another bite, being sure to offer him an eyeful of my masticated food as I did. "I should be spread-eagled by now screaming 'Oh, God'—ironically, of course." I jammed the last of my sandwich in my mouth, muffling my voice to near inaudibility. "So, what's the deal? Do you need my permission to touch me? Is that it?"

The amusement sapped out of his face and he leaned back. "Do you really intend to mock me, Hennie?"

I shrugged and took a chug of my sippy-cup. "I mean no disrespect, D, but I gotta get a grip on this situation before I need an exorcism. You know what I mean?"

"Yes, I do." He grabbed my face, stunning me with the blunt, forceful contact. "To answer your question: No, I don't need your permission to touch you. What I do need is for you to start taking me seriously." The room around us erupted into flames, much like Greg's room had during the exorcism. "If you want this power, then you will have it, but only if you return to me. Defy me again, and I will destroy your life." He pulled me forward and kissed me.

CHAPTER 19

I WOKE TO THE sound of Jess moving around the room, picking up clothes and depositing them in my laundry basket. I could still feel his lips on mine, but he was gone. It was only Jess and me.

"You didn't take your pills with your lunch," she complained.

"Oh." I leaned over to grab my medications and yelped. I looked down at my exposed wound.

"Crap, Hennie, why did you take the bandage off?" Jess moved over to me and patted the bandage shut.

I looked over the lunch tray and found the half sandwich from my lunch remaining on the tray. I noticed the room smelled reminiscent of an autumn bonfire. It couldn't have been a dream because all of it actually happened, but then why did I wake up from it?

"Jess." I touched her arm as she tended to me. She looked up at me, slightly annoyed. "What do you know about the devil?"

She frowned at me. "Horns and a pitchfork. A propensity towards anal sex."

"I'm serious. What do you remember about what we learned in school?"

"Oh God, please tell me this isn't about Sister Aggie and her League of Extraordinary Virgins."

I smiled at the thought of Meredith being referred to as a virgin—however, the extraordinary part might still apply. "No.

I'm just trying to understand the difference between good and evil."

"You really need that explained to you?"

"I'm just saying I've done some pretty shitty things in my life, but I wouldn't necessarily call myself evil. Where's the line? Is there a line?"

"Of course there's a line. It might be a little zigzag, but yeah, there's a line." Jess shifted to sit on the bed with me.

"How do you define it? If I kick a puppy, does that make me evil?" I asked.

"No, but it definitely makes you an asshole." I rolled my eyes, not satisfied with her answer. "Look, the line isn't when you hurt someone, physically or emotionally. It's when you enjoy it."

"I suppose that does sum up the devil pretty well."

"Why are you so interested in Satan?" she asked with a crinkled nose, as if I had suddenly expressed interest in pumping septic tanks.

"I'm considering going back to the convent."

Jess's face melted into disappointment. She folded her hands neatly in her lap before she spoke. "Is that what you want?" she asked quietly, no doubt barely containing her own opinions on the subject.

It was an easy enough question, but the answer was so complicated to me. I wanted nothing more than to be a normal person living my life as benignly as possible. However, that was not what I needed to do. I believed Sister Aggie was right. Somehow, someway, I was connected to this path and the people on it. I needed to see it through to the end—whatever that end might be.

I nodded at Jess, giving her the simple version of the answer.

"Please tell me you're not doing this because of your parents. I know that you somehow think their deaths are your fault, but they aren't. You don't have to punish yourself."

I smiled at her. "I'm not punishing myself, but I do feel compelled to do this. It isn't the end of the world, you know. We will see each other once in a while."

"Yeah, at church." Jess stood and moved away from me. She picked up my laundry basket and headed out the door. She stopped and turned back to me. "I remember having a conversation with Sister Aggie when I was in third or fourth grade. I had similar questions about the devil. I didn't understand what we were learning about in school, because the only devil I ever saw was the red cartoon with a pitchfork. She said to me, 'The only thing you need to know about the devil is that he was the most powerful being God ever created.' Then she asked me, if I had the power to do absolutely anything I wanted, what I would choose to do."

Jess shifted the basket on her hip to grab the doorknob. "That's the difference between good and evil, Hennie. It's having the ultimate power and not letting it control you. The devil wasn't kicked out of heaven because he was evil. He was kicked out because he was a little too human." Jess pulled the door shut behind her, leaving me to contemplate a new definition of evil.

CHAPTER 20

I STOOD OUTSIDE THE old school waiting for the traffic to thin out before I crossed the street. A football game must have let out nearby, because the street was usually empty. Rather than risk my stitches by jogging across, I waited patiently by the bus stop.

I could see Aggie peeking through her window upstairs. I waved at her and she waved back. I motioned to the traffic and shrugged. She nodded and mimed her impression of throwing a football. I smiled and nodded.

The clouds rumbled above and it was starting to rain, but there was still nothing to do but wait for the street to clear out. I looked back up at Aggie and saw her frowning and clutching her rosary.

A darkness fell over my head, and the raindrops stopped hitting me. I looked up at the oversized umbrella and the man holding it. I frowned at my vigilant companion and looked back at Aggie. She was watching me, lips moving in a hyper-speed prayer. I noted she wasn't rushing down to save me. She wasn't standing at the door, beckoning me away from the dark side of the Force. It was still my choice. Always had been. Although perhaps not according to my shadow.

"You'll come to regret this choice. I'll make sure of that," he said. "You are putting them all at risk."

"Why am I putting them at risk?"

"Because I will not lose you to *Him*."

I didn't bother looking at him. I focused on my goal across the street. "Why do I matter so much to you?"

He turned to look at me and I did the same. He snapped his fingers and the world around me froze. Rain drops held in mid-air. The cars crossing the street stopped, the people within pausing as well. I looked over the scene with contained shock. This was beyond anything I had imagined possible with the coven.

"They are nothing compared to what I can offer you. I can give you the power you crave."

"Why do you keep saying I crave power?" I looked back at him. "I never even knew this stuff was possible before I came in contact with the coven."

"It was your choice to be blind, but now that you see it, you won't be able to walk away."

"You're right, and that's why I'm returning to Sister Aggie's coven."

"You'll see soon enough that you don't need them. You can do it all on your own. Join them if you wish, but it isn't you that needs them. It's they that need you. When they see how dangerous it is to play with real magic, they will reject you. Then you can return to me and I will graciously forgive you... again."

"Why do you keep saying 'return' to you, like I left you?"

He chuckled. "It's too difficult to explain to this simple mind, but rest assured, you belong to me, and I won't rest until you are mine once again."

I swallowed hard, my eyes fluttering over his. I wanted it not to be true. I wanted it to be a lie, but it wasn't. There was a connection between us. Whatever it was, I was strong enough to fight it, but for how long? I didn't understand it, but I knew I needed to get away from him.

I stepped forward and stopped at the street edge. I looked back at him, and he nodded. I moved into the path of frozen cars, trusting that he would hold them until I reached the other side. The moment my foot hit the sidewalk, the rain and cars started again. I looked back to see if he was still there, but he was gone.

The door to the school flew open and Sister Aggie held it for me. I walked toward her and crossed the barrier once again and committed to a life I didn't understand, so I could be a part of something I desperately wanted to understand.

CHAPTER 21

I WASN'T SURE WHAT had changed for me, but I wanted to complete the ceremony more than ever. I wanted my life of depression to end and my new life to begin. I wanted to belong to this new family and embrace the power of God. Not because I craved power, as my shadow had said, but because I wanted to do something good with my life. Something useful. Something meaningful.

I felt the minds push into mine just as they had the first time. The pain, the regret, the anger, the shame. I took it all in, with far more bravado than I had in our first session. This time around, I was ready for it. I knew what these women had been through. Meredith's desire and the shame that came with it. Erin's struggle to accept and love herself. Katherine's childhood as a homeless beggar—always cold, always hungry, and *always* scared.

Lynn's memories of molestation were just as hard the second time around, and the betrayal of her loved ones brought me crashing to my knees. Despite the anger that should have lived inside of her mind, she was content. I didn't know how she had come to terms with the abuse enough to forgive them, but I was certain I would never be strong enough to forgive that. Especially since it robbed her of the opportunity to have children.

I looked up at Lynn, wanting to give her more support than my blubbering sobs, but it was she who lifted me back up, she who caressed my face and hugged me.

I didn't deserve to befriend any of these women, let alone carry my pain to them. They had enough of their own. They were all broken, and yet somehow ten times more beautiful because of it.

I wiped my eyes, but the swell of emotion inside of me was turning them into leaking faucets. I just needed to finish the ceremony and add myself as a link in the coven circle. Then I could collapse and cry properly.

Paula stepped forward to take her turn. She stood in front of me and we exchanged our memories. Her wealthy upbringing and lavish childhood had surprised me. She, unlike the others, had not come to this convent under emotional duress. She had quite literally been summoned by God.

Watching her memories was almost as unnerving the second time. It should have been a revelation to me, a confirmation of my purpose with the coven, but what it took for Paula to receive her message was not ideal.

I felt the breeze whipping around my puffy white coat again. I tried to close my eyes, but the vision didn't allow for that. I was skiing down a steep mountainside. I had done it a dozen times already. This time was different, though.

Something, or rather someone, caught my eye as I sped through the snow. I glanced to the edge of the woods and saw the glowing form of a woman... with wings. A creature as mythical to me as Bigfoot and the tooth fairy, yet I knew instantly it was an angel.

I barely caught a glimpse of her before I hit a bump that threw me off my path. I tried to recover, but I was already in the air, heading for a tree.

In the vision, I closed my eyes, waiting for the back-breaking impact. I waited, but it never came. When I finally opened my eyes again, I was staring up at the sky.

I was certain I was dead, but I looked around and saw my surroundings unchanged. I followed the path of my tracks, trying to pinpoint how I had come to land in the snow, unharmed, behind the tree. I looked it over again and again, but I found no reason for missing the tree. No reason for me to be alive.

As I thought back to the glowing woman I had seen, I found my answer—the only answer there was room for: A guardian angel had saved me, bent the walls of reality and manipulated the very physics of the world to protect me. But why? Why me?

I pulled away from Paula and smiled at her. She smiled back at me. She was more than a little pleased to share her inspiring tale. Her life was far from difficult, but then, of course, that made her sacrifice to become a nun that much greater. She squeezed my arm before returning to the circle.

When Ruby stepped up for her turn, I couldn't help but look over the scar on her lip. I was certain the circle could heal the injury and ease her speech, but much like my own damaged wrists, she probably wanted it as a reminder. Of what, I wondered. To never be ruled by a man again? To never be deceived by love? Or perhaps it was just to prevent her from becoming a victim of either.

As I saw the vision of her husband's death again, I wasn't consumed by the trauma of it as I once was. There was a pride in watching her overcome her oppression once and for all. I wanted her to know how I felt.

The raw mental connection was designed and directed by the spell being cast, but I found a way to give her something more than the pathetic memories of my childhood loss. I focused on my pride and pleasure at knowing her. Then I imagined those thoughts as a hug of sorts, a mental embrace that broadcasted my forgiveness and acceptance.

Ruby gasped as I pushed my good vibes through our connection. I didn't really know how I was doing it, but I knew it was safe. I knew I wasn't hurting her.

We fell away from each other and Ruby looked at me with a concern I hadn't expected from my heartfelt gift. "How did you do that?"

"I don't know. I just wanted you to know how I felt, and it came through the connection." We both looked at Aggie for her ruling on the impromptu change to the ritual.

She looked at Ruby and then focused on me. A slight smile played across her face. "Next," she instructed.

CHAPTER 22

WHEN RACHEL FINALLY STEPPED up to bat, she looked terrified. I was not the weeping, cowering blob of emotion I was moments before. I was done crying. I was ready to absorb her pain and give her back the love she needed and deserved. I was being pretty freaking awesome and Rachel didn't like it one bit.

I held back the intensity of my injection and instead let it seep into her slowly. She couldn't handle the dose of love I wanted to give her, and for a number of reasons, I didn't want her to wind up prostrate from the strength of this new magic.

When we finished, she stared at me. She seemed to understand that I had backed off just for her, and she nodded to me. I smiled and nodded back. She slid back to her spot in the circle and I looked around for my next contender.

I felt something shift before I could see it. A coolness spread over the otherwise warm room. The candlelight wavered a little more than it should have without a breeze. I scanned the room for the danger.

The shadows were wrong. Taller than they should have been. They shifted forward, away from the walls. They solidified behind the members of the chanting circle. "What's happening?" I asked, but no one heard me. They continued chanting, eyes locked in a hypnotic gaze.

The dark figures raised their hands, revealing the shadows of their blades. I wasn't sure if it was metaphorical, or if they intended to stab my sisters to death, but I was certain they would die. All of them would die, and all because I hadn't conceded to do the devil's bidding. He was right that I would come to regret my decision to return to the coven.

The hands stabbed downward, and I screamed, but it wasn't my voice I heard.

A coarse, roaring scream disrupted the attack. I looked at the source and saw Sister Aggie glowing with the power she was exerting into the circle. The shadows drew toward her, stretching and expanding, until they snapped and fell into her. All of them.

The ceremony broke and my sisters looked around, baffled by the sudden collapse of the magic. I stared at Sister Aggie as she recovered from her heroics and dropped her head down to her hands. I moved closer to her. "Sister Aggie?" I touched her gently, and she raised her head. The sickly pallid tone of her skin offset the darkness under her eyes. "What did you do?"

"I... trapped them," she croaked.

"What is she talking about?" Paula came to my side, robe freshly on, and one in hand for me.

"Why didn't we finish the merge?" Meredith joined us and placed Aggie's robe over her shoulders.

"There were demons all around us," I answered.

"What did you see?" Paula asked.

"They were shadows. Like the man that keeps coming to me. I could see them behind all of you. They were going to stab you. I tried to tell you, but no one heard me."

"We must have been too deep into the ritual." Paula's eyes fluttered around the room. "Or they were preventing us from hearing you."

"Shadows were going to stab us?" Meredith asked, pulling her robe a little tighter as she checked the location of her own shadow.

"I don't know if they were going to possess you or kill you, but Sister Aggie stopped them. She took them in."

"Took them in?" Rachel said from behind me. "What in blazes does that mean?"

"I trapped them," Sister Aggie repeated.

"Sister." Paula touched her shoulders. "Please tell me you didn't invite them in."

Sister Aggie nodded and Meredith gasped. I looked at her. "What does that mean?" I turned to Rachel, knowing full well she wouldn't tip-toe around my feelings.

"She allowed herself to be possessed."

"But there were eight of them." I looked back at Sister Aggie. She nodded. "No. No. No. How do we get them out?"

"We can't." Paula shook her head.

"Why not? Just one or two at least. We have to try."

"She invited them in," Rachel said. She crossed her arms and shook her head. "She did it to save us, but now she is irreversibly possessed."

"That can't be. There has to be something we can do."

"Even if there was," Paula said, "she would be the only one capable of it. We need all three of us just to get one demon out. We can't get all of these out of her. We aren't strong enough."

"Can't we do it as a group?" I asked.

"No, exorcisms require an individual focus," Paula explained. "We are only there to support Aggie and to protect her."

"It's okay." Aggie grabbed my hand. "I'm strong. I'll fight them."

"You can't fight them forever," I argued.

"Not forever. Just until they kill me."

I frowned at the morbid joke, but she only laughed at me—a deep, guttural laugh that didn't belong to her.

CHAPTER 23

S ISTER AGGIE STARED AT us across the long table in the library. She clenched and unclenched her right hand, embedding half-circle cuts in her palm. Her tongue kept popping from her mouth, licking her lips and her left fingers as they probed the orifice. The body parts each had a life of their own. A puppet with more than one master.

"What do we do now?" I whispered, gawking at the despicable display.

"Why would they try so hard to stop you from joining us?" Paula asked. "What did the shadow man say to you when you came back to us?"

I looked at Rachel before Paula. I dreaded talking to either of them. It was like confronting my parents simultaneously. At any moment, the good cop, bad cop routine was going to turn into lectures and punishments. "He said I was putting all of you at risk by coming back. He said I would come to regret this choice. And I do." I glanced at Aggie, who was gagging on the curious fingers. She bit them and they fled her mouth. The hand slapped her cheek in retribution. "I shouldn't have come back here." I frowned and looked at Paula. "This is all my fault. I'm cursed." I pushed my chair back and stood. "Everyone I care about gets hurt because of me. I should just go."

Rachel grabbed my arm. "Even if you're right. Do you really think leaving now is going to help us?"

"Sit down, Hennie," Paula said calmly. "You aren't cursed. You are, however, a bit of a mystery."

I sat down and tried to ignore Sister Aggie's left hand strangling her throat while she attempted to bite it again. It was comical by any standard, other than the reality of her complete loss of bodily control.

"Let's forget about your past for a moment." Paula touched my hand. "Let's forget about the shadows. Tell me what you did tonight inside the circle. You imbued Ruby and Rachel with something. What was that?"

"It was compassion. I felt their pain for the second time, but I wanted to stop the hurt. I wanted them to feel my forgiveness."

"How did you know how to do that?"

"I just did it. The link was already there. I tapped into it and pushed my thoughts through."

"Bullshit," Rachel mumbled.

"What's the big deal? I'm learning. Isn't that good?"

"Yes, but you haven't been given any power to learn with." Paula dropped my hand and moved to the bookshelf behind her. She pulled an oversized book from it and dropped it on the table in front of me. "Has Sister Aggie ever shown you this book?"

I glanced at the cover, but there was no title, only a cross embedded inside of a pentagram. "No, what is it?"

"Idiot's guide to witchcraft," Rachel answered.

"This is normally where we all start," Paula continued. "It's how we begin to wield the power Aggie draws on. She is like the lightning rod, and we are there to direct it."

"What about the exorcism? You said she does that alone."

"That's because the full force of the power is directed at the task at hand. When we perform spells for permissible miracles, there are usually multiple aspects that need to be taken into consideration. Medical cures involve repairing the body, the mind, and the soul. Preventing events can call for all of us to be in different locations, doing individual spells. The point is, Aggie is the one that provides that ability to us."

"So, I'm drawing from her, and learning as I go without the reading? Yay me."

"But you never connected with her. She was the one person in the circle you didn't complete the ceremony with. If you aren't linked to her, then how do you have the power to exert your thoughts on us?"

My mouth fell open, and I searched my mind for an answer. "Well, maybe I'm tapping directly into—"

"Don't you dare say what I think you're going to," Rachel snapped. "I'll concede that you are some kind of aberration in the magical fabric, but I will not have you presuming to have access to God's power."

I rubbed my face. "You're the ones asking questions. I am just trying to come up with the answers. If you have a better idea, then maybe you should contribute more than insults."

"Stop it, you two. This isn't about ego. However, Hennie, Rachel's right. In order to be directly tapped into God, you would have to be chosen and molded over time. He usually only chooses someone with a deep faith. Plus, as simplistic as it sounds, you simply aren't old enough."

"I'm tapping into power to do this, but you don't know where I'm getting the power from? What did you mean about an aberration in the magical fabric?"

Rachel twisted her mouth before speaking. "There are some people who can tap into neutral power. It's not good or evil. It's just leftovers."

"It's essentially residual power," Paula clarified. "Almost like radiation."

"I'm nuclear?" I scrunched up my nose at her.

"No, stupid, we think you're a witch," Rachel griped.

"Why are you so mean?" I yelled at her, and she scoffed at me.

"Rachel means that you might actually be a witch," Paula said.

"It was the 'stupid' part that bothered me." I stood up to tower over Rachel. "I am just trying to keep up. My mentor is going through a split personality situation, so the only people I have left to guide me are you two. And frankly, her gentle nature is not making up for your bitchy one."

Rachel stared back at me, seemingly unfazed by my explosion. A small smile tipped her lips. "She is a witch," she murmured. My brow dipped, and I looked at Paula, who was nodding in agreement. They both stared at me with rapt fascination.

"Fly, little birdie," Aggie's voice croaked behind me. She sounded more like a man.

"You guys are freaking me out. Why are you looking at me like that?"

Rachel chuckled. "Hey, how tall are you?"

"Taller than you, shortie," I griped at her. Even as I said it, though, I looked around. The room seemed a little smaller than when I had entered. I looked down and saw that my feet were completely off the ground and floating in mid-air. "Holy—"

In Wiley Coyote fashion I dropped like a rock, colliding with my chair and narrowly missing the table. Rachel laughed at my expense.

"Learn to walk before you fly," one of Aggie's alter-egos called down to me.

CHAPTER 24

"**I** FEEL RIDICULOUS," I grumbled about the costume I was being forced to wear. As if I wasn't already scared of mirrors, I was seeing the glimmers of a happy-faced clown on every reflective surface I passed in the hospital hallway.

"Children love clowns," Ruby explained on my left.

"Clowns are creepy," I said, shifting my big red foam nose.

"What's creepy to a dying child is a rosary-toting nun," Rachel said from behind me. I glanced back at her and saw the sternness on her face. Even through her rosy cheeks and painted grin, I could see the frown of disapproval on her face. She took this aspect of her duty very seriously, and I was being ungrateful.

I nodded and stopped fiddling with my ruffled sleeves. I may have looked like a joke, but the task at hand was far from it.

I followed Ruby into the children's cancer ward. She sounded our arrival with the honk of her bicycle horn, and seven beautifully bald heads popped up. Their bright eyes stared at us, wide with anticipation of the fun to come. I smiled as each little mouth dropped open as they took in our brightly colored clown outfits. With faces like that, even I was getting excited about the show.

Rachel brushed past me and tripped on her oversized shoes. I reached to help her, but she rolled and jumped back to her feet with a hop and a skip. The children laughed, instantly appreciating the alacrity of her slapstick comedy.

Ruby joined her and smacked the back of her head. She waggled her finger to lecture her and then pointed to the surrounding children.

Rachel frowned and straightened her oversized tie. She put on a bright smile and bowed to the children. Her hat fell off, revealing her bald cap. Rachel jumped back up with overdramatized embarrassment and then a sad face.

Ruby patted her shoulder and shook her head. She raised a signaling finger to mark that an idea had struck her. She pulled a stuffed toy from her mammoth pocket and placed it on Rachel's head. The children laughed as the toy dog flopped over her ears and eyes. Ruby gestured to the accomplishment, but the children shook their heads and yelled, "No!"

I noticed a pair of bright eyes staring at me and moved over to the little girl. She couldn't have been more than five. I reached for the horn in my pocket and honked it as I pressed my spongy nose. She giggled, and I offered my face for a honk. She shoved her hand into my nose and I honked the horn. She giggled all the more and tenderized my real nose with a few more harsh shoves. I laughed and poked her nose. When it provided the same honking sound, she started to suspect something was up with this trick. Nonetheless, she searched her own nose for the source of the noise.

When I looked back at my fellow clowns, they had resorted to using a baseball mitt to top Rachel's bald head. I noted that they gifted each rejected item to the children.

Rachel caught my eye and nodded to the back of the room. I removed my red nose and placed it on the girl's nose before I headed into the far back of the room. So enamored with the performance, the nurses didn't notice when I slipped behind the curtain of one of the sickest children.

The beeping machines were quiet and plastered with colorful stickers, but they were still dreadful to see surrounding someone so young. The boy in the bed looked to be about ten years old.

I didn't even want to know how long he had fought the good fight, only to end up in this final state.

I doubted there was anything I could do for him. Sister Aggie could heal people, but that seemed beyond my fledgling magic. The bulk of my resume was lie detector, empathic abilities, and levitation. Granted, I was pretty impressed with the latter, but that certainly didn't mean I had any idea how to control it—thus the sore egg on the back of my head.

Paula believed that as long as I directed my power tap toward a specific purpose, I should be able to do anything that Sister Aggie had done. More complex spells would require the entire coven, but apparently healing cancer was a Tuesday sort of spell.

I took the hand of the child before me and I immediately felt a cold shiver pass through me. This boy wasn't just sick, he was dying. I wouldn't have been surprised to see the angel of death standing beside him.

Surely this was too much for me. I thought about leaving and letting Rachel know he was too far gone, but I had a feeling she wouldn't accept that answer unless I was half dead myself.

I whispered the spell Paula had taught me from the book of witchcraft. I barely understood anything I was saying, but it was simple enough to put me into a state of concentration. After that, my instincts kicked in.

I took in a deep breath and my eyes fluttered as something energizing came over me. Every cell in my body stood at attention, ready to direct itself toward a single purpose. I should have been terrified, but it actually felt good.

Really good.

I focused on the hand in mine. I pressed the power I was harboring into him. I injected the breadth of my life into him, burning away the clutches of his sickness. It was faster than I expected. Easier than I expected.

My body tingled from the after-effects of the almost euphoric power rush. I rolled my head back and stared at the ceiling. I bit my lip, trying to drag myself back to reality. When my head finally lolled back to see what my efforts had achieved, I saw the little boy awake and staring at me.

His eyes widened and his mouth dropped open, releasing a horrific screeching scream at me.

The nurses and my fellow sisters instantly surrounded me. The nurses rushed to the boy's aid. As they looked at him and took his vitals, several of them exclaimed, "Oh my God!"

"What happened?" Rachel yanked my shoulders to face her and her eyes froze on me. Ruby gasped and came up behind her. "We need to go."

"Why?" I asked.

"Now." Rachel reached around my back and pulled me forward. She and Ruby shielded me as we left the ward. We had been getting plenty of looks for our clown outfits, but I saw several smiles fade as they locked onto my face. "What is wrong?" I asked again.

Ruby handed me a comically large polka-dot handkerchief. "Wipe your eyes."

I did as she asked and recovered a smear of red with each swipe. I glanced at my reflection as we passed an enclosed bulletin board. Besides the blood dripping down my cheeks, my eyes looked dark. I couldn't even see the whites of my eyes through the blood.

CHAPTER 25

"SO WHAT DOES *THIS* mean?" I asked, motioning to my overly bloodshot eyes. I was happy I could save the child from death, but at what cost to myself?

"We don't know," Paula answered from Sister Aggie's desk chair. It was still strange seeing her there, but it was better than having her multiple personalities trying to run the place. So far, Father Mitchell was buying the influenza excuse for her extended absence, but eventually he was going to want to see her. "We've never had an actual witch in the coven. This might be normal for a spell of this nature. You said that the boy was near death. Perhaps being that close to the edge wounded you."

"But I don't feel wounded," I said. "I feel really good."

"You are bleeding out of your eyes," Rachel said from the chair next to me. She was still mostly clowned up—sans shoes and bald cap. Not that her frizzy red hair did anything to negate the clownish look. I, on the other hand, had shed the outfit and makeup on the ride back. "You shouldn't have proceeded if he was that far gone."

"I considered that," I admitted. "But I knew Sister Hard-Ass wouldn't have accepted my surrender."

Rachel stared at me, jaw clenched but quiet.

"I assume the boy is healed," Paula interjected. "He'll live?"

"Yes," Rachel answered and turned away from me. "The nurses were very shocked."

"I'm sure I'll be getting a phone call or two about that." Paula leaned back in her chair. "Between the doctors and Father Mitchell, we might as well be going to confession for our good deeds."

"Sorry to be self-involved here." I raised my hand. "But could we get back to me?" I leaned forward. "Am I okay to keep doing this?"

Paula frowned. "You just healed a child on the brink of death. Do you really want to stop?"

I chuckled and looked at Rachel. What brief eye contact she gave me wasn't exactly sympathetic. "Look." I turned back to Paula and pressed my hands to the edge of the desk. "I'm not trying to be selfish. I loved saving that kid. It was awesome. I want to keep helping people, but I can't help but feel like we're dabbling in something we shouldn't." I motioned to my eyes. "This can't be a good sign."

"I understand your concern," Paula said. "I'm not asking you to do anything you don't want to do. And truthfully, the only one being selfish in this scenario is me for asking you to experiment with outside magic. But..." Paula glanced at Rachel. "Right now, you are our only access to power. If you don't want to use it, then there can no longer be a coven."

I sighed and leaned back in my chair. I didn't want to be responsible for the coven disbanding. These women needed it. Much like me, they needed to have a purpose and focus to overcome their past. "Maybe we can try to exorcise Sister Aggie's demons? Then she can take over and—"

"No." Paula stood and moved to the door. She shut it gently before returning to the desk. "I don't think that would be a wise idea right now."

"Why?" I glanced at Rachel, but she was just as interested in hearing Paula's response.

Paula reached for her rosary and twisted the wooden cross in her fingers. "There was a fire in the church this morning. Some candles fell and started the altar runner on fire. The damage was fairly insignificant, but it seemed to be... intentional. I wasn't worried about it until I realized it coincided with your spell at the hospital."

"A burned tablecloth worries you?" I asked.

"Father Mitchell was blessing the wine at the time. He wasn't hurt, but it went up so fast that his vestments started on fire. I think it was a warning."

"You think the hell hound is unhappy about my good deeds?"

"It's not a joke, Hennie," Rachel said.

"Oh, trust me, I know it's not." I glared at her. "I'm the one the devil wants to kill, remember?"

"The devil can't actually kill you," Paula jumped in. "He can't kill any of us. However, he can control our surroundings. Much like the way you were tricked into picking up that knife. He can't simply walk up to you and stab you, but he can put you in dangerous situations. He can use your fear to drive you to irrational, detrimental behavior. Behavior that could ultimately lead to your death. And if he can't get to you, he will hurt the people around you."

I rubbed my face. "Everything you're saying tells me I shouldn't be doing this."

"I'm not saying we should stop. At least not yet," Paula conditioned when I objected again. "I'm trying to explain to you why I don't want to help Sister Aggie yet. You've never done an exorcism. Starting with a multiple invasion is not a good idea. We need to let you practice your craft on something less complex."

"Something that won't pop my eyeballs out of my head," I suggested.

Paula blinked slowly at me. "Yes. I think we should try one that we've already done many times before."

CHAPTER 26

Paula pulled the van into the driveway and shut off the engine. I looked over the old dilapidated farmhouse from the passenger-side window. I wasn't sure it was possible for a house to be possessed, but it certainly looked that way. The window of Gregory's room even looked like it was bleeding. I was certain it was only the rust from the old screen dripping down the side of the house after the rainfall, but I had to wonder why it was the only window doing it.

"You don't have to do it if you don't want to," Paula offered when it was clear I wouldn't get out of the van anytime soon.

"Yes, I do. I just wish I understood more about this stuff. Demons and devils, I mean." I looked back at the house and saw Greg standing in his bedroom window, looking out at me. He waggled his finger at me. "Ah, shit," I whispered. "He already knows we're here."

Rachel popped her head up between us from the back seat. "You can do this, Hennie. We already know you're strong enough to bring a kid back from the dead. And we will be right beside you. We won't let anything happen to you." She rested her hand on my shoulder, and I stared at it before returning the awestruck gaze to her. "What?"

"Why are you being so nice? There's a chance I could die, isn't there?"

"No," Paula said. "What Rachel means—"

"I can speak for myself, Sister Paula. Thank you." Paula raised her hand in surrender and she slipped out of the van to give us a moment. "I wasn't trying to scare you. It seemed like a pep talk was in order," Rachel continued.

"You don't do pep talks. You do surly, borderline bitchy comments."

"Yes, clearly I struggle with anger. I am trying to change that."

"Now?"

"I just wanted..." Rachel cleared her throat and adjusted her volume. "Why are you making this so hard?"

"Making what so hard?"

"I'm trying to tell you I have your back." Rachel threw her hands up in the air in frustration and leaned over to get out of the van.

"Rachel." She stopped and looked back at me. "I never doubted you would have my back." I smirked at her. "Just warn me next time before you start being nice. Sometimes the nicer you are, the worse the news is."

She nodded and got out of the vehicle. I unloaded behind her. As I slammed the door, a huge cloud of dust blew in on the wind. We all shielded our faces and pressed forward against the prevailing gusts. "Please tell me this is a coincidence?" I yelled up to Paula.

Before she could answer, a bolt of lightning hit the ground in the cornfield north of the house. The previously scattered clouds had bloomed into thunderheads.

"Come on!" Paula, now safely ensconced on the porch, yelled back at us.

Rachel grabbed my arm and tugged me toward the porch as the rain fell on us in sheets. We ran under the barely adequate roof just as another bolt of lightning hit the driveway not far from where we had been standing.

"Holy crap!" I wiped the rain from my face and glanced at Paula. "Great! How the hell am I supposed to help people if I've got four freaking elements and a big ass lion trying to stop me?"

"It's called faith!" Rachel screamed from my other side. I whipped around to face her and found myself nearly nose to nose with her. "Get some and get over yourself! We're all in this for our own reasons, but if you don't put your faith in something higher than your own agenda, it's never going to work!"

I opened my mouth to rebuke her, but I realized she was right. Ultimately, I wanted to help Sister Aggie. If I had to contend with a little rain to do that, then so be it. "There! Now *that* was a pep talk. Was that so hard?" I yelled back at her.

The ferocity in Rachel's eyes dimmed, and her jaw went slack. Her eyes fluttered over mine before a tiny smile emerged on her face. I smiled back at her.

"Come in out of the rain," Mr. Eady said, ushering us in with the barrel of his shotgun.

Rachel shook her head in an amused reproof and pressed gently on my back to get me moving. The perils of Mother Nature's fervent warnings slipped to the back of my mind as we entered the house, where Greg awaited us with his demons.

CHAPTER 27

T HE SECOND TIME GREG threw me across the room, I chipped the plaster wall with my head. With my fellow sisters pinned to the ceiling, it was just me against the hermit demon.

It was laughable to assume I could complete an exorcism without direct access to God's power. However, I was surprised at just how inadequate I was at the endeavor. I had been concerned I was dabbling in a powerful form of magic I wouldn't be able to control, but my witchcraft was so ineffective against Greg's demons it was almost useless. Perhaps I was getting ahead of myself.

Greg wasn't taking his exorcism lying down. He marched over to me and grabbed a handful of my exposed hair, and lifted me to my feet. His breath smelled like death ten times over. I gagged and coughed, trying to free my tendrils from his grip. I chanted my prescribed spell again, but he just shoved his fist into my mouth, silencing me and choking me. "Foolish little girl! This is not your battle. You should have stayed in the dark."

Rather than continue with the useless effort of the exorcism, I punched Greg in the face. It wasn't much, but it was enough to get his fist out of my mouth. I kicked him in the knee and he threw me across the room again. I slid down the wall behind his bed right along with his framed picture of footprints in the sand. It was so nice of his mother to keep hanging things back on the wall for us to run into.

I landed on the rigid mattress and rolled over to return to the battle. A fit of coughing held me in place long enough to catch a view of my reflection in the framed glass my flung body had only partially broken.

"Why are you doing this?" my handsome shadow asked through the reflection over my right shoulder. "You don't even know what you are doing."

I turned to face him and saw the room frozen around me. Greg's menacing, clawed-finger attack was now a terrifying statue at the edge of the bed. I climbed off the bed to face my perpetually uninvited guest. "It's practice. I have to save Aggie."

He shook his head and clicked his tongue. "Aggie is gone. I have more demons writhing inside of her than a crack whore. You need to give up this fight and return to me."

"I don't belong to you."

"You are nothing without me." He leaned forward, examining me quizzically. "I respect your clout, Hennie. I really do. In the beginning, I actually enjoyed watching you experiment with this ridiculous undertaking, but it's over."

"This ridiculous undertaking? You mean my life?" I shrugged in confusion.

"Exactly."

"If you want to kill me, then do it. But I'll never surrender to you—not while I'm still breathing."

He chuckled. "I'm not going to kill you, but soon everyone around you will be dead. I'll be all you have left. You do see that, don't you? That I'm the only one you can truly depend on?"

I shook my head, refusing to believe it. "Please, just leave me alone."

He stepped forward to a claustrophobic intimacy. "You don't want that." He grazed his finger beside my face, not quite touching me. A coldness came over me, making me shiver. "You want me back and I want you."

"You can't control me."

"You can't live without me."

"And how could I live *with* you?" I narrowed my eyes at him. "You're the spawn of evil. A traitor to your own. What could possibly draw me to a detestable creature like you?"

His subtle smirk died away, and the cool shiver I had felt before set deeper into my bones. His eyes, that I had once thought contained a sparkle of red, now contained slender slit pupils. I frowned and backed away from him. "Yesss, indeed," he hissed, as if he had developed a sudden lisp. "What could draw you back to such a hideousss beassst?" He stepped past me and put himself into position behind me, nearly touching my back as he spoke close to my ear. "I've given you more than enough warnings, Hennie. I'm not sure what would possess you to defy the spawn of evil, but if you want a war, then you will have it."

He moved away, and by the time I could turn to look at him, he was gone. Everything had returned to normal—the normal of a botched exorcism, that is.

Greg growled as he leaped across the bed and landed on me. He pressed me to the floor with his heavy body. His overly long fingernails pinched into my neck as he gripped it and repeatedly slammed my head into the wood floor.

I saw stars, and I knew I was about to pass out. That brought on a feeling of lightness in my body. When I no longer felt my head hitting the floor, I opened my eyes.

I was levitating. Judging by how Greg was shifting to find balance on my suddenly floating body, I gathered he wasn't in control of this particular magic trick.

We rose to the ceiling, where Rachel and Paula remained pinned. They took advantage of their proximity and reached out to grab his arms. They pried him off my neck and hugged his forearms to their chests with all their strength. Their chants took on a new fervor.

I focused on the words and delved into the same magical energy I used in the hospital. I touched Greg's chest and his heart raced. The demonic voices within him bawled and howled in pain. They wanted to be free, and Greg's meager tortured existence was as close to it as they could get—an eye staring through a keyhole, desperately trying to unlock the door. A door that had long since been shut on them.

Instead of fighting the demons, as the exorcism was designed to do, I reached out to them. My mind merged with them, drawing the evil to me, not unlike the way I had bonded myself to the coven.

"What are you doing?" Rachel yelled at me. "Don't let them into you!"

"I can take them away," I babbled and closed my eyes, feeling their minds absorb into me. With no true body to ground them, that was all they were: angry minds, tortured souls, and autonomous energy.

Energy. Power. Sweet, sweet power.

I drew them into me, one by one, with an astonishing speed and a feeling of gratification I was certain was very, very wrong. Especially since I was essentially killing them. I didn't understand any of it, but I understood that. It felt as second nature to me as drinking a glass of milk. I had no guilt for the act and no empathy for their diminished existence, but when I reached Greg, I stopped.

As I floated beneath the pitiful man, I debated if I should end his life. It would have been a blessing. His existence up to that point had been hell. Even if he was free of demons, I was certain his body was far too damaged to live much longer, anyway.

However, it still wasn't my decision to make. I had already trespassed into God's territory by giving a life. I wasn't about to fill in for the Grim Reaper as well.

I released him, and we drifted down to the floor. The sisters followed right behind me, with Greg draped between them. We touched the ground, and they looked at me fearfully before assisting the confused man back into his bed.

Once he was in position, Paula returned to me. "Are you okay?" she asked. "It felt like you were inviting the demons in."

I nodded to her.

"What, now you're possessed too?" Rachel said from Greg's side.

"No. I'm fine."

"How?" Paula asked.

"I'm not sure. I think I'm immune to demons."

Paula was about to say something, but Mr. and Mrs. Eady rushed into the room, interrupting our conversation. They fawned over the boy before encompassing Rachel in their all-inclusive hug. They waved Paula over to take part.

"You should head out. Your eyes are bleeding," she whispered and motioned to the door before obliging the Eddies.

I moved to leave, but first checked the corners of the room for any more *spiders*. Just in case there was a queue of evil waiting to make a home in Gregory Eady. I found a particularly dark spot that seemed to have no reason for a shadow. As I stared down at it, I saw the darkness shift and churn as if it were a living, liquid entity.

I leaned forward and whispered, "Boo!" The blackness absorbed into the wall and the corner returned to normal. I smiled introspectively and headed out to wait for the Eadys to release my sisters from their engaging gratitude.

CHAPTER 28

"Wipe your face again." Rachel handed another tissue up from the back seat. "I can't believe you don't feel anything."

I laughed and wiped a fresh batch of blood from my eyes. "I feel good, Rachel. Don't tell me you're actually going to start worrying about me now." I glanced at her in the back seat of the van. "I don't know if I can handle this new nice version of you."

"I'm not..." she huffed and shifted back in her seat.

"You are bleeding out of your eyes." Paula volleyed her eyes from the road to me. "It's not natural."

"I know, I know, it's creepy, but let's face it: I'm tapping into some weird stuff. If there weren't any physiological effects, I think I would be more concerned. Didn't Sister Aggie ever have some issues with her gift?"

"Migraines, blackouts, and dizzy spells," Rachel mumbled.

"See?" I raised my hands. "I think a little blood in my tears is justified."

"This isn't good," Paula said.

"I'll be fine," I insisted.

"Not you, look." Paula pointed out the windshield toward the emergency vehicles parked in front of the school.

"Why are the cops here?" Rachel popped forward to stare at the flashing lights outside the convent.

"And an ambulance," I pointed out.

Paula pulled over to the side of the road and we all jumped out. We scrambled through the melee of people and found Meredith standing with Lynn on the grass in front of the building. I reached them and tugged Meredith to face me. Her eyes were red and full of tears.

"What happened?" Paula pushed in front of me and I stepped back to let her question the girls.

"She didn't come to the prayer circle," Meredith whimpered.

"Who didn't?"

"Erin. I went to look for her and found her... hanging there." Meredith broke into sobs. Paula hugged her and patted her back.

"Oh, no." I looked at Rachel and found the same shock in her eyes.

Lynn scooted closer to us and whispered. "It was suicide."

"No." I shook my head. "This is him. That bastard is responsible for this. I don't know how, but—"

"We all know she was suicidal," Rachel pointed out reluctantly.

"And we all know she was tough as nails," I reminded her. "She wouldn't do this. Not now." I saw the paramedics wheeling a gurney out of the building with a black body bag. I ran towards them. One police officer dutifully tried to stop me, but I raised my beaded rosary as if it were a press pass and he let me through.

The paramedics conferred a moment before stepping back to let me perform my last rites. I made a good show of the sign of the cross before unzipping the body bag. There was a shift to stop me, but I pressed the cross of my rosary to her forehead and mumbled an Our Father. I was amazed by how much they permitted me to do under the guise of religious freedom.

I pulled her hand up and kissed it. I noticed the bruising around her neck where the noose had strangled her, but I also saw scratches on her wrists. A mortician would record these injuries as failed attempts at wrist-slashing. Nothing she hadn't tried in the past. I pulled up the sleeve of her robe and found more bruising, this time in the shape of a handprint. This was new and recent.

"Sister, you'll have to let us take her now," one paramedic said. They pushed in and zipped up the bag before I could determine if her fresh cuts were indeed claw marks.

Paula came to my side to watch the stretcher being loaded into the ambulance. "What is it?" she asked.

"She didn't commit suicide. She was attacked." I shook my head and looked back at the convent. "I don't know what to do, Paula. I'm endangering all of you by being here. He is making good on his promise to hurt the people around me."

"You can't give in to him, Hennie," she insisted.

"But this isn't singed arm hair. This is murder."

Paula nodded. "Then we will have to figure out how to defend ourselves."

CHAPTER 29

"NO, AGGIE, DON'T BITE." Ruby flinched, but finally removed the gag from the sister's mouth.

"Insipid little trollops," Sister Aggie growled from her spot at the library table.

Sister Aggie lunged to bite Ruby. She yelped and scampered to the other side of the table with us. "How is she going to help us like this?"

"I've read every book I can, biblical and ceremonial," Paula complained. "The only person we can ask is God, and since she is still our only link to Him, she will need to tell us."

"God is still in there?" I asked.

"Of course," Rachel answered from behind me, where she was leaning on a bookcase. "He wouldn't abandon her now."

"I get that, but she already has so many voices in her head. Wouldn't one more just add to the chaos?"

"With so much influence from demons, how can we trust anything she says?" Ruby asked after she was situated across from Paula.

Paula motioned to me at the head of the table. "Hennie, here is a human lie detector."

"Really?" Ruby turned to me for confirmation.

"Just a little something I've always been good at. I didn't know anyone else knew about that." I glanced at Paula and she gave me a small smile.

"Everyone lies!" Aggie burst into the conversation. One of her wandering hands pushed into her mouth, making her gag. She vomited on the table in front of her.

"Uck," Ruby moaned. "Why do demons have to be disgusting?" She moved to the bookshelf behind us and grabbed a newspaper to lay over the mess until she could clean it up properly. We were all on cleanup duties these days. Caring for Aggie had become a full-time job: bathing, feeding, bathing again.

Once Ruby had returned, Paula shifted to face her former leader. "Sister Aggie, how can we protect ourselves against the demons?"

"Open your legs and mouths." Aggie licked her lips.

"I'm going to assume that's a lie." Paula glanced back at me and I nodded. "How do we defend ourselves against a predator we can't even see or touch?"

"Pray, pray, pray." Aggie chortled. "God's not home!"

"God is everywhere," Ruby rebuked her.

"Then why are you still searching for Him!" Aggie yelled back at her in a gravelly voice.

"I'm not!" Ruby insisted. "I've already found Him."

Paula reached over and pressed her hand over Ruby's. She grimaced and leaned back, unable to respond to the accusation. I didn't bother to mention that Ruby was lying.

"Aggie, I know you are in there," Paula continued her interrogation. She kept her voice low and controlled. "I know you want to get a message to us. Tell us how to protect ourselves."

Sister Aggie paused, and several groaning noises came from deep in her throat. "Cleanse him." The words creaked from her throat, barely loud enough to hear.

"Cleanse him?" Paula looked at me.

"That's her." I sat up straight. "That's Sister Aggie speaking."

"The warrior," Aggie continued as we all leaned in to hear each and every strangled word. "Safeguard... find him."

"Who?" Paula whispered, as if the demons might not hear her if she did. "Who is the warrior?"

Aggie's body lurched back, stricken with a paralyzing seizure. She let out a moaning exhale and her hands grappled at the newspaper in front of her. All at once, she began to laugh and relax. "Nope, nope, nope. Bad, bad girls." She clicked her tongue at us and shook a finger.

"Damn," Ruby whispered.

"Trying to sneak past us." Aggie let out a snorting snarl.

"This is a dead end," Rachel grumbled behind me.

"I don't think so," I said. "Look at how hard she is clenching that newspaper?" I nodded to Aggie's right fist, which was brimming with a scrap of the newspaper Ruby had laid in front of her.

Rachel approached her and tried to rip the paper from her hand, but Aggie bit her reaching hand and started hitting her with her left hand. "Ouch!"

I rushed to her aid, trying to pin Aggie's aggressive arm, but she was abnormally strong, and I was only offering her more fingers to bite. Paula joined the struggle, but Aggie stuffed the page in her mouth and swallowed it instead of letting us get the upper hand.

"Son of a..." I bit back my curse, despite it being extremely applicable to the situation.

"Can't we just look at this one?" Ruby asked. She had moved to the shelf she had taken the original from. "It's the same day."

"Yes." Paula chuckled at her. "That should do it." She took the paper from Ruby and laid it across the table to examine the front page. "It has to be this Pratchett guy. That's his picture." She shifted the paper around so I could read it from my side of the table.

I examined the large photo. The man was broad-shouldered, with ample biceps, and surprisingly no tattoos. He might have been mistaken for the boy next door at one time—tight-cropped ash-blond hair, denim blue eyes, and a smile to die for. Unfortunately, people *had* died for that smile.

"You've got to be kidding me," I said. "This guy can't be our protector."

"Why not?"

"Don't you guys remember who this is? Pratchett the Hatchet." I air-quoted the moniker. "He's a serial-murdering rapist."

"That's why she said we have to cleanse him," Ruby said.

"I think this guy is beyond rehabilitation," I said.

"He is probably a little more hardened than our usual clientele," Paula said. "But we've done it in the past for prisoners who wanted to reform."

"Done what exactly?" I asked.

"All his animalistic tendencies will be cleansed, balanced. We will reconnect him with his moral compass."

"He's a psychopath. He doesn't have a moral compass." I looked around to see if everyone was seriously considering bringing a serial killer into our group under the guise of *protection*. "Even if this cleanse is possible, he's still a man. How is he going to fight demons?" I looked at each of their puzzled faces, frustrated that I had more questions than they had answers.

"Aggie wouldn't steer us wrong," Paula said simply.

"Whatever." I huffed and shook my head. "It doesn't matter, anyway. We still can't use him."

"And why is that?" Rachel crossed her arms.

I shoved the newspaper back around toward her so she could read it. "Because he's going to be executed... tomorrow."

CHAPTER 30

"**W**HAT THE HELL ARE we doing?" I barked beside Meredith as we walked down the prison hall behind our escorting guard. The guard glanced back at me and I gave him a warm smile that was meant to instill the love of God in his heart. The minute he turned back around, I aimed my miffed grimace at Meredith. "This is insane!" I hissed at her.

"It isn't insane, just very, very risky," she said, mollifying me.

The inmates along the row took notice of us, hooting and hollering about wanting to take our virginity. A few others yelled defensively about having respect, but I doubted they would do as much if they were alone with us.

"I was on board for flying nuns," I whispered. "But teleporting nuns is a little too far."

"Shame, shame, I'm telling Paula that you're doubting the power of our supreme and almighty God."

"Oh, I don't doubt Him. After what I've seen lately, I am all aboard the awesome God train. But we aren't getting on His choo-choo train. We are relying on my hackneyed traveling medicine show."

Meredith smiled at me. "You don't trust yourself much, do you?"

"No, and neither should you. This brain doesn't exactly come with an instruction manual. I've never done anything like this before."

"Which means you have no idea for certain whether you can or can't. Worrying about it isn't going to change the outcome. Just let it happen."

I opened my mouth to respond, but I couldn't argue with her Zen logic. Unfortunately, it didn't take the knot out of my stomach or stop the thumping of my heart. We were about to help the most hated man in ten counties break out of jail via a very complex transference spell. If I failed, we would lose the opportunity to defend ourselves against the incorporeal threat in our midst. If I succeeded, we would have a serial murderer inside the walls of the convent.

"Stay close," the guard advised us as we entered the next section. "Don't go near the doors. Don't talk to them. Don't even look at them."

We stepped through the section break and followed his instructions to a T, heads down, moving fast, and staying close to him. When we reached the tail end of the hall, he pointed to the door. "This is him. Do your blessing."

"We will require contact with his body," Meredith said.

"Are you f— kidding?" The guard grimaced at her.

"It's so hard to explain to a civilian." Meredith touched the guard's shoulder. "The contact between two human beings is so important." She moved closer to him. "It's the only way we can truly see one another as equals. Flesh to flesh." She dragged her hand down his arm, letting it touch the bare skin of his forearm. "Do you see what I mean?" She gazed at him, batting the eyelashes of her beautiful gray eyes—a love spell in their own right.

He cleared his throat. "I'll have to handcuff him. The window is small, but his hands are lethal." He moved to the door and banged on it. "Hands out, Pratchett!" A pair of meaty hands pushed through the bars of the window, and the guard handcuffed them to it. "There you go, ladies—err, sisters."

"Thank you." Meredith leaned over and kissed his lips. When the slightly long kiss ended, the man stared at her in shock and guilty attentiveness. "Go with God, my son. Let us bless this wretched beast in private. We will call when we're ready."

"But... I..."

"Trust in God." She touched his face. "He will protect us."

The guard backed away, dumbfounded by Meredith's semi-flirtatious religious coaxing. "I'll just be through those doors. Yell if you need me." When he was through to the next section, Meredith snorted and turned back to me.

"I never get tired of that. I swear, as long as you have a habit on, you could get even the most loyal husband to drop his pants. It's as if God is commanding them to cheat. They don't know what to do with you."

"I'd know what to do with you." A deep bass voice spoke from within the cell ahead of us.

Meredith peeked in at Pratchett. "No, you wouldn't. You only know how to get what you want from a woman, never mind what she wants.

"I've never had any complaints after I was done."

"Only because you killed them all," I blurted out, drawing his creepy blue eyes over to me.

"I'd be happy to prove you wrong," he said with a dulcet tone that reminded me how handsome he was... and dangerous.

"Why are we even doing this?" I asked Meredith. "He's a sadistic bastard. He rapes and murders women for fun."

"It's not for fun," Pratchett interjected. "It's because I was born to do it."

"Great, a man *destined* to be a serial killer. That's so much better than the regular kind," I sniped.

Meredith touched my shoulder. "Believe me, I agree with you. I would love nothing more than to watch this guy fry like a fucking fishcake."

"What church are you from?" Pratchett's face scrunched with confusion.

"But I trust in Aggie," Meredith continued. "And I trust you. We can break this piece of shit."

"Orthodox?" Pratchett asked.

"But first... we have to save him," Meredith said.

Pratchett chuckled from behind the bars. "God can't save me now, sisters. The noose is already tightening around my neck. The devil is already in the shadows."

"You have no idea how right you are," I grumbled.

He looked back at me, scanning the minimal features he could see outside of my habit. "I've done a lot of bad things, it's true, but I bet you can't guess what my favorite part was."

Meredith scoffed. "Slitting your victims' throats," she said as she laid out a circle of stick crosses behind us.

"No." Pratchett glared at her even though she wasn't looking at him.

"The orgasm at the end of the rape?" I suggested, already suspecting his sadistic response.

His lips curved up into a devastating smile that could fund a campaign all on its own. "I never raped the women," he said with smooth conviction.

The sarcastic smirk dropped from my lips as I heard the truth in his words.

"Yeah right." Meredith pulled another handful of little stick crosses from her pocket and started tossing them through the barred window. "And I'm still a virgin," she mocked his claim. Pratchett's brow dipped at her and then he examined the odd little additions to his cell. Despite his assurance that God could not save him, he shifted to allow her to drop them in. "You can't lie to Hennie," Meredith boasted on my behalf. "She can sense deception."

"Is that so?" Pratchett asked, his eyes narrowing with curiosity. "Hennie," he added, as if he was letting me know he knew my name.

"What was your favorite part?" I asked, not wanting to admit to Meredith that his title of rapist may have been unwarranted. Then again, interpretation was everything in a lie.

"My favorite part was how easily I could convince them to take me back to their homes." He leaned forward. "I know exactly what a woman wants to hear. Even if she doesn't know it herself."

"And what do I want to hear from you?" I asked.

"You want to know why I did it. You want me to tell you that there is some redeeming quality inside of me, so you know you aren't wasting your time."

"Is there?"

Pratchett simpered at me, but didn't answer.

"Okay, let's do this," Meredith said.

"Do what?" Pratchett asked.

"We're going to save your life," Meredith answered.

His brow dipped low. "Don't you mean save my soul?"

"Eventually—maybe." Meredith shrugged. "But first we need to keep you out of the electric chair."

"Why would you do that?" he asked.

"Because we need you." Meredith flicked holy water at him and he flinched. I expected it to burn him like acid, but alas, he wasn't a demon, just a really bad man.

"This is new," he said, licking the holy water from his lips. "I hope you ladies have something more helpful than those beautiful breasts stashed under those robes, because this is a high security prison. There aren't enough Hail Marys to get you past armed guards."

"As far as you are concerned, Pratchett"—Meredith squeezed her breasts—"these knockers are your saviors."

He glanced at me. "You aren't really a nun, are you?"

"Depends on your definition," Meredith said. "I am an instrument of the Lord."

"And what about her?" Pratchett pointed his pinky at me.

Meredith glanced at me and smirked. "She's the hammer."

Pratchett looked me over again, as if he had missed this hidden strength on his initial evaluation. I ignored him and reached for Meredith. She took my hand and squeezed it. I looked at Pratchett and raised my hand out to him. He tipped his head to one side and smirked as he reached out for me.

I waited for him to grab me with a wrenching strength. Perhaps even try to yank me toward the cell, but instead his fingers dragged lightly along my wrist, caressing the skin. It should have disgusted me and sent shivers down my spine the same way that my shadow did, but it didn't.

I tried to tell myself it was only because Pratchett was a beautiful man, and I wasn't fully allowing myself to accept the monster he truly was. I told myself it was a normal bodily reaction to the pressure of a strange hand, but as his fingers slid into place, cupping my palm in a handshake embrace, I wondered if it was more.

I stared at him, and he stared back. I waited for him to smirk at me, or do something despicable with his tongue, but he didn't. He glanced down at the connection between our hands and then back to me, as if he were feeling the same thing I was.

Meredith began the spell, and after a moment to collect myself and refocus my thoughts, I joined in.

Even across the span of two counties, I could feel the link between me and my fellow sisters. They were doing the same spell at the convent, backing up my power on the other end and waiting for our arrival.

"What are you doing?" Pratchett started to release my hand, but I squeezed it tighter. He stopped pulling and tightened his grip on me as well.

I pushed in deep, trying to tap into the burst of energy I had enjoyed so much the last time. It took a moment, but I felt something tug through my connection with Pratchett. My eyes darted over to look at him. A darkness surrounded him. Not the shadows of demons, but something different. Something dark from within.

It called to me, demanding for me to destroy it. I reached out to it and my mind almost instantly connected to his. Memories of his past leaked through the link, but I ignored them and pushed deeper toward the source of his strange shadowy outline. I reached it and latched onto it, trying to draw it in. The darkness bent toward me, but it wouldn't release itself to me as the demons in Greg's mind did.

"What the hell is this?" Pratchett winced as I ripped at the aberration. Something horrible and awful was living in him, but it wasn't a demon. He tried to pull his hand away to break the connection, but even I couldn't let go. "Stop!" he yelled, but I ignored him and tugged again. "Please!" he begged. The darkness wouldn't budge. I suddenly realized that the abnormality wasn't a stain I could simply wipe away. It was a part of him. The stain I was trying so desperately to extract was his soul.

Meredith squeezed my hand as she chanted. I looked at her and she raised her brow. I nodded, turning my attention from Pratchett, who slumped against the bars, recovering from my procedure. I refocused my thoughts on the transfer.

After a moment, I felt the spell take hold, guiding the energy I had accessed. The power poured through me, just as invigorating as the first time. I saw the double vision of a ring of women around us, and I knew we were right on target.

Pratchett must have seen the same vision, because he tried to pull away again. Luckily, his handcuffed wrists were keeping him within reach. I gripped him tighter, pinching my nails deep into his skin. I could barely see him through the double world, but I knew he wasn't happy about this strange new reality of witchcrafty nuns.

The euphoria of the final movement challenged my balance. I faltered, but Meredith kept me up with her firm grip on my hand. The prison finished fading around us and we were inside of the convent basement. My fellow sisters surrounded us, their voices tapering off as they saw us solidify before them.

I looked at Pratchett, standing in front of me. He looked thinner than his photo in the paper. The prison diet had thinned out his cheeks and shoulders. He still looked like the boy next door, but his face was a little overgrown. There were dark circles under his eyes, as if he hadn't slept for a few days. No surprise being on death row.

Much to my disappointment, the transfer has not included Prachett's most distinguishing trait—the all-too-important locked door that had separated us in the prison. The handcuffs were our only protection now, but I doubted that would be enough to keep him on his best behavior.

He surveyed his new surroundings, and the strange unfamiliar faces circling him, quietly chanting. His gaze finally landed back on me. "What the fuck did you just do?"

"You are in Mount Grace's convent." Paula stepped up from behind me and pressed me to one side so she could face the man. I wasn't sure how she was managing to do it so fearlessly, but I was more than happy to let her take a front-row seat to this maniac. "Your life has been spared, so you can be cleansed and become a servant of this coven."

"A servant?" Pratchett perked his brow at her.

"You are the destroyer!" Katherine blurted out from the sidelines as if she were announcing his arrival in royal fashion. "And the protector!"

Everyone looked over at her, but as was common in these moments, no one gave it more than a moment's pause. Except Pratchett, who was frowning at the odd woman.

"Will you cooperate with us?" Paula asked him.

Pratchett looked back at her, then to me. "That was a pretty nifty trick, Hennie. I don't think it was the right choice, though."

"And why is that?" Paula shifted to further block me and get his attention back to her.

He looked at her and smiled, giving her the same once-over as he had Meredith and me. "Because I think it made your little chickity sick."

Paula looked back at me and her eyes widened.

I slumped my shoulders and shook my head. "What, more blood?" I touched my eyes, but my fingers came back clean. I felt something dribble on my lips, like I had a runny nose. I touched my nostrils and found blood. "Oh, crap." I leaned forward and blood drizzled onto the floor beneath me. Meredith pulled off her veil and graciously allowed me to bleed all over it.

"Are you okay?" Paula asked.

"I think so," I said through my pinched nose.

"I'll let you ladies take this from here. Hennie, thank you for the ride. Sisters." Pratchett gave a slight bow before stepping around Paula to make his exit. When he reached the edge of the circle, he raised his knee to step over the chalk-drawn circle. His leg stopped before he could get it over the line. He looked around, trying to propel his body forward, but nothing, not even brute strength, was getting through our circle.

"You aren't going anywhere, Mr. Pratchett." Paula moved to face him again.

He chuckled and lowered his leg away from the impassable line. "I don't really think you have a choice about it."

"You aren't leaving this circle until you agree to be cleansed," Paula said.

"Wait, why does he have to agree?" I asked, still pinching off my faucet nose. "Let's just do it."

"No." Paula glanced back at me. "We need his permission."

"Are you kidding me?" I complained. "He kills women for kicks. Why would he agree to help us?"

Pratchett leveled a glare at me. "I'm not going to play this game much longer, ladies. As you might imagine, the wick to my temper is pretty short. Release me from this Ouija board party or I will start getting unfriendly."

"This isn't a physical barrier, Mr. Pratchett." Paula tipped her chin up. "You can't break it."

"Oh, I suspected as much, but I can break you." Pratchett threw a fast punch at Paula and she dropped to the floor, adding her blood to my own.

"Paula!" Meredith scrambled to help her, but Pratchett kicked her in the face. She fell back against me, knocking me to the floor along with her.

"Break the circle!" Pratchett yelled as he leaned down over Paula. I could see the girl's eyes flitting between all of us, searching for the right answer, even as they continued to chant. Pratchett yanked Paula's veil off and pulled her head up by her bobbed coffee locks. "You better release me, or I will kill her."

"Don't break the circle! No matter what he does to me!" Paula called to the other sisters.

Pratchett clicked his tongue and shook his head. "Not a good idea, Sister. I'm not going to go easy on you just because you're a nun. In fact..." He shoved her over to her back and kneeled down beside her. "I might give it to you a little harder because of it." He punched her again in the face and then again in the stomach.

Paula coughed and sputtered as she curled into a ball. Pratchett stood up again and kicked her in the stomach.

"You son of a bitch!" Meredith stood and dove at him. She jumped on his back and put him in a headlock, but it didn't take him long to throw her off again.

He eyed me on the floor next. I was cowering from the fight. I should have been jumping up like Meredith, but it seemed hopeless. We had made a mistake. He wasn't going to be our champion. He was going to be our doom.

He stepped toward me, and I stared at him fearfully.

"Hey, prick!" Meredith yelled, ready for another round. "You want a fight or not?"

Pratchett ground his teeth and went after her. She ducked his first two punches, but soon enough, he had her wrapped up in his handcuff chain. "Release me, you witchy bitches."

I crawled to Paula and checked on her. She was alive, but out cold. I looked around at the frightened faces. I knew Pratchett would have to kill one of us to get the girls to break the circle, but that seemed like a senseless sacrifice when we could just let him go.

I looked at the chalk line that allowed the circle to be larger than the reach of hands. I searched through Paula's pockets and found the chalk she had used to draw it. I shuffled around her, drawing a circle around her and linking it to the outer circle. The girls nodded profusely, overjoyed with my protection plan.

Unfortunately, I didn't think Pratchett would take a time out so I could help Meredith.

"Hey, you rapist asshole!" I yelled at him.

He turned back to me and glared at my stubborn statuesque stance in the middle of the circle.

"You ready for me now, Hennie?"

"Are you ready to be cleansed?"

"Cleansed of sin? Really?"

"No, cleansed of *her*."

Pratchett slowly let Meredith drop out of his stranglehold. He stared across the circle at me, curious and suspicious. "Who?"

"Tell me something, Pratchett. Did you enjoy having sex with her?" I asked.

His eyes narrowed, and he tipped his head forward, narrowing his vision on me. I was skirting into territory I shouldn't, but there was no sense in letting my knowledge of his past go to waste.

I could see Meredith clumsily drawing herself into the circle with a piece of chalk the girls had tossed in to her. I should have ended my distraction and just drawn myself an escape route as well, but I knew Pratchett wouldn't submit to a cleanse unless he had a very good reason to.

"Answer me!" I yelled as forcefully as I could. "Did you enjoy having sex with your mother?"

The shock was there and gone, replaced by cold, murderous hatred. "How the fuck do you know about that?"

"Did you?" I taunted him.

I could see him shaking. The anger was boiling up inside of him. I was playing with emotions tangled up in childhood sexual trauma, and if I wasn't careful, I was going to lose.

"No," he seethed.

I smiled, giving him a broad, cocky smile. "And that's a lie."

Pratchett ran at me like a bull. I had gone too far and had nowhere to run. I cringed and waited for the punishing impact, but it didn't come. His body stopped and levitated as if in an invisible Jell-O mold over the floor.

I hadn't noticed the subtle change in the chant. The same chant that had protected Aggie from my death blow.

I watched Pratchett struggle against the magical pause button. I breathed a sigh of relief and circled around him. He cussed and frothed, blaming me for every injustice in his life and threatening to kill me.

At the completion of my slow exploration, I reached out and touched his face. There was nothing on his part to compel my compassion. Much like petting a snapping turtle, it was entirely for my benefit.

"We can make it better. Take away the pain. Make the anger subside." Pratchett finally stopped his ballistic rant and looked at me. "We can get her out of your head." I caressed his cheek again, but this time, he pulled away.

"How do you know about her?"

"Do you want to be free, Dane?" He stared at me. As startling as everything he had witnessed was, I seemed to be the greatest mystery to him. "Do you want to be cleansed?"

His eyes dimmed, and he swallowed hard. "Yes."

CHAPTER 31

"**O**PEN THE FUCKING DOOR." Dane slammed his hands against the cage that usually protected the convent's supply of toilet paper from wandering students. Now it was protecting us from the piece of shit trapped inside.

It was a miracle we had gotten him in it in the first place. After two days, though, the fog of magical transportation, levitation, and promises of assuagement had worn off. Now we were just a bunch of bitches holding him hostage in a chain link cage. Adding to us not having the key to his handcuffs, and we had the makings of a very cranky serial killer.

"I am going to cut out your lying tongue! And that's not a metaphor!" Dane raged, pressing his face into the fencing.

"Does that mean you don't want breakfast?" I asked, trying not to show my fear on the surface.

Dane looked down at the plate of eggs I had brought him. He frowned at it and pushed away from the door. He sat down on the bed we had brought down to make the cage a proper prison.

"Just take it." I shoved the plate into the makeshift food slot. While designed for mail, the small opening accommodated my hand and a plate. "After two years of prison food, I know you'll enjoy a home-cooked meal." He didn't move to take the food. Much like he hadn't eaten the last four meals we had brought him, most of which ended up on the basement floor. I sighed and blew on the plate, wafting the smell over to him. "I know you're hungry. Starving yourself isn't going to change the situation."

He turned his head to point his glare at me. "You said you would make it all go away."

"We will," I said.

"The lethal injection would have made it all go away."

"Did you really want to die?" I asked.

He looked away. "Can you really tell when I'm speaking the truth?"

"Yes."

"What if I don't know what the truth is?"

I shrugged. "Not every lie is all lies. Not every truth is completely true."

"So you know I didn't *really* enjoy my mother's abuse?"

I frowned and nodded. "Yes, I know. It doesn't count if it's forced. I'm sorry, I said otherwise. I just got caught up in the moment."

He shifted to reach for the plate of eggs. He bypassed the meal and grabbed my wrist. I yelped as he yanked my forearm farther through the narrow mail slot. My elbow got jammed up, and I dropped the eggs to the floor. I screamed for help, kicking myself for dropping my guard.

"That's why I didn't rape them," he said casually between my screams.

His admission silenced my shrieks, and I looked at him. He moved forward, pushing himself against my hand. I glanced down at the intimate proximity to his crotch. It made no sense for him to proposition me, since it was putting him in a far more vulnerable position than me.

"I wanted them to enjoy it for real," he said. "The police called it rape because I was a murdering bastard. They never had any proof, they just wanted to add to the charges. Every woman I have ever been with has wanted me." He pushed my hand into his crotch. "Aren't you curious to find out what they found so enjoyable?"

I frowned, feeling him harden against my fingertips.

"Why did you kill them?" I asked in a whisper.

"I wasn't killing them. I was killing her. I enjoyed it so much the first time, I wanted to do it again. And again."

That was the truth.

I knew from the brief glimpse into his mind that he was reliving the murder of his wretched mother over and over again, because it was the only way to satisfy the intense anger he felt for her. His feelings for her were so twisted he couldn't even let her stay dead. He had to keep digging up the horrid memories of his abuse and wallow in them. When it was too much to stand, he would kill again. Although consensual, the sex was actually a way for him to emotionally flagellate himself with the guilt of his incestuous pleasures.

Dane Pratchett was not born to be a murderer. He was just a little boy, trapped inside of a nightmare he couldn't and wouldn't wake up from.

He released my hand, sliding his fingers up my wrist and over the soft underside of my forearm. I stared at him and he at me, as he tickled the skin with his talented, seductive touch. I frowned and pulled my hand out of the mail slot. He let me withdraw and walk away without any further aggression, much as I suspected he would. After all, he wasn't a rapist—just a murdering bastard.

CHAPTER 32

DANE STARED AT THE circle of women around him. His predacious stare was enough to unnerve all of us—except Meredith and Paula. They both bravely stepped into the circle, facing him with the bruised faces he had caused. They marched right up to him and began disrobing him.

He smiled and watched them tug at the sleeves of his jumpsuit to get them over his jumbo-sized hands. He didn't seem remotely concerned about undressing before an audience.

"We should have left the cuffs on," I murmured to Rachel. I had taken to huddling next to her, like a scared child. Despite her endless attitude, she projected a bravado that comforted my chickenshit side. I was still reeling from my previous encounter with Dane and I fully intended to hide behind the nearest black robe if he came after me.

"He needs to enter the ritual of his own free will or it won't work," she said, almost bored.

"Damn that nuisance free will." I cleared my throat after the girls tugged down the bottom half of Dane's jumpsuit, revealing his commando preference. He smiled all the more, no doubt perfectly comfortable putting his fine physique on display for a room full of women. Not that he had one square inch that could elicit any objection from me. "Why does he have to be naked?" I frowned.

Rachel glanced at me. "Nudity, much like in your ritual, is a symbol of surrender. In this case, it's also a catalyst for his rebirth. He will awaken cleansed, like a newborn babe. Just as God intended him to be.

"What if God intended him to be this way?"

"God doesn't create murderers. That is a free will choice."

I sucked in a breath between my teeth and looked at her. "I'm not sure I entirely agree with that. I think the pain one is subjected to in life has a lot to do with it."

Rachel turned to me, almost glaring at me. "That is where one free will choice compromises another. Just because someone hurts you doesn't mean you have the right to hurt someone else."

"I agree," I said, matching her tone of condescension. "But it doesn't follow that one doesn't have a right to seek retribution against the one who hurts them."

"That depends on if the retribution is designed to teach a lesson or just outright return the pain, because I assure you there is a difference."

I shivered, remembering the vision of Rachel's father burning alive, his blackened skin cracked and bleeding. I shook away the image and stared at Rachel. Her glare was gone. She was questioning my sudden shift in mood. I nodded at her. "Yes, there is a difference. I see your point." A tiny smirk played over her lips. It was probably only the second time I had seen her smile at me during our acquaintance. I couldn't help but smile back at her, but her demeanor quickly turned sub-thermal, and she looked away.

For the first time since I had met her, I actually felt wounded by the dismissal. We were obviously both combative personalities, and strongly opinionated. I doubted we could ever have a conversation without a debate of some kind. For once, though, we were in agreement. We were having a legitimately friendly accord, and she retracted from it.

Did she truly not like me?

I looked away from her, trying not to focus on the sting of rejection that reminded me so much of high school.

"What kind of ritual did you have planned, ladies?" Dane reached out and smacked Meredith's butt as she moved away from him. She turned back, ready to barrel into the man.

"Meredith!" Paula scolded her, and she reluctantly turned around again.

Dane laughed. "Down, girl. Good dog." He barked at her and panted. Meredith's snarl twitched as she twisted back to face him. Dane smirked and leaned his head down to gaze at her from under his brow. "I know you want it, Sister. That sweet ass has been waiting a long time for a pounding. How long has it been since your last taste of heaven?"

Meredith reached into the pocket of her robe. She pulled out a switchblade and flipped it open. The room shifted incrementally, as if we were all preparing to jump up and stop the potential violence.

"Meredith." Paula shifted to her and touched her arm.

"I vote we make this a blood ritual." I couldn't see Meredith's face, but I could hear the grit in her voice.

"Blood ritual!" Katherine barked from the sidelines. "Shed the blood, drain the sins!" she continued, though no one was paying attention to her.

"We don't do blood rituals," Ruby interjected.

"It won't be necessary." Paula pressed on Meredith's hand.

"Blood ritual?" I turned to Rachel.

She nodded, not taking her eyes off the scene. "Pain is another symbol of surrender. It accelerates the cleansing. We rarely get into anything resembling blood sacrifices."

"Too barbaric?"

"Too messy." Rachel scrunched up her nose.

"Are we going to do this or not? I'm getting cold." Dane grabbed his member and shook it. "Don't want to misrepresent myself."

"Meredith." Paula pressed on her arm, urging her to put the blade away.

"Will it increase the potency of the ritual?" I asked loud enough for everyone to hear.

Paula looked back at me and frowned. "Yes, why?"

"Maybe you should let her do it."

Meredith glanced back at me, but she didn't take her eyes off Dane too long.

"Why?" Paula asked.

I glanced at the inquisitive faces around me. I didn't want to admit the truth. At that point, everyone was thinking of my skills as a power source. Just plug in and point it with a spell. However, the pleasure I received from using it was kind of freaking me out. If I could do anything to speed up the process and keep myself from becoming a magic junkie, I was all for it.

"You said you've never cleansed anyone as messed up as him. Maybe we should get all the help we can."

Paula looked at the other girls. She got a few nods until she reached Ruby. They looked at each other a moment before Paula turned back to Meredith. "Okay, we'll do a blood ritual." Meredith stepped forward, but Paula pressed her back. "*I* will do the marks." Meredith frowned at her, but placed the switchblade in Paula's extended hand.

Meredith moved around behind Dane. He tracked her movement, keeping her on his fringe until Paula approached him. He eyed the blade in her hand before looking up at her face.

"This will sting a little. I would advise not moving." Dane repositioned, widening his stance and puffing up his chest, as if the manly militant position would lessen the pain. Paula pressed the blade against his chest, drawing blood to the surface. He clenched his teeth and watched her etch a bloody cross over his heart.

Paula lowered the blade and finished drawing a pentagon over the cross using the blood. She moved away, but Dane grabbed her wrist. Meredith jumped forward and grabbed his arm, but it wasn't enough to release his firm grip. "This better work," he said to Paula. "I don't like being used."

Paula nodded. "Trust in God."

"I am not trusting in God!" His volume stilled the room. After a moment to contain his rage, he spoke again. "I am trusting in you and your flock. Don't disappoint me." He released her and yanked his arm away from Meredith. They both moved away and joined the circle.

We began the chant, and I immediately felt my power percolate to the surface. It was getting stronger, as was the pleasure I got from it. I lost track of the chant, and my eyes rolled back into my head.

I felt a pair of hands grip my shoulders and a face pressed into mine, touching my cheek to his. "You can't tell me you aren't enjoying this," my shadow murmured into my ear. I knew it was in my mind. A conversation inside of a wakeful dream, but with real consequences. I leaned into his neck, despite my usual distaste for him. It was difficult to hate anyone while I was enjoying myself this much. "I can feel it coursing through you." His lips touched my ear, tracing the ridges before he drew my earlobe in for a gentle, playful bite. "As much as I want to see you wallow in this, you need to stop."

"Why?" I asked.

"You aren't designed for this type of magic. You're going to hurt yourself."

"I have to fix him."

"You can't. He was designed to be broken. He's a puppet, just like your precious Aggie. God's little marionettes. Dancing and singing, just for him."

I opened my eyes and looked at Dane in the center of the circle. He had dropped to his knees, writhing under the intensity of the ritual. It was supposed to be draining his aggression and relieving his pain, but it wasn't working. It was hurting him more than helping him.

"You can only break him further."

I knew my shadow was telling me the truth, but I couldn't change the ceremony now. I certainly wouldn't stop it just because the devil on my shoulder was telling me to.

"You're going to get hurt, Hennie."

I turned and looked at him. "What does it matter to you?"

His brow dipped and his eyes flickered over my face. "Your pain is my pain. Don't you see that yet? I only want you back, safe and sound. Is that really so wrong? Am I selfish to want what belongs to me?"

"I don't belong to you." I spoke the words, but it was getting harder to deny his claim. Every time he touched me, I wanted to sink into his arms, feel him, breathe him.

"Yes, you do, and the longer you tread in these deep waters, the harder it will be to stay afloat. When you finally start to drown, I will be the only one who can rescue you. No matter how hard you try, you can't survive in the light, Hennie."

Dane screamed and slammed his head into the hardwood floor beneath him. He did it again and again, as if he could remove the voices in his head. His conscience was in overdrive, and without being able to repair the damage his mother did, he would be driven insane by his guilt.

When Dane's forehead was bloody from his punishment, he lifted himself on all fours, panting and gritting his teeth. He looked up at us. His eyes bore into all of us, declaring without words that we had failed him.

His eyes roamed to me and his snarl diminished. Through slit lids, he focused on me—but not me. Something just over my shoulder.

He bared his teeth again, and I felt my shadow shift away from me. I looked, but he was gone. I turned back to Dane and found him watching me. Evaluating me with new eyes. And I did the same to him.

CHAPTER 33

"**Y**OU LIED!" DANE THREW another desk across the room, disrupting the perfectly piled junk in the other corner of the room. Paula barely had enough time to dive out of the way before it crushed her skull. "You said the pain would be gone!" Dane screamed. "I can still hear her voice!"

Meredith jumped in front of Paula, shielding her from the wrath of his words. "We did the ritual right! Maybe you're too fucked up to be helped!"

"Maybe you're right." Dane approached her and grabbed her chin, squeezing her cheeks tight. We all took a preemptive step forward, but no one wanted to be the first to combat the psychopath. "Maybe I should go back to what I'm good at."

"Which part?" Meredith slurred through his grip. "The raping or the killing?"

"Let her go!" Ruby's usually tempered voice screamed.

I turned to look at her, as did everyone. A successive gasp circled the room as we saw Ruby's trembling hands on the hilt of a revolver. I wasn't sure where she had gotten it, but by the looks on the surrounding faces, it was as much a shock to them as me.

"You don't touch her!" Ruby yelled, even as tears dribbled down her cheeks.

"Ruby?" Paula stood slowly and put her hands up as she approached her. "That's not how we do things."

"He's hurting her! He hurt you!" Ruby clenched her teeth, not taking her eyes off Dane.

"We aren't killers, Ruby," Paula beseeched her.

"I am," she whispered. "And so is he."

Dane released Meredith, giving her a shove to keep her out of his way. He shifted closer to Ruby. "Do it," he goaded her.

Paula glanced back at him and shifted to block her aim. "No, Ruby," she pleaded. "This isn't what Sister Aggie wanted."

"Don't listen to her, Ruby! I'm a murderer! I'm a rapist!" Dane came forward again and shoved Paula out of the way. She landed at my feet and I ducked down to hold her when she tried to get up again.

"Hennie, let me go." Paula sloughed me off.

"Wait," I whispered and grabbed her again. She glanced back at me, but my gaze remained fixed on Dane and Ruby.

"I killed them all." Dane took another incremental step and Ruby took a step back rather than fire. "I will kill you too! I will rip out your throat!" Meredith jumped on Dane's back, trying to strangle him, but he flipped her off with ease. He slammed her against the floor, leaving her out of breath.

Paula shifted to join the fight, but I tightened my grip on her. "He's lying," I whispered to still her.

"Kill me!" Dane roared. Ruby jumped at his volume, but she didn't fire. "Shoot me, you pathetic little bitch! Kill me!" He took one last step, but he still hadn't attacked her. "Please." I could barely hear the whisper, but it was enough to still the room.

Ruby stared at Dane. The shake in her hand was gone. The snarl on her face looked more piteous. She slowly lowered the weapon to her hip.

Dane growled and came at her. Paula shoved me away to intercept him, but she was too far away.

Dane reached Ruby and ripped the gun from her hand. She cringed away from him as he raised it. The muzzle passed her by as he turned it back toward his own head. He pinched the trigger.

"No!" I screamed, and raised my hands as if I could will the bullet to stop.

Time and space around me slowed to a near stop. I could see what I was doing, and the power that allowed it. Waves emanated from my hands, ballooning out, the same way the bullet warped the air as it penetrated the sound barrier.

My tidal wave of energy flowed forward, driven by an invisible force. It collided with the bullet and shattered it. The tiny pieces, no bigger than grains of sand, pelleted Dane's face.

Screams followed the sound of the gunshot. Dane yelled and tumbled back from the stinging sensation of a thousand tiny but benign bullet fragments. Paula arrived and yanked the gun from his hand. Rachel joined in and punched him in the face while Meredith pinned his arms back to get the handcuffs back on.

Everyone slowly took on a befuddled expression as the events leading to Dane's miraculous survival registered. All eyes eventually turned to me. They stared at me, taking in my appearance.

The panting and wheezing I thought Dane was responsible for was actually coming from me. I could feel the blood dripping from my nose and eyes already. I touched my face and drew back a hand full of blood.

Before I could question it, I keeled forward and retched a puddle of blood on the hardwood floor. Somewhere between that, and the intense pain in my forehead, I blacked out.

CHAPTER 34

D ane slammed his head against the bars, holding the chain link. Repeatedly, he bloodied his forehead, making his already dappled and bruised face look worse.

"He won't stop," Ruby shouted over the noise of his penance. I grimaced at the sight, but I still wasn't sure why she had brought me down to see him. What could I do that the ritual could not? "I don't think we should have done a blood ritual," she mentioned more quietly.

"It wasn't the ritual, Ruby. Something's wrong with him. Something that God couldn't fix."

"God can fix anything. You just have to give Him time."

I didn't want to get into the semantics of free will, so I nodded. "Maybe He wanted something different from what we expected."

Ruby nodded in agreement and looked in at Dane. He was done trying to yell and scream at us. He wouldn't even talk to us. His only interest was in fighting himself and the demons with beating hearts.

"Can you help him?" Ruby asked.

I glanced at her. "Me?"

"I know Paula said you shouldn't do any more magic until she figures out what it is doing to you, but... maybe you could knock him out for a while."

I grimaced. When did I become the resident magician?

Oh, right, when my mentor got hijacked by a dozen plus demons, thereby clogging everyone's access to power.

I took a breath and sighed. "Okay, open the door."

"What if he tries to hurt you?"

I looked in at Dane. He was about two more hits away from being on the floor, but he was too dizzy to find the poles. He was just going in circles. "I'm going to put my money on not, but if you wouldn't mind hanging around with that taser..." I motioned to the device in her hand. It was the only concession Paula would make since she had taken Ruby's contraband weapon away.

Ruby unlocked the door and stepped inside the cage. I touched Dane's arm, and he whipped around to face me. He grabbed me by the arms and shook me. "Where is he?" he asked, frantic.

"Where is who?" I glanced back at Ruby. She was already opening the door again, but I waved her off.

Dane stared at me. "Who are you?"

I shook my head. "Hennie," I answered. "Did you forget?"

Dane pulled me forward. "I can't make it go away. It hurts so much. I feel the fear and the pain, and I can't undo it. Is this my punishment?"

I frowned and nodded. "I think so."

"When will it go away?"

"When you let go of the anger."

"All I have is anger!"

"Then that's all you'll ever have." I brushed his hands off my shoulders, and he backed away. "Let me fix your forehead. Ruby, would you hand me that first aid kit?"

Ruby handed me the first aid kit through the slot and I pointed at the cot for Dane to sit. He sat down and watched me as I prepared my nursing arsenal. I reached to dab the alcohol on his wound, but paused. "This might hurt a little."

"Why are you being so nice to me?"

"I'm treating your wounds. That hardly classifies me as Mother Teresa."

"Don't you detest me?"

I thought about that a moment before dabbing the cotton on his forehead. He cringed, as I knew he would. It was one thing to bash your head into a steel post until it was numb, but antiseptic always stung like a bugger.

"I think you deserve that, but no, I don't detest you."

"Why not?"

I shook my head. "I don't know. I guess I feel sorry for you."

"I don't want your pity."

"You'd rather I detest you. Isn't that what this is about? Now that you know how much of a monster you are, you want everyone to see you as a monster."

"I'm more than a monster. I'm the devil."

"No, I've met the devil. I would rather deal with you." I dipped my brow, thinking back to the darkness inside of him. "Whatever you are, you aren't nearly as bad as all that." Dane leaned forward and sniffed my chest. I backed away from him. "Excuse you."

"You're wearing perfume."

I glanced at Ruby. "It's probably my soap."

"Why would a nun wear perfume?"

"Can I finish this? Are you done sniffing?" I paused before returning to apply a bandage.

"Did you really stop that bullet?" he asked.

I looked over the speckled scabs on the side of his face. After a lot of scrubbing, most of the shrapnel was out of his skin. "Not technically. Or didn't you notice your face?"

"I noticed the lack of bullet in my skull and fiery pitchforks around me." As soon as the bandage was in place, he shifted away from me and lay down on the cot. "You should have let me die."

"Probably," I mumbled.

"Why didn't you?"

I wasn't sure why I had done it. It was too fast of a reaction, too instinctual to analyze. There must have been a part of me that didn't want him to die. It probably wasn't a testimony to anything he had shown me, but rather a testimony to myself. Perhaps I wasn't as bad as I had once thought. Maybe the rebellious teenager who picked fights was all grown up. If the pain of my parents' deaths no longer incited my vengeful anger, then I suppose I was finally at peace.

"I need you." I gave him the only answer I was sure about.

Dane lifted the hem of my skirt with his finger. "What do you need me for?"

I batted down the fabric. "*We* need you."

"All the better." He eyed me.

"We brought you here to protect us."

Dane shook his head. "I'm not a hero."

I couldn't help but smile. "I think we know that, Dane, but regardless, Pratchett the Hatchet is gone."

"You know that for sure?" He sat up abruptly, making me jump. He pressed his hands to my hips, holding me in place. "Maybe I should take a lie detector test, just to be sure."

"Hennie?" Ruby questioned my safety. I glanced at her and shook my head.

"I think that's a great idea." I tried to push his hands off me, but he refused to let go. He shook his head and drew me forward between his knees.

"Where shall we start?" His mammoth hands easily cupped my hips with room to wander into other territory.

"Do you want to kill me?" I asked the first question on my mind.

"No."

I breathed a sigh of relief. "Truth." I perked my brow, impressed he was being honest. "Are you planning to kill any of us?"

"No." He looked at Ruby. "Ask her the same for me."

I sighed and turned to her. "Are you planning to kill Dane?" I waited for her to dismiss the idea, but she didn't. She looked between the two of us, unwilling to answer. "Ruby?"

"He's a killer, Hennie."

"I can't argue with that, but I do know everyone has a breaking point. He just couldn't put himself back together again."

"That's no excuse," she whispered and glared at Dane.

"You're right, but that's between him and God now. Sister Aggie sent us to him. We will follow her lead, and short of that, Paula's, but neither of us will harm him unless it is self-defense. In that case, you can direct me to the other gun you have stashed."

Ruby's eyes lit with shocked fear. I hadn't actually known she had another gun. I had just guessed, but now that I knew, I would be on the lookout for her hiding place, lest someone get killed.

Ruby slunk away from the cage. She walked a short distance away, close enough to listen, but she apparently didn't want to look at me anymore.

Dane's hands slid down my legs, stopping just above my knees. "I miss pantyhose." He touched my black tights. "Why don't women wear them anymore?"

"Some do. Could you not touch me so much? I know you aren't technically a rapist, but you are clearly confused about the meaning of personal space."

He scoffed and released his hands. "Why does rape offend you more than murder?"

"It's a girl thing."

He leaned back against the cage wall behind his cot. "She's right, you know. I'm a killer."

"You were a killer."

"Still am."

I frowned, hearing the truth in his words. "How do you know you're still a killer if you don't want to kill any of us?"

He smiled and stood up. I backed away to give him space. "A lion can be trained to jump and sit, but he never loses the instinct to hunt."

He corralled me back into a corner. "Ruby." I gulped. "Open the door, please."

"Relax, Hennie," he purred. "I don't want to hurt you, but there is something out there I do want to hurt."

I narrowed my eyes at him. "What do you want to hurt?"

He shrugged. "I don't know, but..." He dragged his finger up my arm and rested it on my shoulder. "...whatever it is. I think it's afraid of me."

My eyes flickered over him. "Yeah, well, it's not really a stretch." I shifted under his arm and ran out the door before he could grab me. Ruby locked the door behind me and I took the key from her. She questioned me, but I pocketed it. "I'll hold on to this for now." She glared at me and stormed off.

When I looked back into the cage, Dane was staring out at me. The hard stare of an animal caged in a zoo, anticipating the feeder to mess up. "There's something about you. As much as I don't want to hurt you, I still want to hunt you."

"Seriously, you're flirting with me? You were barely 24 hours from the electric chair when we met. That's not an attractive trait in a man."

"I'm not flirting with you, Hennie. I'm warning you." Dane moved back to his bed and I walked away, trying not to think about what he had just said.

Truth.

CHAPTER 35

"**S**ERIOUSLY?" I SQUAWKED AT Paula from across Aggie's desk. "I'm being grounded because of a nosebleed?"

"You puked up a pint of blood, Hennie!" Rachel argued from beside me.

I turned and looked at her. "Why are you here? You are always here when there is bad news to give."

"I'm trying to protect you from yourself!" Rachel yelled at me.

"Who asked you to?"

"You don't have to ask. We're sisters!"

"That's freaking beautiful, but I don't want to stay here alone!" I sat back and crossed my arms.

Rachel shifted uncomfortably and, after a moment, she looked at Paula. "Maybe she could ride along."

Paula sighed and leaned forward over the desk. "Hennie, I would love to bring you along, but I think all of us are underestimating the toll this magic is taking on your body."

"But I feel fine."

Paula raised her hand to silence me. "You're like a child saying you aren't tired when clearly you are."

"But I'm helping. This is working. Why did you ask me to do this if you were only going to cut me off?"

Paula lowered her eyes a moment before answering. "I was willing to ignore the traumas when I thought it was transitional, but I think your initial concerns were accurate. Every time you have used your magic, the impact on your body has been more significant."

"Great. Now that I'm starting to get the hang of this, you dump me."

"We are not dumping you," Paula assured me. "We just need to try to reconnect the coven with an external source of power. I'm afraid if we bring you along, you won't be able to help yourself, and it will impede our efforts."

"Your efforts to separate yourself from me."

Paula frowned and leaned forward over the desk. "We are not going to leave you behind, Hennie. You are a part of this group now, but as you well know, sometimes we have to change our paths to suit the situation. I won't argue about this any longer. You will stay here to monitor Pratchett and Sister Aggie. The rest of us will be doing a prayer circle elsewhere."

"Fine." I walked out, not wanting to fight with her. It didn't matter how many times she denied it—I was being squeezed out of the circle. It was nothing new, but I thought a convent of all places would be above shunning.

As I reached the stairs, Rachel caught up with me. "Hennie, wait."

"What now, Rachel?" I turned to face her a few steps up from her. "I'm really not in the mood for your criticism."

She narrowed her eyes at me. "You know we're just trying to protect you."

"Yeah, but as I've said a dozen times. I feel—"

"What part of this is not freaking you out? You're tapping into more power than we have ever seen before. You stopped a bullet, Hennie."

"That's nothing compared to teleportation and levitation."

"Teleportation spells take the concentration of an entire coven over the course of several minutes. You stopped that bullet by yourself—instantaneously." She frowned at me and came up another step. "Aren't you scared?"

I couldn't tell her I wasn't scared. What sane person wouldn't be a little unnerved by bullet-shattering power? Then again, who wouldn't be thrilled by it at the same time? I honestly felt a little indifferent about the prospect of being a super witch.

I clunked down a few steps to meet her. She shifted back to the wall, and I leaned against the railing. "The only thing I'm afraid of is going back to being the freak."

Rachel scoffed. "You're not a freak."

"When I came here, I was a screw-up with no future, but somehow I fit. Now, I'm some sort of a lightning rod for magic. So, yeah, I'm back to being a freak."

Rachel moved forward and gripped my shoulder. "That doesn't make you a freak. It makes you special."

"What's the difference?" I shrugged.

She smiled at me. "Freaks don't have a sisterhood to back them up." I smiled back at her, but as I did, I saw her lips flatten out. Her hand slid off my shoulder and she started back down the steps. At the bottom step, she turned back to face me. "Hey, you be careful tonight."

"I'll stay away from the knife block."

"No, I mean around Dane. I don't trust him. I don't like the way he looks at you."

"Mmm." I nodded in agreement, though I knew his leering observations were mostly harmless. "I'm not nearly as worried about babysitting him as I am about Sister Aggie."

CHAPTER 36

"A GGIE, NO!" I WAILED as Sister Aggie bit the head off a dead mouse she had found under one of the bookshelves. The desiccated little blob had probably long since died from rat poison, but that was hardly my concern when I asked her not to eat it.

I gagged as I heard it crunch. "Oh, damn! Why?" I bellowed at her. "Why would a demon want you to eat a dead mouse? It's not scary. It's not symbolic of evil. It's just gross!"

Aggie groaned and chomped away. Her demons were pleased as punch she was making me sick to my stomach.

"So, the grilled cheese sandwich you threw up, but *that* you can keep down." I shook my head in exasperation. "Where were we?" I flipped back to the Bible verse I was on. It wasn't my preferred bedtime story, but since Aggie's faith was based on the text, Paula insisted it would be important to read it to her regularly.

I began reading the yawn-inducing litany when a blob of something smacked my cheek. I looked at Aggie and saw her grinning with furry teeth. "No." I stared at her. "Tell me you didn't just spit that on me!" Aggie laughed from deep in her throat.

I stood up and set the Bible down gently, lest I throw it at Aggie. I knew she was not truly responsible for any of this, and in fact was probably keeping the more violent acts under control, but it was getting harder to resist retaliating against her.

I stopped beside her chair and leaned over her. "Eeew!" I yelled in her face and stomped out. Despite it accomplishing nothing, I was still glad to have done it.

I went down the hall to the bathroom and scrubbed my face much harder than necessary. It wasn't so much about cleanliness as relieving my aggression, so I didn't hurt my ward.

Satisfied with my timeout, I headed back to the library to read to her again. As I neared the end of the hall, I could see Aggie through the windows. She was mostly behaving. I wasn't sure I had done the Bible any good by leaving it in her possession, but I supposed I could find another copy. I was in a convent, after all.

I stood outside the door watching Aggie rip the book apart with her teeth and hands. She made it a point to shove some pages into her pants. I scrunched my nose, already anticipating it might not be a symbolic use of the text as toilet paper.

As I watched the disturbance, dreading the clean-up it would require, I felt a shift in the air. Not unfamiliar with the creepy-crawly sensation of someone watching me, I turned to see if anyone had arrived back early. No one was there. Not behind me. Not coming up the stairs.

I listened for the sound of anyone's feet pattering downstairs, but it was quiet. There were no signs of darkness in the branches of the t-section either, no spiders or lions lurking about.

I looked back at Aggie in the library, and immediately noticed the figures behind me reflected in the glass. I screamed at their proximity and whipped back around to see who was there, but the hall was empty. Reluctantly, I returned my gaze to the glass and saw that the shadows were closing in on me.

I moved toward the stairwell, monitoring their movement through the windows. The shadow reflections turned toward my path of retreat. They were following me.

I counted six as I backed away. When I reached the staircase, I took a breath before turning my back on them and losing my only visual. I didn't want them behind me any more than in front of me, but I had to get away from them.

I jetted down the steps, nearly toppling, as I swung around the banister corner to take the next flight to the basement. I could feel them at my heels, like a monster under the bed. There was no stopping now. Not until I was under a sheet clutching my teddy bear. Or in this case, a hired gun.

Once I hit the concrete floor, I sprinted to the other end. I reached Dane's cage and pulled the key from my pocket, but my hands were shaking and I dropped it. Tears made their way to my cheeks as I grappled to get the damn thing back in my hand. I was going to die like a pathetic, clumsy side-character in a horror flick.

I jammed the key into the lock and twisted. The door popped open, and I ran inside. I slammed it behind me and backed deeper into the cage. After a moment of hyperventilating, I looked at Dane.

Stretched out on his mattress, he stared at me. I was certain I looked like I had lost my mind, but he seemed wholly indifferent to my interruption except that it was interfering with his sleep.

I took in a breath to gain control of my faculties. Pissing myself or passing out would accomplish nothing. Rather than try to explain the lunacy of my experience, I reached for his hand.

Dane looked at the strange offering, but sat up and clasped my fingers. I instantly felt better at the human contact. The fact that he was a serial killer didn't seem to make a difference to me. I tugged on his hand and he stood up. He looked me over, but didn't ask me why I was sniveling like a child.

I didn't ask him to come with me. I just moved toward the door and hoped he would follow. I led him out of the cage and across the basement—a good deal slower than my arrival.

He shifted his hand around, linking his fingers between mine as if we were taking a stroll as a couple. I glanced at our hands, but didn't object. I didn't really care how he held my hand, so long as he stayed close to me.

We reached the stairs leading to the first floor and stopped. It took me a moment before I realized I was the one stopping our ascent. I squeezed his hand and forced myself to move forward. He climbed the stairs beside me and we stopped on the main floor.

I looked around the hall, peeking in framed pictures for shadows, but they hadn't come down. Part of me thought maybe they were staying near Aggie, but I didn't know if that was true.

As we went up the next flight, I lost my will to move. I had no way of knowing if Dane could actually help me. He had done a good job scaring my shadow away. I was hoping he could do the same to these.

Dane glanced over at me and then at the floor above. He stepped up to the next stair tread, urging me on. He tugged on my arm, now leading me to the second floor.

When we reached the top, I clutched my other hand around his forearm and led him to the windows in front of the library. At first, I saw nothing, and I thought it would just be another one of my stories to tell, but something shifted in the air again, making me uncomfortable.

I angled my view and found the shadows just down the hall, staggered and attentively guarding our doorways. I tried to count them, but I already knew that there would be one for each room. Except for Erin's room. Her demon had already completed his duty.

"Do you see them?" I asked Dane and pointed to the glass.

"Yes," he answered, but he wasn't even looking at the reflection with me. He was looking behind me into the long branch of the hall.

I turned around and looked at the nothingness behind me. "You can see them?"

"Yes, I can see them, hear them." He stared down the hall with rapt fury. "I can smell them. I can even taste them." He dragged his hand free of my needy grip and looked at me. His eyes sparkled with sinister intent and he smiled. "Let's see if I can touch them."

He looked back over at them, his expression turning feral as he moved away from me. A few steps later, he stopped and shook his head. "I think you have me confused with someone else," he said. After a brief pause, he chuckled quietly. "Let's find out for sure."

Dane grabbed at the thin air and threw a punch at it. Though the enemy was imperceptible to my eyes, I could see his fists catching with each impact. I felt a shudder inside of me as one opponent retaliated, causing Dane's lip to split open and bleed.

I turned back to the window to watch the fight unfold in the glossy reflection. Two shadows jumped on Dane's back, but he seemed indifferent to the weight. He continued to punch his current victim until it split in two and melted into the floor.

He flipped his backpack attackers off, but three more took their place. I got the impression from their squirming, almost humping motions, that they were actually trying to get inside of him, to possess him like Aggie's demons had. Instead of absorbing into him, they bounced right off him.

Dane caught another shadow and ripped it apart with as little effort as ripping a tattered cloth. The next adversary lost what might have been his head, if that actually applied.

One of the piggy-backing shadows leaped off Dane and came straight for me. I wanted to run, but a voice pressed into my mind. "Stay!" The word demanded, and I couldn't ignore it. I couldn't even call out for help.

The dark form came up behind me, clouding my thoughts and blocking my view of Dane. It loomed over me and spread its shadowy wings. I stared in fascination at the creature, even as my mind reasoned for the necessity of distance.

It was so clear I wasn't even sure it was the reflection I was seeing anymore, or if this was a dream I might wake up from. *Please, God, let me be sleeping.*

The clawed fingers trickled over my shoulders, gripping me before slithering down to my chest. My heart raced and I could hear the monster's rasping breath—or perhaps it was my own.

I felt the cool black fingertips pushing into me. A feverish cold hit my blood, and I wanted to give in. I wanted to let the creature take me over, but it stopped. Its head turned slowly to one side, and I followed its gaze along the windows of the library.

I saw my shadow reflected in the hall with us. He was as clear to me as when he was standing in my bedroom next to me. He was glaring at the creature behind me. The winged demon growled and my shadow hissed. The demon released his grip on me and backed away.

Before I could question the reason for the creature's retreat, it arched forward and roared. A trickle of light peeked through his torso and grew until I could see Dane on the other side, rending him in two. His face contorted and he let out a long, arduous groan. The demon let out one last shriek before it shattered into oblivion.

Dane stared at me through the reflection, panting and sweating. His gaze shifted, and he looked at my shadow. My shadow looked back at him curiously. I wondered if he had ever expected that I would have backup.

Dane marched over to him, and my heart leaped with concern for him. Did he even understand whom he was facing? Dane was strong enough to fight demons, but could he fight the devil himself?

Dane stopped halfway between us and stared at the devil before him. He turned his attention to the floor and then back at me. I feared the worst—that the whispers of a dark angel would compel him to kill me. Dane's eyes narrowed on me, but then he turned back to his real opponent.

My shadow smiled and tipped his head. "Aren't you just the luckiest man alive? Treading the waters between worlds. You and Hennie have so much in common. A gamble, if you ask me, but then again, He always was a bit of a risk-taker."

"Leave or I will—"

"Will what?" my shadow asked. "Rip my head off? I think we both know you won't do that. After all, you don't want to hurt poor Hennie, do you?"

Dane looked back at me and I shook my head. "Do it." I motioned for him to commence the decapitation.

He shook his head. "I can't." He looked back at my shadow. "What do you want? Why are you even here?"

"I just want what's mine. Hennie has taken her games too far this time. Once I have her, this will all go away." He motioned to the scene of carnage that fortunately did not leave any bodies behind. "Until then, people will continue to get hurt."

"Not if I can help it," Dane said.

My shadow smiled. "As much as I like you this way, Pratchett, I really did prefer you with a hatchet."

"Fuck you!"

My shadow chuckled. "You kiss your mother with that mouth?"

Dane lunged at him, but before he could reach him, my shadow was gone—returned to the depths of hell where he belonged, or perhaps just back to my nightmares.

CHAPTER 37

I WALKED DANE BACK downstairs to his cage. We had spoken little about what had transpired. He seemed at ease with the recent developments in his reality. Far more than I would have expected. If I wasn't mistaken, killing the demons had actually put his mind at peace in a way that therapy and prayer never could have.

I wanted to ask him what he had seen, and why he didn't attack my shadow when he had the chance. I wanted to know what he knew about me that I didn't seem to understand. Why was the devil on my shoulder so resistant to letting me go?

I had surmised that my power, my connection to magic, was of value to him, but why? Surely demons had enough power. They didn't need to borrow from witches.

In the back of my mind, I wondered if belonging to him referred to a union between us. Was I his wife? Did I marry the devil and just not remember? Was there such a thing as divorce in hell? And if so, what would it cost me to get it?

Dane pushed past me to get into his cage. He turned back to look at me, and I at him. He had saved my life. He had probably saved everyone's lives. If they had come home to demons on their doorsteps, we would have gone down in history as the suicide pact sisters.

I looked down at the door I was holding open and the key in my right hand. He wasn't running. He wasn't hurting anyone. Did I really need to cage him up any longer? He wasn't the hero, but he wasn't the villain of this tale either. Not anymore, at least.

I looked back up to Dane, but before I could suggest a probation, he grabbed the door and swung it shut, clanging it hard against the metal post. "Lock it," he said and dropped onto his bed.

I did as he asked and left him alone. I may have trusted that he was reborn into a life without senseless murder, but he obviously didn't.

CHAPTER 38

I TRUDGED BACK UP to the main floor with the weight of the world on my shoulders. This had gone too far. I had gone too far. This twisted little experiment into the world of *double double toil and trouble* was turning into exactly what my shadow wanted. We were at war with hell. With our access to God shut off and our only ringer being a former murderer, what chance did any of us have of winning, let alone surviving?

I did a quick check in the office windows for demon reflections before I headed back up to the second floor. As I reached the top step, I could feel the air go stagnant. Every sound, from the creak of the wood at my feet to the hum of the fluorescent lights overhead, was gone. The chill in the air was more visceral than literal, but it still made me shiver.

"You should not have done that," Sister Aggie warned me. She was standing at the entrance of the library, watching my arrival. It wasn't her voice, but it so seldom was anymore. "She doesn't like losing."

Against my better judgment, I moved closer to her. "That's tough shit. Wait. Why did you say *she*?"

Sister Aggie tipped her head. "The devil has many faces. She, he, it."

"So we're talking about a she now. Not the lion or my shoulder puppet." I checked Aggie's reflection in the library window and saw tentacles of black waving all around her. She was inundated with parasitic demons. "And what exactly is this she-devil pissed off about?"

"Your little coven has power."

"But they always had power. What difference does it make now?"

Aggie snorted and laughed, but her mouth barely reflected the amusement. "Oil and water. Fire and ice. Your witches were firefighters in an inferno."

"What are they now?"

"Fire to fire." Aggie bit her lip hard and lapped up the blood she drew with her tongue.

I heard a scratching sound behind me and turned to see where it was coming from. I couldn't see anyone or anything in the hall. I turned back to Aggie.

"Fire with fire? Are you saying that my power is the same as his?" Aggie offered a non-committal gurgle, or perhaps it was a growl. "He was telling me the truth, wasn't he? My shadow. Somehow we're connected."

"Run. Run. Run away." Aggie danced her fingers, playing with imaginary marionettes. "Hide and seek's your favorite game. Blind and deaf, dumb and weak. All for the chance to lose the blame."

"What blame?"

Sister Aggie laughed.

"What blame?" I screamed at her.

The phone rang in the office downstairs. The muted sound sparked my concern, since only people with the convent's number called.

"You might want to get that. It might be important." Sister Aggie smiled broadly.

I frowned and ran downstairs. I pushed open the office door and picked up the receiver. "Hello."

"Hennie," a voice whispered on the other line. It was barely loud enough to hear.

"Paula?"

"Help me," she rasped.

My heart fell as I recognized the voice. "What's wrong? Where are you?" The phone clicked, cutting the connection. "Jess!"

CHAPTER 39

I HUNG UP THE phone and ran back out of the office. I smacked into Rachel on the way out. "Easy speedy." She took in my panicked face. "What's wrong?"

"Jess." I looked back at Paula and the others trailing behind her. "She's in trouble."

"Who's Jess?" Meredith asked.

"My friend. I gave her our number in case of an emergency. She's hurt, I think."

"What happened to her?" Rachel asked.

"I'm not sure. She was cut off before I could find out more."

"Satan's wrath is upon us," Katherine uttered. Despite the rabid nature of her words, I knew she was right. I had pissed the devil off and now poor Jess was in the crossfire.

"I need to find her." I started toward the door.

"Wait." Paula grabbed my arm. "I'll go with you."

"Me too," Rachel added.

"The rest of you stay here," Paula instructed. "Stay by the phone and call us if you hear anything more from her friend."

Paula led the way back out to the van and got into the driver's seat. I took shotgun while Rachel climbed into the back. I could feel my anxiety raise my heart rate as I gave her a summary of the directions to Jess's house.

I rocked in my seat and tried to fight away my tears. "This is all my fault. I never thought... Not her."

"Why are you so worried? You don't even know what's happened to her." Rachel leaned forward.

"I do." I looked back at her. "I made him mad."

"How did you do that?" Paula asked.

"I let Dane out."

"What?" Rachel squawked. "By yourself? How stupid are you?"

"He's a weapon. I used him and he... He's amazing," I admitted and glanced back at Rachel. She narrowed her eyes, still distrusting of my evaluation.

"What did he do?" Paula asked, not taking her eyes off the road.

"He fought the demons that were waiting outside of everyone's doors."

"There are demons at our doors?" Rachel asked.

"Not anymore." I turned to her and shook my head. "I don't know what he is. I don't know what we did to him, but he can see them. And he can fight them."

Rachel looked at Paula. "Is that what Aggie meant for him?"

Paula's jaw twisted, and she nodded. "We have to assume so. Did he hurt you?" She finally afforded a glance away from the road.

"No. He saved me."

"I still don't trust him." Rachel leaned back in her seat.

"Agreed," Paula seconded. "But we can't keep him locked up like an animal forever. If he's an asset we intend to use, we'll need to come up with an excuse for him to be around the convent."

I nodded. I wasn't about to seek Dane out socially, but I also wasn't likely to be out of danger anytime soon, so he was the best solution to the threats in my life. Whether I liked it or not, he was about to become a member of our coven.

As Paula rounded the last corner on our journey, I recognized the surrounding houses. Years of riding my bike down the sidewalks had impressed the image of each house number into my memory. I pinpointed every aberration, from new siding to a missing tree. The most obvious change, of course, was the blazing fire at the end of the cul-de-sac in front of us.

I stood up before the van stopped and bumped my head on the ceiling. I scrambled with the door handle as Paula slowed to a stop behind a police car. I leaped out the door, ignoring the hollers from Rachel that I should wait.

I ran toward the two-story inferno, past the police line, and into the path of firefighters. My habit may have bought me some time with the police, but the firefighters weren't about to let me near the house.

A strong arm barricaded me and practically shoved me to the concrete. "Stay back!" the fireman yelled from behind a thick plastic face shield.

I looked at him and saw a familiar face in the reflection of his mask. "Where is she?" I screamed.

"Who?" the fireman asked.

"Jess!" I answered him, in case he actually knew the answer.

"We haven't been able to get inside. This heat is relentless. Are you family?"

"A friend."

He frowned. "Are you sure she was inside?"

"She called me." I glanced at the reflection of the man standing behind me for conformation, but my shadow wouldn't answer.

"I..." the fireman faltered. "I'm sorry, Sister. I don't think anyone could survive this." The fireman slunk away, leaving me to come to terms with his honesty.

I felt a hand rest on my shoulder and I shrugged it away.

"Hey," Rachel yelled over the roaring fire and popped up beside me. "Let's get away from here." She pressed on my back, strongly urging me to move.

"He's doing this to her because of me. I put her in danger. I have to stop this somehow."

"I know you want to help, but I don't think you can." Rachel reached down and squeezed my hand. "If this really is part of his revenge, your magic won't be any good against it. He is too powerful." She tugged my hand, but I didn't move. "Come on, let's move back. It's hot as hell up here."

"Hot as hell's fire," I murmured. "There's only one thing that can fight a fire this hot."

"What?" Rachel leaned her head towards my mouth to hear me better.

"I don't think I'm a good witch, Rachel."

"What are you talking about?" She leaned back to look me over and search my eyes for the reason behind the statement. She frowned and shook her head. "Yes, you are."

"Why do you believe that?"

"Because..." She shook her head again. "I don't know, Hennie. I just do. Please, come away from the fire. Let these people do their jobs."

I stared across the road at the burning house. The firefighters were drawing back from the blaze. The only rescue efforts they were making now was keeping the fire from spreading to other homes.

"Hennie, let's go!" Rachel finally returned to her tried-and-true anger to get me to budge.

"Not yet." I yanked my hand from hers. "I need to save, Jess."

CHAPTER 40

I SPRINTED ACROSS THE concrete, feet pounding, robe swishing around my legs, and my rosary beads rattling against my chest. Rachel screamed behind me. She was on my heels, ready to tackle me if she got the chance.

Since the firefighters had drawn back, I had a clear path to the house. However, as the emergency workers noticed us running toward the fire, they jumped into action to save us from our own stupidity.

I heard angry bellows as several brave men tried to intercept us before we could reach the house. They moved with shocking speed despite their heavy protective attire. They tackled Rachel and dragged her away, but they were too late to catch me.

The air rippled in front of me as I reached the front stoop. The exterior walls were blistering from the heat within. The home was groaning as the structural components weakened and threatened to collapse. The fire was several hundred degrees hotter than I should have been able to withstand, but I could also feel something cold waiting for me inside.

Whatever it was, it was allowing me to get close. Taunting me, daring me to come inside after Jess. It was a trap for sure, but what else could I do? Jess was my best friend. She was innocent in all of this. I needed to save her.

As I reached for the doorknob, to push the front door open, it opened on its own—another bad sign that I was being baited.

The flames within subsided so I could enter the foyer without catching fire.

I entered the home, which was only a glimmer of its former beauty now. The blackened walls and melted carpets were unrecognizable. Despite the bright blaze devouring the dining room and front room on either side of me, the center passageway seemed dark.

I heard a holler behind me, and I looked back. Two determined firemen were coming in after me. The flames rose behind me, forcing them to dive away from the heat. Just to ensure their departure, the front door slammed shut behind them.

"Hennie!" Jess's voice carried down the stairs to me.

"Jess!" I yelled back up to her and ran up the staircase. I reached the landing just as a wall buckled behind me. The charred studs fell across the stairs, blocking my option to turn back.

"Hennie, help!" Jess called to me.

"Jess! Where are you?" I continued up the stairs to the second level. I looked left and right, listening for another outcry to tell me which bedroom she was in. "Jess!"

I heard a muffled plea from her bedroom and I ran toward it. The floor squeaked and cracked beneath my steps. I hit a weak spot and the wood gave way beneath. The carpet caught my foot, preventing me from falling through the gap.

I climbed back up and called to Jess again. I ran to the last bedroom and opened the door. Black smoke wafted out of the room, choking my lungs. I peeled off my veil to use it as a filter on my mouth before stepping into the room.

"Jess!" I yelled, ducking away from the flames rippling across the ceiling above me.

"I'm here! Under the bed!" Jess yelled.

I moved through the blinding smoke until I reached the bed. I ducked down to see her and found her under her mattress, shielding herself from the heat. There was a pair of panties looped around her neck and covering her mouth so she could breathe.

"Hennie," she whimpered. "Help me."

"I'm here. Let's get you out of here." I pulled her out from under the mattress and helped her to her feet. She yelped and fell against me. "What is it?"

"My leg." She pointed. I leaned down to examine her bleeding leg and found four long gashes in her calf. "There was something in the house. Before the fire."

I pulled Jess's arm over my shoulder and pulled her along. "Don't worry about all that. We need to get out of here. Have you tried the windows?"

"Yes, they won't budge." Jess limped alongside of me, hissing with every step. We moved out into the hall and shuffled back to the stairs, but flames engulfed the steps. "What do we do now?"

"Let me try something," I said. I closed my eyes and tapped into a fire of my own. The sensation of magic poured over me, making me tingle from head to toe. I focused my power on the barrier of flames, smothering them. When I opened my eyes, there was a path for us to descend through.

"How did that happen?" Jess asked as I helped her down the steps.

"I'll explain later," I said.

We reached the main floor and wobbled toward the front door. I couldn't believe I was being allowed to save Jess. It was too good to be true.

As we passed the living room, Jess gasped. Her body was ripped from my grip and dragged across the burning room. She screamed as her arms were jerked upward. Her body floated in mid-air over the fireplace in a crucified pose. Her skin began to steam as the intense heat started to cook her.

"Let her go!" I screamed at the hidden entity. I used my power again to reduce the heat in the room, but as I got it under control, my back erupted in searing pain.

I yowled and dropped to my knees. I reached around to feel the wound and returned with blood on my hands. I stood and turned to face my enemy, but there was no one to see.

Pain raked across my belly and I bent over, cradling the second injury. I noted the four rips in the cloth of my robe. The beast was no longer trying to make my death look accidental.

"Leave us alone!" I screamed at the torrent of flames in the dining room. The fire swirled and bent, forming a mouth of sorts.

"Surrender!" The voice was as much the creaking in the house as an actual vocalization. The swirling fury feigning a mouth opened and spewed a fireball at me.

"Stop!" I yelled and raised my hands to protect myself. Time slowed down, just as it had when I stopped the bullet from killing Dane. The wave of my power crashed against the flaming ball, eating it away to nothing.

The fiery mouth roared, and I was thrown back into the living room under Jess's hanging body. I heard her moan and I looked up at her. She wasn't sweating anymore. The intense heat was dehydrating her. Her skin was bright red. If I didn't stop this beast, I was going to lose her.

I stood up and raised my hands. I willed myself to summon as much of my power as I could. It sprung to life, trickling through my body like a morphine shot laced with Ecstasy. The euphoria that flowed through the connection evoked a moan from me that was out of place for an impending battle.

The magic coursed through my veins, opening my mind and evaporating my fear. I stared out through what felt like new eyes. The room was no longer an inferno. It was dark, blackened by the evil that was staring back at me from across the foyer. Red eyes peered out at me, threatening to attack at any moment.

I had no idea how to fight the beast. Fire against fire made little sense until I reached out with my mind. I latched onto the power feeding the blaze. Rather than fight the pervasive energy,

I did the same thing I did with Gregory's virulent intruders: I drew it in.

The fuel of nightmares soaked into me, adding to my overwhelming enjoyment and dropping me to my knees. Had I been capable of thought beyond the concept of "more," I might have realized how unbelievably stupid I was being, but my power-hungry brain was in overdrive.

Inside my mind, the beast roared, overloading my connection to it with visions of bloody, barbarous acts. Murderous thoughts poured into me, bringing old angers to the surface. Pain pilfered the pleasure of the magic and robbed me of my control.

I screamed, and the connection snapped. I fell to my hands and knees, panting and crying blood. I could no longer feel the icy presence of the beast. I also couldn't feel the heat of the raging fire.

I looked around and took in the charred remains of my friend's family home. The unnatural hellfire had diminished to nearly nothing. I could hear the din of hollers outside the house as the good men of the volunteer fire department took it upon themselves to finish what I had started and tamp out the remaining flames.

Water from the fire hoses poured down on what remained of the roof. It soaked through the second-floor carpets and trickled between the floorboards above me, giving me a shower of black rain.

I turned back to check on Jess, to see how much harm these devils had done to her, but she was gone.

I heard a soft, patting clap from the doorway. I looked over and saw Jess leaning on the frame, applauding me.

"Jess! Thank God you're okay."

She chuckled and crossed her arms. "Oh, I wouldn't be thanking Him for that just yet."

I frowned and wiped the excess water from my face. "What are you...?" I trailed off as I noticed her skin was a perfect creamy peach and her leg was no longer bleeding. "Who are you?"

"You did a good job, Hennie." Jess smiled at me. "The beast is not an easy mind to connect to. If you were anyone else, you would be insane by now."

"You're *her*, aren't you?"

"Her who?"

"*Her* her. The third one. The beast, the snake, and the..."

"I am generally referred to as the goat or the ram. I'm the one with the horns." Jess poked her fingers up beside her head.

"What do you want?"

Jess tipped her head left and right. "I want you back on a leash, where you belong."

"So you support the snake agenda?"

"It's a matter of cohesion, really. He and I are rather like-minded. You should be glad I'm not supporting the beast. It wants you dead." Jess shrugged. "Although it wants everyone dead. It's really a rather raw creature. Not much in the way of higher thought, as you might imagine."

"So, if I agree to surrender, will you release Jess?"

"Release her?" Jess furrowed her brow. "Oh." She frowned. "You think I'm inside of her? Controlling her?"

"Aren't you?"

"No, Hennie, I'm not a demon. I'm in a corporeal form. I can appear as anyone I want."

"Don't tell me you *are* Jess." I blanched at the thought of my best friend being the devil all along.

"Oh, I would love to tell you that." Jess leaned forward and winked at me. "But unfortunately, you've only started getting interesting recently."

"Then where is she? What did you do with her?"

Jess sighed. "Oh, you foolish girl, she's dead."

"No," I whispered.

Jess chuckled. "She was already dying when you picked up that phone." Tears sprung to my eyes, and I hyperventilated. I looked around the room for proof of what she was saying, even though I knew it was true. "You never even had a chance of saving her," Jess mocked my pain.

"You monster!" I screamed and charged at her. She just laughed and disappeared into thin air. I scrambled in circles in the foyer, looking for another trap to snare me, but the devil was gone.

CHAPTER 41

O UTSIDE THE FRONT DOOR, I heard Rachel and Paula calling my name. The firefighters were trying to break down the door, but part of the floor upstairs had collapsed in front of it.

As I waited for them to figure out a new entrance option, I wandered back through the dining room. I crunched through the charred wood and melted carpets until I reached the ceramic tiles.

The kitchen looked worse than the rest of the house. The entire floor above it was gone, leaving it completely exposed to the night sky. The marble countertops still looked fine, but the wood holding them up had collapsed. I could see the phone melted on the back wall beside the fridge. The receiver was missing, dangling by the threads of bare wires.

I moved around the island and saw a blackened leg sticking out from under the toppled island. I knew she was dead. There was no denying it. I needed to see her with my own eyes.

I kneeled down to lift the heavy marble top as best I could. I was only able to shift it a little, but I managed to unveil Jess's body.

I expected the rest of her to be charred black, but it wasn't. The stone counter top had protected her from the flames. She was a bright red with streaks of dark red where the blood of her many gashes had dried.

Her eyes were open, staring at me through the foggy haze of her dried corneas. They accused me of doing this to her. For bringing this harm on her. As guilty as I was for my part, I was also furious. More than ever I wanted revenge, and it wasn't because a devil was whispering in my ear. This was my own human thirst for retaliation.

"How could it do this?" I asked as two pairs of crunching feet entered the room.

"Oh, Hennie," Paula whispered behind me. "I'm so sorry."

More feet crunched over the debris behind me. "Sisters, you can't be in here," the muffled voice of a firefighter commanded them. "It could collapse at any moment."

"Holy shit. She's still alive," a different muffled male voice said. "We need to get her to the paramedics."

"I'm fine," I said. There was a scuffle behind me and one of the firefighters lifted me up from under my arms. "I said I'm fine," I stated more strictly and looked back at him.

The fireman immediately drew back from me, eyes big with shock. Rachel gasped and covered her mouth. Paula made the sign of the cross and clasped her rosary.

I could see in the firefighter's face shield that my eyes were now pure black. There was no blood this time, just a darkness from within.

"Leave us," I ordered the men. They conferred with each other a moment before fleeing the room.

"You can't keep doing this," Rachel chastised me the minute they left the room. "You are pushing yourself too hard. You're hurting yourself."

I stepped around the debris to face her. I could see her eyes fluttering over my face, trying not to look at my eyes. "For the last time, I feel fine. The magic isn't hurting me." I dismissed her concern and turned to Paula. She held my gaze faithfully, but squeezed her rosary tight enough to make her knuckles white.

"I thought the beast couldn't kill us. How did he do this?"

Paula's brow pinched. "I'm sure the cause of death will ultimately be smoke inhalation."

"But that thing caused this fire! This wasn't an accident. This was murder. Just like with Erin."

Paula's eyes watered as she gazed over me. "I don't have the answers you want, Hennie. I'm sorry. All I can do is share the blame for your friend's death and hope you will forgive me."

"You aren't responsible for this," I seethed. "This is all because of her."

CHAPTER 42

"J ESS HAD NOTHING TO do with this!" I grabbed Aggie by her collar and pulled her halfway over the table. Paula and Rachel were grabbing me, but I was only vaguely aware of the effort they were exerting.

"She had everything to do with this!" Aggie's creepy voice yelled back at me. "You have betrayed your master and now his beast is seeking retribution."

"What is she talking about?" Rachel asked.

Aggie clicked her tongue. "Shame, shame, shame, Hennie. Keeping secrets."

"What secrets?" Paula asked, still trying to undo my fingers from Aggie's collar.

"Tell them. Tell them the truth."

"The truth about what?" I let go of Aggie and she dropped back into the chair. She smiled at me, tongue licking across the edge of her teeth.

"Tell them how much you like it."

I stared across the table at Aggie, horrified by this revelation. I wasn't sure how she knew, or they knew, but they did. I slipped back off the table and stared at my sisters. Rachel narrowed her eyes on me, already asking the question I didn't want to answer.

"What is she talking about?" Paula asked.

"I don't know."

"Yes, you do," Rachel said.

"She's talking about the magic. When I use it... I sort of get a high from it. I enjoy it." I stared at Paula and Rachel as they exchanged glances.

"What kind of high are we talking about?" Paula asked. "A caffeine high? An endorphin high?"

I cleared my throat. "All of that plus a semi-erotic, psychotropic rush."

They both stared back at me. I could see the concern and disappointment in their eyes. They had no doubt assumed that the magic was more of a burden. Perhaps even painful at times, given my aftermath of bleeding.

"Why didn't you tell us this?" Paula asked.

"At first I thought it was normal. But then it got stronger, and... I didn't want to lose it."

A chuckle rumbled deep in Aggie's throat. "I guess you're no better than the rest of us after all."

I glared at her. "I'm am nothing like you."

Aggie waggled her head and pointed a bent finger at me. "You are just like us. You've always been like us. You were just never any good at it. You never much cared for your powers before you left. Maybe you're getting homesick. Or maybe you're realizing you can't be someone you're not."

"What are you talking about?" I shifted to lean over the table again. "What do know about me?"

"I know where you get your power from. Didn't you know you've been sucking off the teats of hell this whole time?"

"No. No, it can't be." I backed away from the table and looked at Rachel and Paula for their agreement, but they were on the same path of shock as me. "He said I belonged to him, but that's not true. I'm not a demon. I would know if I were a demon. Right?" Paula's mouth gaped, but none of her supportive words came out. "I am not some minion of hell!" I screamed at Aggie, though it was mostly for my own ears.

"Of course you're not a servant of hell," Aggie yelled back. "You're one of the masters."

CHAPTER 43

I STARED INTO NOTHINGNESS in the cafeteria and tried to come to terms with some aspect of who I was—*what* I was. Despite Aggie's revelation, I still didn't know any more than I did before.

Was I really some powerful demon?

I looked down at my body, touching the skin on my arms. Why did I look human? Was this even me? Was the real me just an apparition riding inside of this form?

When did I get inside of it then? I had memories as far back as anyone could. Kindergarten. Preschool.

News of my evil resume had quickly made the circuit around the convent. I was already getting strange looks because of my black eyes—which I wasn't sure were ever going to clear up. Now everyone was watching me for a new reason, as if I had suddenly grown horns out of the top of my head. Perhaps a vestigial tail was forming, too.

I had intentionally sat at a different table to keep everyone comfortable during our meeting, but it wasn't really working. They were just peering between each other and glancing over their shoulders to catch a glimpse of me.

I caught Dane's eye as they escorted him into the cafeteria with the rest of us. He froze and narrowed his eyes at me. Even the hardened criminal was looking down on me. I wiped away another cascade of tears from my cheeks and moved my focus to the floor.

"What's going on?" Dane asked as Meredith sat him down at the table with the other girls.

"One of Hennie's friends was killed tonight," Paula explained from the head of the table. "She is being targeted because of her magical strength. Among other reasons," she added, delicately avoiding the topic of my apparent runaway status. "The devil is trying to disillusion her by going after her loved ones."

"Good thing my parents are already dead." I snorted even though it wasn't funny and drew more tears from my eyes. Everyone looked at me with a piteous discomfort.

"In addition to that threat," Paula continued, "we found scratches on her bedroom door."

"Scratches?" Dane asked. "Why does that matter?"

"Claw marks, slightly burned, three groups of three."

Dane looked around the table. "I know I'm not the best with biblical numerology, but isn't three a good number? Six is the bad one, right?"

Paula nodded. "That's correct, but nine is a number that represents finality. Given the nature of these recent attacks, we feel that this might be a final warning."

"Warning about what?" Dane looked at me. "What does the big bad wolf want to do with our hen?"

"To take me back to hell," I answered. "He told me I belong to him. He told me if I don't go to him, people would get hurt. They have."

"Giving yourself up isn't going to make her come back," Rachel said.

"No, but it might save the rest of you. Did it ever occur to you that there are nine of us? Erin is gone, but now Dane is here. The devil is just letting me know who his next targets are. I'm not the only one in danger here."

"What do you want us to do? Just give up on you?" Rachel asked.

"This isn't an exorcism. This isn't a spell. You're talking about taking up arms against the biggest bad of them all. It's not just suicidal, it's pointless."

"We can handle it. We have been fighting this war for a long time," Ruby said.

"Yes, to save the humans. That doesn't really apply here." I pointed at the blackness draping my eyes. "This is not what Sister Aggie intended. She shouldn't have brought me here. I'm a wolf amongst lambs."

Meredith turned her chair to look at me. "What if that's the point?"

"What do you mean?" I asked.

"What if that is precisely why she brought you here? You were a wolf in lamb's clothing. Maybe she saw an opportunity. Or maybe... Maybe she saw you were wounded. A wolf that, for whatever reason, doesn't want to hunt anymore. Whatever you were, it doesn't matter now. You are one of us."

I looked around at the others to see if they agreed with that. I got a few nods. "Do you realize how ridiculous this sounds? You want to fight the devil to save a demon. You're fighting evil with evil."

"Sounds about right to me," Dane said. Everyone shifted to look at him, but he only shrugged.

"As much as I hate to agree with Pratchett," Paula said, "he has a point. We've never been in a fight quite like this. The only chance we have against a power this great is by using someone equally as powerful."

"The only reason this war is coming at all is because of me. I should just turn myself over to him and save all of you."

"You're not turning yourself over to him," Rachel insisted.

"Is that what you want, Hennie?" Paula leveled a hard stare at me. "Do you want to go back to him?"

The question hit me like a pop quiz, and suddenly I realized I hadn't studied. I looked over the faces of my sisters before landing on Dane. His eyes narrowed on me and he shook his head slightly.

"No, of course not," I told Paula, but I directed the words to Dane. I wasn't sure why, but I felt he deserved to know where my loyalties lay. "I don't want anything to do with him."

"I'm glad to hear it," Paula said. I did a double take on her as she stood from her chair. She had just lied to me. She wasn't glad to hear it. I wondered if she was secretly hoping I would turn myself over and save them all the trouble.

"This is no longer a decision I can make on my own. We need to make this decision as a coven. What we are facing is something unimaginable. It will take everything we have and everything we are to fight this. It very well could take our lives. It's not a decision to make lightly. It's also not a decision we can make based on what we assume Sister Aggie wanted. We have to decide this on our own. Hennie is our friend and our sister. Please stand if you consent to follow me in this battle of your own free will."

I watched as the faces bounced to one another, searching for the answers in different eyes. One by one, they all stood to support me.

The only one left seated was Dane. Slumped back in his chair with his arms crossed, he watched them all agree to their suicidal mission with disinterest.

"You too, Dane," Paula said.

"I'm just the muscle. I don't make the big decisions."

"I hope you didn't think we saved you from execution for your witty banter and cynicism? Whether you like it or not, you are a part of this group, which includes being a part of the risk. Either you agree or you don't."

"Sounds like a pretty good time to me." Dane looked at me and nodded. "I'll fight for Hennie." With his return loyalty established, I couldn't help but feel a little safer.

I looked over my friends and my sisters with swelling pride and growing guilt. They were ready to fight the devil himself on my behalf. I didn't bother to mention *I* wasn't ready to fight him.

CHAPTER 44

REGARDLESS OF WHAT I said to convince them otherwise, everyone was on board with the new plan. We were staring into the face of hell with the equivalent of fluttering fingers pinned to our noses. Our childish attempts at rebellion were not likely to impress him.

I still didn't understand why everyone would risk their lives to save me. At least when it was under the orders of Aggie, it made sense. Now, however, they were just doing it for me. It was flattering, of course, but it was a lot of weight to carry on my conscience.

We were once again back to the basics. Our circle of eight witches and one bodyguard was all that stood between us and annihilation. I put my faith in my sisters. I may not have believed in myself, but they did. The murmur of chanting began, and I felt a wave of pleasure trickle into my veins.

I looked at Dane, where he was leaning against the wall, watching me. He had seen something in me from the very beginning. Something he didn't understand. Something he wanted to hunt. I supposed the fact that he hadn't killed me said something about my character.

I closed my eyes and tipped my chin to the ceiling. I let my guilt evaporate with my magical euphoria. I opened myself up, wider than I've ever done before. I allowed the power to not just flow through me, but into me.

Even as the magnificent force of power settled into my bones, I felt a chill that went even deeper. I felt intangible hands wrapped around my shoulders, pressing down on me. I could feel breath against my neck. As wrong as it was, it felt right.

"This is too much, Hennie," my shadow purred into my ear. "You've gone well beyond your boundaries. I won't allow you to stay here much longer."

"And what will you do to stop me?"

"I've told you what I would do."

"You've told me what you would do to others to get me back. You've killed my friend. You've killed my sister. Yet I am still here. If you were capable of taking me back by force, you would've done it by now. It's as I've always suspected: You have no real power over me."

"I have more power over you than you realize. The only reason I have not punished you is because it would hurt me as well. I told you before you're a part of me. I want you back. At my side. Loyal to me."

"If that's true, then you can do nothing to me."

"I can destroy your coven."

"You can try." With an elegant wave of my hands, the power inside of me spread, trickling through the bond that connected me to my coven. The sisters gasped as they received my magic.

"No," my shadow rasped. "Don't do this."

"I just did. If you want me back, you will have to get through the entire coven to get me."

"You have no idea what you've done."

"I've given them a part of my power."

"It was not yours to give away." I felt his hands slip away. "I wonder... I wonder what you'll choose once this power has changed you."

"I am only using this power to get away from you."

My shadow chuckled from somewhere behind me. "Foolish girl. The more you use this power, the closer you get to me." I heard him laugh again, somewhere in the distance, but it faded away, as did the euphoric feeling of the magic coursing through our circle.

I open my eyes and looked around at my sisters. They were alight with enthusiasm for my gift. Dane, on the other hand, seemed furious. His narrowed eyes were fixed on me; his jaw was set, and his fists clenched.

"What did you just do?" Rachel asked, staring at me.

"I used our bond to plug you into my power. Now you can access it anytime you need, in or out of the circle."

The sisters glanced at one another and laughed.

"You were only supposed to put a protection spell on us," Paula said as she examined her hands. "Why did you do *this*?"

"Because I want to free Aggie from her demons."

"Can we do that?" Meredith asked.

"I think we can now." I smiled.

"No," Paula interjected. "We need to focus on the threat at hand."

"But we could use her. We need her help."

Paula frowned and glanced around at her fellow sisters. "I know all of you want to save Aggie, but there's so much evil inside of her. I'm afraid that if we try to help her now, we may find ourselves getting dragged under with her."

"She's right," Rachel said. "We need to save ourselves and then we can save her."

I sighed, unhappy that Paula was still keeping me from doing the one thing I wanted to do with my power: save my mentor. Rather than argue with her logic, I nodded my head along with the others.

CHAPTER 45

"YOU DO REALIZE HOW ridiculous this is?" I asked Rachel as we walked the grounds of the school, spreading salt, holy water, and a mixture of herbs intended to hold back the avalanching threat of hell.

"It's just a precaution. We need all the help we can get," Rachel insisted.

"No, not the salt. I mean... Fuck, Rachel, it's the *devil*." I threw my hands out expectantly. "We can't actually win. All we can do is piss him off."

Rachel threw down her bag of salts and turned to face me. "Just what the hell do you think we are going to do? This is why we do this. We were *always* fighting the devil. The only difference between now and then is he's actually started taking notice of our fight. We were flies before, buzzing in his ears. Now he sees us. Now he's actually worried about us."

"And you think that's a good thing? The devil seeing you? I don't want you to get hurt." Rachel frowned at me. "I don't want any of you to get hurt. This just seems like too big of a fight. Not when I can stop it."

"It's okay, you know." Rachel took a step forward and pushed a piece of my hair back into my wimple. "We aren't going to blame you if things go bad." She rested her hand on my shoulder and smiled. "We've all had difficult lives. We've hurt people, and they've hurt us. We know we will get hurt again, but it doesn't mean you stop moving forward." She moved her hand to my cheek, stroking her thumb along the skin. "This is our destiny. This is why we were all drawn here. It's not about survival at this point. It's about completion."

Rachel stared back at me, holding her small smile without retreat. For a moment, I thought I saw something in her eyes. As unusual as our friendship was at that point, I wasn't sure that was quite what I saw.

"What are you girls doing out here?" Dane's voice interrupted the awkward moment, and we backed away from each other. We each took our turn looking at the ground before turning back to Dane. "Don't let me interrupt."

"I'll finish the circle." Rachel snatched up her bag of salt and continued to sprinkle along the fence that skirted the property. I suddenly felt guilty, but I wasn't sure why.

"She likes you." Dane moved up beside me, scanning the perimeter. His new skill set had put him on permanent guard duty.

"Only sometimes." I shrugged. "We haven't quite made it to friend status."

Dane chuckled and looked over at me. "I don't mean that she wants to exchange friendship bracelets, Sister. I mean, I think she wants to exchange tongue lickings."

I scoffed and looked away. "She's not gay."

"How would you know? You've never even had sex. How would you recognize when someone wants to be with you?"

"I'm not a virgin," I snapped before I realized what I was admitting to.

"Oh," Dane drawled. "One of *those* nuns, huh? The ones that go in post-poppin."

I gritted my teeth and shook my head. "You are so disgusting. Can you say anything that doesn't sound rude or hypocritical?"

Dane considered that for a moment, dipping his head in thought. "Didn't you like it?"

"Like what?" He smirked at me and winked. "Oh." I sighed, thinking about the last time I had delved into a relationship. "I liked it just fine."

"Then why become a nun?"

"I'm not really a nun." I glanced at him to see what he thought of that. He narrowed his eyes at me. "Sister Aggie needed members to join her coven. Not everyone gifted in magic is willing to take the vows, so we just go through the motions with our fingers crossed and a few prayers of penance."

"So, which of you are actually nuns?"

"Sister Aggie, Sister Paula, Sister Rachel—"

Dane hissed. "Oh, too bad for you. That might've been a nice love story."

I frowned and looked over at Rachel. She was still dutifully surrounding the premises with salt. I was curious whether he was right. I wasn't sure it mattered, but I wondered whether her irritation for me stemmed from the frustration of an attraction. Or perhaps I really was just as annoying as she thought I was.

"It doesn't matter, anyway. I'm not gay," I mumbled and looked back at him. A small smile creased his eyes. "I have to finish sprinkling these herbs." I lifted the brown bag as if proving I wasn't just running away. I moved down the fence, adding a second layer of protection to our property. I glanced back and saw that Dane was following me. I wasn't sure why, but I got the impression it wasn't to keep me safe.

CHAPTER 46

I WOKE IN THE middle of the night to the smell of burned flesh. I flung my blankets off and jumped out of bed. I opened my door, glancing up and down the hallway. I listened for the sounds of screams, but I couldn't hear anything.

I moved down the hall door to door, sniffing for the source of the odor. The lingering scent seemed to run away from my nose as I moved.

With no more doors to sniff, I moved downstairs. The main office and the classrooms were locked up tight. There was no sign of fire, no source for the smell, and no reason for alarm, and yet I felt on edge. Something was wrong. I just wasn't smart enough to figure out what it was.

I moved down to the cafeteria in search of the only open source of flame I could think of. I cringed, thinking of what could be going on to cause such a smell. Visions of Hannibal Lecter's dinner parties popped into my head, and I nearly gagged.

As I stepped into the eating area, I noted the empty chairs surrounding the tables. The steel buffet line separating the dining room from the kitchen was empty. No sign of fava beans or anything else. Except for the emergency lighting, the room was dark.

I heard a grunt and some movement from inside the kitchen. I moved past the buffet, treading into the territory of yellow stained linoleum. I zeroed in on the noises and determined they were coming from the pantry. I moved forward, prepared to yank open the door and save whoever was on the other side from a horrible death.

Just before my hand hit the knob, another grunt and a lamented moan stopped me cold. I paused and listened to the definitive rhythm of the movement. I heard panting, and then Meredith's voice declared a verbal consent to her partner for the activity. My mouth dropped, and I backed away from the door before I could make an unusual situation embarrassing as hell.

I knew Meredith wasn't chaste. I was also aware she wasn't a stranger to a prolific sex life. However, it had never occurred to me that she would sneak her suitors into the building at night. Then again, how else was she going to maintain an active heterosexual lifestyle with an all-female coven?

As I backed away from the door, I thought about my conversation that afternoon with Dane. I had revealed to him that some of the nuns—nearly all, at that point—were not celibate. I frowned at my prediction regarding the identity of the man behind the pantry door. It had not taken Dane long to coerce Meredith's hatred for him into lust.

I wasn't sure why it bothered me so much. Perhaps it was a jealousy of sorts. Dane was far from a suitable boyfriend, given that he was a serial murderer and all, but at that point, he was the only man to even consider. I suppose that little side of me that imagined a connection between us was pouting.

I headed back out of the kitchen. A hard body swung around the corner in the dining room and I smashed into it. A pair of arms wrapped around me, lightly bracing me in case I fell. "Whoa, careful, chickity."

I looked up at Dane's face and smiled, stupidly revealing my relief for his exterior position to the pantry. "What are you...? I thought you were...?"

Dane's brow perked as he found some small amusement in my confusion. "Midnight snack?" he asked.

"No, I was checking on something." I frowned as I heard the entertainment in the pantry get a little louder. "We should get back to bed." I pushed him back as if I could simply corral him away.

"What is that?" His eyes darted toward the kitchen. Instead of moving backward, he moved forward.

"Dane, don't." I tugged on his T-shirt, trying to stop his movement like a bridle on a horse. "It's nothing."

"Is that what I *think* it is?" He snorted and tiptoed into the kitchen where I had just been. The sounds from inside the pantry were coming to a close, and therefore much louder and enthusiastic. "Who is that?" he asked.

"Meredith," I whispered. "I don't know who the man is."

"Lucky guy. Although it doesn't sound like she's faring too bad herself."

"Please, Dane." I tugged on his shirt again. "Don't embarrass her. Or me." He glanced down at my hand twisted in the cotton of his T-shirt. I couldn't tell if my attempt to bully him amused him, or if he was amused by my familiarity.

He took a few steps back and listened to the finale. I caught him watching me, no doubt finding great amusement in the bright blush that had formed on my cheeks because of the pleasureful moans coming from inside the pantry.

He smiled and touched a lock of my hair. For the first time since I met him, my hair was fully exposed. Not to mention I was in a nightgown. It wasn't the sexy type that men preferred; it was more or less a prison-issued, old-lady flannel. However, since it wasn't a black robe—symbolic of a marriage to God—and offered at least some view of my figure, it was probably an improvement in his eyes.

I rested my hand against his stomach and felt the taut muscles beneath the thin layer of cotton. I wasn't sure if the background noise, or my proximity to his body heat, inspired it, but I couldn't keep my eyes from roaming over his body, examining the hard curves.

By the time I reached his face, I was panting as if I were the one inside the closet. He looked at me in the same fashion, with a sort of hungry intrigue. We stared at each other, our baser instincts hanging out like slobbering tongues.

I hadn't even realized our background music had shut off until there was a scuffle inside the pantry. We both snapped out of our reverie and retreated behind a shelf that masked the sink from view of the dining room. Despite being safely screened from view, Dane pressed me back a little farther, as if Meredith's rendezvous was a threat we were hiding from.

Meredith's man complimented her body and begged to see her again. She agreed, but only on the condition that she call him. I heard them kiss and footsteps moved away from us.

I breathed a sigh of relief and after a few seconds, I came out of hiding to leave the kitchen. I heard Dane laugh behind me. "Wait a minute." He moved up behind me and snaked his arm around to block my path between the metal buffet and the wall. He repositioned in front of me, his jaw twisting in smug satisfaction. "You thought *I* was in there." He motioned back to the pantry.

"What?" I tried to move around him, but he shifted to block my path. "Move."

"You did, didn't you?"

I shrugged. "Of course I thought you were in there. You're the only man here."

He licked his lips. "Yeah, but you smiled when you saw me."

"No, I didn't."

"Yeah, you did." He pointed his finger at me. "You took one look at me and smiled. You didn't want me to be the guy in that closet."

I looked back at the pantry and then at him. "It doesn't matter." I tried again to bypass him, but he just weaved in my way, trying to keep eye contact with me even as I evaded it. "Please move."

He moved, but only to come closer to me. I took a step back, but he stayed right on top of me. "Look at me," he whispered.

I swallowed and looked up at him. His satisfied smirk was gone, replaced by a discontented frown. He shook his head. "Why would you want to be in that closet with me?"

"I don't." He leaned down and kissed me. I froze as he willed my lips to part for him. I finally surrendered, and he devoured my lips, summoning a whimper of shocked pleasure from me. When he moved away, he looked at me with the same unhappy surprise.

"Why did you let me do that?"

"I don't know."

"I'm the bad guy, Hennie."

"Not anymore."

"I'm a bad guy with a purpose. That's not the same thing as being innocent." He narrowed his eyes. "Why would you even consider lowering yourself to be with me?"

I shrugged, not really sure myself. "Haven't you heard? I'm a demon."

He chuckled and lifted his hand to my forehead. He pushed aside my hair, examining my scalp. "I don't see any horns here."

"Then you're not looking hard enough."

He nodded, pondering on that thought a moment. He braced one hand on my shoulder as he reached around me with the other. Before I realize what he was doing, he lifted my nightgown over my buttocks. "Nope, no tail," he declared as I ripped away from him.

"Very funny." I smoothed down my gown. "You're quite the charmer. I can't imagine what you did to get all those women to sleep with you." He chuckled and waved a hand over his fit body. "Besides that. You had to have said something or done something that inspired them to take you home."

He smirked, although I could see there was a little sadness in his eyes. He didn't remember his triumphs as proudly as he once had. "I just told them they were beautiful."

"That's it?"

"That's all you need if you say it right. And if you mean it."
He stepped close to me again and brushed my hair away from
my face. "Would you like me to tell you how beautiful you are,
Hennie?"

I gulped and shook my head. "Actually, I'd rather you tell me
I'm not a bad person."

He took a breath and grabbed my hand. "Let's not get ahead
of ourselves now. Bad can be pretty fun." He took a step
back, drawing my hand forward. He paused before turning and
tugging me onward.

I let go of my thoughts and the reservations that were hanging
on to the idea of Dane's previous life. I followed him without
question, much as he had followed me once before to battle my
demons.

We descended the stairs to the basement and walked down
to his cage. He pulled open the door and released my hand.
He leaned on it, waiting for me to enter. Without the physical
cajoling, my feet remained frozen, unprepared to make a
decision, let alone deal with the consequences of that decision.

Dane scoffed quietly and stepped inside his cell. He looked
back at me and slowly closed the door. I had a feeling if I was
on the other side when the metal clanked, he wouldn't open it
again.

Before it latched, I pressed my foot in its path. He glanced
down at the doorstop, then back at me. A sinister satisfaction
settled into his face and he backed away, giving me room to step
inside. I closed the door behind us, even though there was no
privacy in the cage. The two levels between us and the other girls
were the only thing securing our privacy. I imagined it was more
than enough distance to mute my moans of pleasure—or my
screams of pain if I was wrong about Dane's rehabilitation.

He sat down on his bed and reached out for me. I stared down
at his hand, contemplating the complex emotions leading me
into the arms of a murderer. He leaned forward and took my

hand, tugging me gently towards him. I shuffled over to stand in front of him. With no further encouragement from me one way or another, he slid his hands up the backs of my legs, under my nightgown, and over my buttocks. He tugged on the fabric of my panties, drawing them down to my feet so I could step out of them.

He drew them up with a single finger and waved the black lace in front of me. "These don't look like the panties of a good girl."

"Then catch me on laundry day."

He paused his cool, calm, collected sex-beast mode. His smug smirk momentarily twisted into an outright lopsided grin.

He shook away the distraction and removed his shirt. My heart raced at the sight of his smooth skin and perfectly corrugated abs. Why did the bad guys always have to be so damn hot?

He undid his pants and shifted them down to reveal the broad length of masculinity that had been missing in my life since my first and only boyfriend dumped me. I wasn't sure the male member could ever be described as beautiful, but if it could, Dane was a contender for the compliment.

He used my panties to massage the length of his shaft. I stared at the display with rapt fascination. I had never been envious of my panties before.

"See something you like?" He groaned from the enjoyment of his own touch.

"Why are you teasing me?"

"I'm not teasing you. I have every intention of letting you have me. I just want to make sure you can't blame me for seducing you tomorrow. You can still be a good girl and go back upstairs with the rest of the nuns. Or you can be a bad girl and climb onto my cock."

There was no question of what I was going to do. I reached forward and ripped my panties from his grasp. I tossed them to the floor where they belonged and took my rightful seat on Dane's lap.

I gasped as his exquisite girth slipped into place. His eyes shut and he bit his lip. I moved against him, and he opened his eyes. He leaned forward and pulled my nightdress up over my head.

He reached around my back, pressing my breasts to his mouth. He grabbed a fistful of my hair and yanked my head back. He kissed my neck, dragging his tongue up to my chin. He gave the skin a playful bite before releasing my hair again.

His movements stopped all at once. I looked down at him and found him frowning. With any other man, I might have assumed he had already finished without me. In Dane's case, I assumed far worse things. "What's wrong?" I asked.

"Nothing." He looked up at me. "This feels right. This feels... normal."

"Isn't that a good thing?" I kissed him and drew back to look at him again. When he still looked befuddled, I raised my hand and touched his cheek. "Are you okay?"

"Yes, I think I am."

"You're not going to hurt me, are you Dane?" I asked, just to be sure.

He shook his head slowly. "No, I don't want to hurt you, Hennie. I only want to give you pleasure."

I heard the honesty in his statement, and I relaxed my defenses. I moved again, drawing his attention back to our initial purpose. I wasn't sure what illumination our joined bodies had provided him—other than the fact that it felt fantastic—but he seemed relieved by it, as if the feelings of confusion and resentment linked to his childhood abuse were no longer clouding his enjoyment of our intimacy.

Dane's enthusiasm revived and he continued with the act, unencumbered and without distraction. As we found our rhythm, the sexual argument began, me rising on his length, and him pulling me back down again. All the while, the friction ignited us. My ebullience left me bellowing wildly, and his grunts of ardor sounded as animalistic as mine. United in a climactic euphoria, we groaned, and I collapsed against him.

Panting and sweating, I held onto him, allowing my heart rate to come down and reality to seep back in. The romanticism passed, and we were just two naked bodies, slightly more acquainted than when we started. He moved beneath me and I shifted off him.

He sprawled out on his cot. Once he was situated, he directed me down beside him. I tucked into the crook of his arm and watched him watching me. He played with my hair; pulling a strand forward, he frowned at the blackened tips. He showed it to me as if it was the first time I might've seen it. "What's that?"

I smiled. "A phase."

He chuckled and released the hair. "Cute," he muttered. I wasn't sure how black-streaked hair qualified as cute. If anything, I had done it to remove the description of cute from my appearance.

"Are you comfortable?" he asked as he laid his head back and closed his eyes.

"Yes, but I should probably go back upstairs."

"Mmm-hmm," he mumbled an agreement and squeezed me a little closer.

CHAPTER 47

I ROLLED AWAY FROM Dane, nearly falling off the cot. I scrambled to get up and get dressed before anyone could walk in on us. Not that anyone came down to the basement besides me, but still.

As soon as my feet hit the floor, something felt wrong. As wrong as it did when I had woken last night to the smell of burning flesh. This time I was sure of it.

Dane woke and saw me struggling to get my pajamas back on. "It's barely sunrise. Come back to bed."

As tempting as the request was, the pull to get upstairs was far stronger.

"What is it?" he asked, seeing the distress on my face. He sat up in bed. "What's wrong?"

"I don't know. Something is very wrong." I moved toward the door, but he grabbed my arm.

"Wait for me," he said and pulled himself out of bed.

"I can't."

"I said wait," he said forcefully.

Despite my urgency, I waited for him to throw on a pair of pants and a T-shirt. We ran along the basement floor, our bare feet slapping against the concrete. We reached the stairs and thundered up and as a united pair. After the second rise, I found the source of my urgent instincts.

The sisters had gathered in the library, still in their pajamas like me. I cursed and ran toward them. I flung open the windowed door, alerting everyone to my presence. Several sad faces stared back at me.

I moved forward, passing tearful eyes as I sought the reason for their distress. I was already shaking my head as Paula stepped into my path. She blocked my view of the table where Aggie had spent most of her time since her possession began.

"Hennie, I don't think you should see this."

"What? What is it? What has happened to her?" I yelled.

"She's dead."

"What? No!" I pushed past her, refusing to allow her to censor the level of my grief. As my view cleared, I saw Sister Aggie sitting in her chair. The vacant, dull expression in her eyes was proof alone that her body was without life, but it was her position that declared her death a malicious act. Her neck was partially severed, leaving her head to loll back over the back of the chair. Her glassy eyes stared back at me from their upside-down position.

I moved forward, and nearly everyone reached for me, ready to catch me before I could step in the massive pool of blood that was still congealing in the shallow carpet around her chair. I avoided the bulk of the blood and leaned over to pull up her sleeves. I had expected to see claw marks, but her arms were only bruised.

Aggie wasn't killed by the same hateful creature that had killed the others. This was not a well-planned accident and it certainly wasn't suicide.

It would be easy to blame her death on the parasitic demons, but I was certain they wouldn't dream of killing their host. What would be the fun in that?

This was outright murder—something that the devil in any form was incapable of. Aggie had been killed by a human. Someone with a taste for blood.

I glanced back over the faces surrounding Aggie, each distraught by her death. Everyone except Dane, who was observing the scene of carnage with indifference.

CHAPTER 48

"**W**HAT EXACTLY ARE YOU saying, Hennie?" Paula asked.

"Is there any way that the devil could have done this?"

"No. It goes against the will of God for him to kill humans."

"Her demons wouldn't have killed her. They were having too much fun. Killing her would have robbed them of their host. That means she was killed by a human being."

"Don't you think it's more likely she did this to herself?" Paula moved back to Aggie and examined her body closer.

"You're kidding, right? There is no way that cut is self-inflicted. She would have bled out before she could get close to that deep. Not to mention, where exactly did she get the knife?" I asked. "And more importantly, where did she put it after she slit her throat? She hasn't moved from the chair."

"But if this happened overnight, you're saying that someone here did this, aren't you?" Meredith asked. She glanced around the room, as if somebody might raise their hand and admit to the crime.

"The blood of the visionary has been spilled," Katherine whispered. "God will call another to take her place."

"No one here would do this," Ruby said. "We all loved Aggie. Unless... Are you saying that this was an act of mercy?"

"This is far too vicious for an act of mercy," Rachel said. "This was outright murder."

"And we all know who is capable of murder," Dane pointed out.

One by one, our heads turned to look at him. I was grateful I didn't have to point out the obvious. However, since Dane was staring at me, I was fairly certain I hadn't kept my concerns as obscure as I thought.

"There is more than one murderer here." Paula moved back to us and crossed her arms. Her right hand fiddled with her rosary that was perpetually within reach, apparently even at night. "Hennie has a very valid point. And if this was murder, it was probably done by someone with access to this room. That, unfortunately, includes everyone." Paula looked around the room. "And we all know how to fish out liars around here. I'll start by stating that I did not slit Sister Aggie's throat. Hennie, am I lying?"

"No," I answered.

"Good. Meredith, are you responsible for Sister Aggie's death?" Paula asked.

"No, I am not," Meredith answered forcefully, as if she needed to enunciate the words to keep me from getting a false positive.

Paula posed the same question to each of us, and we all claimed our innocence. In the end, it was down to Dane. "Are you responsible for Sister Aggie's death, Dane?" Paula repeated.

Dane smirked at me and shrugged. "You believe whatever the hell you want."

"Dane, just answer," I pleaded. I was ninety-nine percent sure couldn't have killed her, but I didn't like that he wasn't cooperating.

"I'm not answering that question," Dane said.

"Why?" I asked.

"Because it doesn't matter. Any one of us could have done it and not remember. It's not a lie if you believe what you're saying is true."

Paula looked at me. "It is possible that one of us was coerced into performing this act by the devil, but it would take a lot of work to override our free will. Does anyone remember anything strange happening last night?"

"We were sleeping," Ruby said. "How would we know?"

"What about a trip to the restroom? Was anyone out of their rooms last night?" Paula continued to prod.

Meredith blushed and looked down at her feet.

"I was out of my room last night, but I have an alibi," Dane readily admitted as he stared me down, threatening to reveal our impromptu tryst to get back at me for my accusation.

"And what's that?" Paula asked.

"I saw him when I got up," I answered. "I thought I smelled smoke early this morning. I went down to the kitchen to check, and I ran into him on the way out."

"That only proves he was up and around," Rachel said. "Where did you go after that? There was plenty of time to step in here and slit Aggie's throat."

Dane licked his lips, as if he was relishing the idea of wallowing in my embarrassment. "I can't say much for after that," he said. "I slept pretty well. That's all I know."

I stared at him, grateful and guilty. It was a minor concession and one that still left him as a potential suspect, but I couldn't help but wonder why he was up to begin with. Did he follow me to the kitchen, and if so, how did he know I was going there unless he was already awake?

"This is my fault." Meredith's face scrunched as she looked back at Aggie's body. "I brought in someone last night. A date. I must not have locked the door. Someone must have gotten in."

"Meredith, you know how we feel about that," Rachel said.

"I know. I know. I just needed a break. A little stress relief."

"Let's not jump to any conclusions," Paula said. "Let's look around for the murder weapon. That might give us more answers."

We piled out of the library and searched our rooms. As demeaning as it was to be playing *Clue* with my own sisters, it was even more difficult to consider that the man I had just slept with could be responsible for Aggie's death.

One by one we searched the rooms, finding nothing but minimal contraband: candy bars, condoms, and clothing catalogs. Nothing that was going to get anyone killed.

After the last room, everyone milled about, glancing at Dane. No one wanted to suggest that we check his area. The only thing more dangerous than accusing a murderer of murder was standing next to him while you did it.

"Alright, let's head downstairs," Paula announced. She didn't seem to be afraid of Dane. Even after being his punching bag, she didn't seem to view him as good or evil, just a necessary tool.

Our slippers and bare feet plodded downstairs. We made our way across the basement and clustered around the cage while Ruby and Rachel searched it.

Since Dane had no belongings, it was only a matter of ripping the sheets off the mattress and flipping it up. Beneath the bed cushion was a bright gold letter opener with a wooden handle.

I frowned and looked at Dane. He shook his head. "I put that there for my protection. I didn't kill anyone with it. Not yet, anyway," he added, diminishing his credibility further.

"Will you answer the question now?" I asked Dane.

"I went straight to bed after I bumped into you. Is that a lie?" Everyone turned to look at me for the answer.

"No."

"I have no desire to hurt any of you. Is that still true?" he asked me.

"Yes." I nodded.

Dane shifted past the girls to stand in front of me. "Then why the fuck do I have to keep answering that question?"

"What if you were possessed?"

Dane tapped his forehead. "There isn't room for any more up here. I got all the demons I can handle right now." He brushed past me and moved farther down the hall. He stopped and turned back. "And for your information, there's no way anyone could cut her throat with a damn letter opener. Your murderer either had something sharper, or they were using magic to do it."

CHAPTER 49

DESPITE MY SUSPICIONS OF Dane and the laundry list of reasons I had for not being with a former murderer, my mind kept wandering back to the memories of last night's encounter. I couldn't stop thinking about his chiseled features, soft skin, and powerful arms. I wanted nothing more than to slip out of my bed and crawl into his.

However, aside from the visceral attraction I felt toward him, I wasn't sure there was anything else between us. I wanted to believe he was a changed man, and I did, but I wasn't sure he was the right man for me. I had spent my whole life struggling to fit in, and being a demon wouldn't help that any. The last thing I wanted to do was add 'death-row boyfriend' to my quota of strange.

Somewhere after midnight, I couldn't take it anymore. My lust was getting the better of me, but I wasn't sure I cared. After all, I hadn't taken a vow of celibacy. I pulled my feet out of my covers and pressed them to the cold floor of my tiny room.

Just then, I heard the doorknob twist. My heart leaped, hoping it might be Dane, yielding to his own desirous quandary. The door creaked open and a shadowy figure stepped inside. My disappointment was immediate; it wasn't my new lover's large physique in the doorway, but rather my petite sister.

"Rachel?" I asked. She shut the door and moved toward me. She kneeled down in front of me. "What are you doing here?" She latched onto my knees, and I instinctively pressed my hands over hers. I could see through the moonlight streaming in my window that her eyes were puffy and red. "What's wrong?" I frowned and touched her face.

"Please, forgive me," she said in earnest. "I begged it not to be true, but I can't deny it now."

"Can't deny what?"

She reached up and pressed her palm to my cheek, mimicking my own gentle caress. I thought back to what Dane had said about her being a lesbian. I blinked at the movement and took a deep breath. "Rachel," I whispered and shook my head. I wasn't entirely sure how to reject her attraction without dismissing her feelings. "I don't think—"

"I killed her."

My eyes widened, and I pulled my face away from her touch. "What?"

She drew away from me and pressed her rosary between the palms of her hands. "I don't remember it, but I know I must've done it."

"Why do you say that?"

"I woke in the morning from a terrible nightmare. I thought the visions were a premonition, so I ran to check on Sister Aggie, but she was already dead."

"Just because you found her doesn't mean you did it. Maybe the dreams were premonitory, but you didn't wake in time to stop it."

Rachel shook her head and looked up at me. "After we looked for the knife, I went for my morning shower. When I disrobed, I found blood splattered on my arms."

I took a breath, trying to rationalize the finding. I wasn't sure why I wanted it not to be true, but I needed to know Rachel was innocent. Perhaps it was because she was a true nun—one of the few of us who would actually commit to this life and to God. It needed to be Dane, or it needed to be someone of questionable morality. It couldn't be her. "Maybe you touched her when you found her—"

"I also found this." Rachel pulled up the sleeves of her robe, revealing bruises on her forearms. The size and shape resembled that of hands, as if the devil himself had latched onto her and guided her to murder her mentor. "More than that, I feel it." Rachel pressed her hand against her chest. "Something's happened. Ever since we left that night... The night Jessica died, we performed the ceremony. It was meant to focus us, to help bring us back together, and give us guidance, but I don't think it did what it was supposed to do." Rachel opened her hand, showing me her rosary. "It doesn't feel right anymore."

"What doesn't feel right?"

"The crucifix." She pinched her fingers around the small silver cross and released it. "It hurts to hold it."

I took a breath and placed my hands on my forehead, rubbing away the forming migraine. My eyes prickled with the threat of tears. It needed to not be true. I knew enough about possession to know that the possessed did not prefer to be near religious artifacts.

"I've always struggled to control my desires." She sat back and touched my knees again, squeezing the muscles behind them. "The last few days, I've been unable to focus on my prayers. All I can think about is satisfying my cravings." She panted just speaking of the cravings. "At first, I thought it was a test. Or that the proximity of this evil was bringing my endurance into question." She squeezed my legs painfully. "But they are no longer cravings that a human should have."

"What does that mean?" I touched her hands, silently begging her to release the blood flow to my legs.

"I mean, I am no longer craving food or sex. I am being compelled to drink blood, and eat dirt, and..." Rachel pinched away the tears flooding her eyes. "I saw a dead rat in the basement, and I had to force myself not to eat it." I winced as she pinched my legs hard enough to dig her nails into the skin. "That is not the behavior of a human. I am carrying a demon inside of me. I don't know when he arrived and I don't know if he will ever leave, but before I can no longer control him, I need you to know I am no longer to be trusted."

I forcefully pulled her claws from my skin and pressed her hands together. "What can I do?"

She shook her head. "I don't think you can do anything. We need the power of God, but there is more evil here than good. We've been outplayed. You need to get out of here. He won't stop until you're dead. Until one of us kills you." Rachel looked at me gravely. "I don't want to be responsible for another death."

Swallowing hard, I looked down at the crescent imprints her nails had cut into me. I felt the fear I was possibly much too late to act on. I had feared for the safety of my sisters when the devil had threatened to harm them, but it never occurred to me that he would use them as a weapon against me. It was the ultimate offense, because even with the threat of my death, I didn't want to hurt them.

And the cherry on top of the devil's plan was me imbuing my potential murderers with my power.

CHAPTER 50

I REACHED THE FRONT door and noticed the chains leashing the handles together. The heavy padlock was not something that was going to give way easily. I tried to use my magic on it, but it was bound with a spell that couldn't break—a spell created with the strength of a coven.

I smelled fire and ash permeating the air in the hall. I could feel the weight of silence pressing down on me. There was always noise in the old school—creaking and settling, old pipes clanking and bad ventilation—but now everything was quiet.

I ran to the office and unlocked the window Aggie used to conceal her smoking habit. I ripped off the screen and maneuvered myself out of the slanted opening. I was halfway out, tasting the humidity of the night air, when a scream froze me in place.

It was a deep, harrowing cry for help, and I immediately knew it was Dane. I also knew it was a trap. He was the only one that the demons couldn't get into, but that didn't mean they couldn't get to him through the sisters.

If it had been a day earlier, I wouldn't have thought twice about cutting my losses and jumping out the window to freedom. As it stood now, however, Dane was my lover, and he deserved at least some consideration.

As I hung through the window pane staring down at the grass below, I weighed fear and self-preservation against a one-night stand. I wasn't sure I could even save him. And there was, of course, the chance that I would die trying. Was it worth risking my life for a serial murderer?

I was nearly ready to bolt for freedom when I remembered what Jess had told me about the devil. The difference between good and evil was how you behaved when you were given great power.

With some effort, I climbed back inside the office and shut the window behind me. Resigned to my duty as the unofficial heroine, I followed the sounds of Dane's agonized screams in the basement.

CHAPTER 51

I DESCENDED INTO THE darkness of the basement. I could hear the chants of my coven, but I couldn't see them. Their litany was normally a welcoming sound to my ears, but now it sounded ominous.

The candlelight circle set in amongst the concrete pillars offered a perfect view of Dane's naked form writhing on the floor. There was no visible source of his pain, yet new gashes were being rented across his chest. His body lurched upward as if his heart were about to be ripped out of his chest.

I moved forward cautiously and kneeled at the edge of the circle. He turned and looked at me. The fear in his eyes was more than his fear of death or pain. He had seen the beast, and he knew what torments awaited him in hell.

"Get out!" he yelled at me. "Get away from them!"

I felt as much as saw the darkness shift. The robed figures of my sisters stepped out of the darkness, blocking my path back to the stairs.

"Let him go!" I yelled over their spell. I turned to each one of them, begging for his release. "Please don't do this. You can fight your demons."

Paula stepped out of the ranks and paused in front of me. "I don't think you're going to want to stay for this, Hennie." She stepped into the interior of the candlelit circle and stood next to Dane.

"Stay for what?" I asked. "What are you going to do to him?"

"I'm not going to do anything to him. The beast, however, has different plans."

"Paula, you have to stop this. You have to fight what's inside of you."

"Oh Hennie, you foolish girl. I'm not possessed. There is no Sister Paula. I am the ram. Remember?" She smiled and poked her fingers up alongside her head.

I frowned, looking over her features in a new light. She had been the epitome of religious grace to me, the balance between Sister Aggie's matriarchal brusqueness and Sister Rachel's rigid devotion. There was nothing to indicate she was marked or driven by evil intent. "You've been here the whole time."

She chuckled and nodded. "The whole time."

"Even before me."

She leaned forward and whispered, "They never even suspected me. Standing right next to them, helping their cause, all the while subtly directing them. I've been doing it for years. Mostly just to observe their activities. When you showed up to this misfit group of witches, I knew I couldn't stand by and watch anymore."

I looked back at my sisters and found Rachel's face. She was crying despite the glazed look in her eyes. I reached for my power, drawing on the connection between us. I could feel her trying to fight the voices inside of her.

"It's no use, Hennie. You can't help her. You can't help any of them."

"They are stronger than you think."

"They are indeed, but they have surrendered their free will to follow me," Paula said.

"They would never do such a thing!" I turned back to face her.

"They did it right in front of you."

"What?"

"I asked if they would follow *me* in this battle of their own free will." I grimaced, remembering the agreement they all made to support me. It was all in the phrasing. "They may not want to do this, and some of them are fighting very hard, but they *have* to do this."

"Will you let them go if I agree to come with you?"

Paula looked back at them. "No." She simpered. "They belong to me now. I will use them until they are driven insane. Besides, it's been a while since I've done a bulk possession. I miss it."

"And what about Dane? Will you release him?"

Paula clicked her tongue and shook her head. "You have always been a pain in my ass, Hennie, but this abomination you created is far worse." She wheeled back around and circled Dane. His cries had become more subdued and his lurches less forceful, but I got the distinct impression it was only because he was wearing out, not because the pain was lessening. "I never thought it would be possible—a free-will soul partially transformed into a demon. He belongs in hell."

"No, you want me, not him. Just let him go and you can have me."

She smiled. "I'm afraid it's not that simple. You have given him the ability to kill demons. You have declared war against me, and this is your banner. I don't take that insult lightly."

"You and your beast declared this war. I've been trying to get out of this ridiculous situation since it began. You were the one who talked us into it."

"Free will." Paula leaned her head to one side, like the phrase made her nostalgic. "It's all a matter of perspective." She leaned down and touched Dane's cheek. He flinched at her gentle touch. "For example, from my perspective, Dane is more of a problem than you." She stood back up and tipped her head to examine me. "He's been generous with you. If I'd had my way, I would've killed every member of your family the day you were born."

"What?"

"Oh, didn't you realize? Your mother's accident... Not an accident."

"You couldn't have done that."

"You think it was that hard to convince a man to get drunk and drive recklessly? Not the most difficult whispers I've done."

"Don't tell me you're going to claim that my father's cancer was caused by you?"

"What cancer?" She smiled deviously. I stared back at her, frightened to ask for more information. "It's not the disease that killed him, it's the cure. That one was a bit more difficult—a few clumsy hands switching charts. By the time anyone realized the mistake, it was too late and, as you might imagine, no one was willing to take the fall for that one."

I cussed and put my hand over my eyes, willing my tears to go away. There wasn't time to mourn for the loss of my family in a different way. They were gone, never mind the how or the why. They weren't coming back. I couldn't save them, but maybe I could save Dane and the others.

I was vaguely aware of the power percolating through my body and into my extremities. It wasn't until I saw the irritation on Paula's face that I knew I was doing something bad. I threw the power at her, focusing on pain as much as raw energy. The force threw her across the basement. Her body slammed against the concrete foundation and flopped to the ground, unconscious.

I jumped into the circle and wrapped my arms around Dane, pulling him upward. He gurgled up blood as he spoke to me. "No, you have to get out of here."

"I need to save you."

"You can't. You can't fight this."

"Clearly I can." I nodded to Paula's slumped body at the end of the basement.

"Not her. It," he rasped and stared at something behind me.

A low growl vibrated my eardrums. I could feel hot breath on my neck and shoulders. The smell of fire and ash permeated the air, joined by sulfur.

I closed my eyes and brought my power back to the surface once again. The action spurred another growl from behind me. Dane continued to stare at it, his eyes as wide as they could go. He seemed unable to take his gaze off the ominous creature.

I considered turning around and blasting it with my magic, but the pressure of a gargantuan paw vaulted me out of the circle. I barely glimpsed the cracked skin over molten rock before I hit the ground.

As my eyes came back into focus, the blurry images of my sisters came into view. Their hands came at me from all around, grabbing my arms and legs, dragging me back into the circle. "No," I said. "Stop this! You have to fight her!"

Their glassy eyes stared away from me, concentrating only on their goal—doing the bidding of their new master. The indistinct murmur of chants bled into one another, creating a background noise that was as indistinguishable as chatter at a party.

They set me down inside the circle beside Dane and backed away, creating a secondary ring of bodies behind the candlelight. I frantically searched for the beast. I could feel its presence pressing down on me, far more than a tingling on the back of my neck. More like he wanted to rip my neck in two.

Off in the distant corner of the basement, within an unnatural darkness, I saw glowing red eyes. Hunched over on all fours, it still had enough height to loom over me. With each tiny movement, the cracks in its skin shifted, revealing the lava coursing beneath.

I jumped up and tried to barrel through the candle-lit circle and my surrounding coven, but more than their physical presence was keeping me there. I bounced back and landed on the floor again.

I searched my sisters for some sign of awareness, but each one of them had a shadow looming over her shoulders—a demon guiding them to go against me.

"Let them go!" I screamed.

"I appreciate you giving them a dose of your magic," Paula said from behind me. I looked back and saw her standing in the other corner of the basement, opposite the beast. "Now they are strong enough to keep you under control."

"I was trying to help them," I whimpered.

"I told you, Hennie," my shadow said. I whipped around and found him inside the coven circle with me, his handsome face daring to show sympathy for my situation. "Everything you have done from the beginning has only brought you closer to me."

I looked back at the beast and Paula. "Which one of you is real?"

"We all are," Paula enlightened me. "You've heard of the Holy Trinity. Think of us as Hell's Trinity."

I turned back to my shadow. "You're the same being?"

He tipped his head. "My mind, my body, and my rage. We are the same, but different."

"How is that possible?"

"Anything is possible if I will it to be so," he whispered, his voice as much in my head as in my ears.

"Why are you doing this, then?" I wailed. "How could one escaped soul be of any consequence to you? Can't you just let me live my life to a natural death?"

Paula and my shadow laughed; the beast growled, or perhaps it was its attempt at laughter. "You still don't understand what you are, do you, Hennie?" My shadow purred as he stepped inside the candlelight circle. "You don't belong here. This is not your body; you've stolen it from a dying mind."

"No, I am not a demon." I looked to the shadows hovering over my sisters. "I'm a good person. I'm not the best person, but I'm not evil. I *know* I'm not."

"You're right, you're not a demon," my shadow assured me. "You are not a human either. You are like nothing I have ever seen before."

"Is that why you want me so badly? Am I something special to you? Something so special you had to shadow my existence all of my life?"

He laughed again and looked at Paula. She nodded to him as if it was time to reveal the secret he had been holding just shy of my comprehension since he arrived. "I am not the shadow to your existence, Hennie. You are the shadow to mine."

I blinked and stared at him. I still didn't understand. I looked between him and Paula, gauging the sly, indeterminable expressions on their faces. "I don't understand. What does that mean?" I finally asked.

My shadow smiled and stepped away from me, looking down at the floor. I followed his gaze to the concrete beneath my feet. The room was dark, but the candlelight threw shadows everywhere. It was hard to tell where one shadow began and ended.

He raised his hands, bidding the candle flames behind him to rise up into torches. The extra light offered a definitive shadow between us. There was something odd about the way it stretched, overlapping my feet. I shifted to one side to examine the remainder of it, but it followed me, bending unnaturally. I looked behind me to see where my shadow would lay, but there was nothing there. No matter how I shifted, I couldn't block the light in any way to create one.

I shook my head and looked down at his shadow again. The elongated mass met my feet, but even when I stepped back, nothing more of it was revealed, as if the darkness vanished inside of me. "Tell me what this means!" I yelled at him.

"I have split myself into parts as a mockery of our Lord. But there were fragments of myself I preferred not to retain. Memories of a father I cannot deny." He stepped closer to me. "Desires I can't cover with my bitterness and rage." He reached up and grazed his finger along my cheek, touching so lightly that I wasn't sure whether it was actually his hand or just the warmth of it. "My sweet Hennie, you are the last shred of my soul, the only part of me I could not fully destroy."

"Your soul?" I backed away from him, nearly burning myself on a set of candles. "You can't possibly have a soul."

"I was given free will just as man was. I am the ultimate rebel."

"How is this possible? How can I be a part of you and yet separate from you?"

He motioned to Paula and the beast. "I pushed you away as far as I could until you were nothing more than a shadow at my back."

"I'm your shadow? But I'm flesh and blood."

"You were so pained and lonesome that you chose to flee my body rather than endure the darkness any longer. You became human."

"How? How did I get here?"

"The same way God brought Christ to earth. He took over a human body."

"You're not seriously suggesting what I think you are. Christ was not a demon!"

"No, of course not. He was a sliver of our Lord, placed inside an unborn child. The angel that visited Mary that night wasn't just delivering a message."

"That's ridiculous. You're saying that Christ was just a puppet for God."

"Not quite." My shadow narrowed his eyes on me. "Christ had permission from the child. You, on the other hand, injected yourself into this body without permission. In truth, you shouldn't even exist."

"I stole this body?" I looked at Paula, searching for some counsel despite her no longer being the woman I thought she was. My fears that I was a demon now seemed more appetizing than my current diagnosis.

"Your escape into this world has mocked me from the very beginning." He paced before me. "Without even trying, you have tapped into my power and used it against my will to help people I have no wish to help. This useless endeavor of being human is over. I want you back."

"You want me to die?"

"It's not quite that simple. You are connected to this body, and I to you. You must separate yourself from it. You must claim allegiance to your one true master."

"And how do I do that?"

"Simple," Paula interjected. "You must kill your coven. All of them, including your lover."

CHAPTER 52

THERE WAS NO DENYING that my life had taken an interesting turn. I had relegated the usual questions of identity and purpose to the backseat, while the incredible discovery that I was the devil's shadow took shotgun. In the already dark recesses of hell, I was the only opposition to his anarchy, the few fragments of light that remained of his tattered, broken soul.

And the devil was Peter Pan, frantically trying to find his shadow, to catch it and reunite it with himself—a fairytale that had far more meaning to me at the moment than it should have.

I was even starting to understand my power. As much as it dismayed me to know that the source of my magic was coming directly from the devil, I also found it somewhat cathartic to know that I had saved several lives with it.

Jess had told me that the devil was the most powerful being ever created. Short of God's will, he was an unstoppable powerhouse.

What did that mean for me? Was I as powerful as him?

I looked down at the knife that had appeared in my hand. Sister Aggie's blood still stained it. The blood they had forced Rachel to spill. My mind fumed with thoughts of vengeance. I wanted justice for my friends, and I wanted the devil to pay for his cruelty to all of us.

If I was the devil's soul, then I had the same free will he had. He had chosen to be bad, to go against God. And I had chosen to go against him.

The four of us were probably due for a long conversation about the dangers of split personalities in all-powerful beings, but I wasn't interested in getting back in their good graces—if there was even such a thing when dealing with the rulers of hell.

I looked at the devil before me and shook my head at him. "You know I will never do that." I closed my eyes and let the floodgates open.

Power.

Appointed by God. Transformed by the flames of hell. And stolen straight out of the grip of the most powerful being on earth.

I could feel the darkness overtake me, bleeding into my eyes, as my mortal body tried to endure the endless reserves of magic I was drawing from.

The beast growled, and the smell of sulfur and ash surrounded me. My sisters' chants hastened, their magic pushing against me, trying to keep me contained. Their power was strong, but since I was the one who had given it to them, it was easy to turn the tables. Their chanting ceased, and for a moment I felt the fear and confusion. I pressed the thought into their minds to run, and the circle disbanded. Their feet scurried away from me and I breathed a sigh of relief that they were at least a little farther from danger.

"You don't want to do this, Hennie."

I opened my eyes and saw my shadow through a new distortion of power. Tiny serpentine scales overlaid his handsome features. His eyes were yellow with slit pupils. I could see fangs in place of his canines.

"Oh, I think I do," I said.

"You'll never be able to resist me if you take on this much power."

"Resist you? I'm going to destroy you."

"You can't kill the devil," Paula said.

"That's a lie," I pointed out. "Where there's a will, there's a way. Obviously, I have the will, and since you have provided the way..."

My shadow laughed, and I caught a glimpse of his forked tongue. "Let her," he said with a smile. "I want to see this."

I felt a grip on my leg and I looked down. Dane was practically climbing my leg, trying to hold me back. "Stop this," he groaned. "You're playing right into his hand."

I didn't bother entertaining his warnings or calming his concerns with promises of loyalty. I just waved my hand, sending him skidding through the circle of candles and onto the sidelines. He wasn't any safer there, but at least he wouldn't get trampled in our battle.

CHAPTER 53

THE BEAST ROARED, AND I screamed right back at him. One swipe of his giant paw and I nearly lost my head. The gash across my neck bled profusely into my nightgown. I touched my hand to the wound, burning it shut.

He dove at me again and his horns gored my side, forcing blood to eject from my mouth. I shoved my knife into the blackened skin, burning my fingers on the heat contained within. I poured magic into the blade, the unquantified power I had drawn upon.

Instead of rearing in pain, the beast almost purred. I whipped my hands away, and he withdrew his horns. I healed the two holes they left behind.

Paula arrived in the beast's place, tipping her head with curiosity. "Did you really think that would work?"

"Fight fire with fire," I responded.

"That's all well and good, but that only works when you're not flammable." With a flick of her wrist, she ripped my knife from my hand and caught it mid-air. Before I could defend myself, she threw it back, plunging it into my leg. I gasped and stumbled backward to get away from her. "Translation, foolish girl: you're still human. You can change that, though."

I fell to the ground and struggled to get the knife out. It was in so deep I could feel it tugging against the bone. Paula approached me, chanting a spell as she slobbered black ooze from her mouth.

She lunged at me, but Dane came out of nowhere and tackled her to the ground. I grimaced, knowing he wouldn't get very far with her. A few punches and she melted the skin on his fist. He wailed, and she threw him off toward the stairs.

I noticed my sisters huddled under the steps, clustered in a circle with hands linked. Their lips were moving, praying furiously, no doubt for *my* benefit this time. As pleased as I was that they were still willing to fight by my side, I would have preferred they just run away.

Paula returned to me to continue our fight. With so few of the candles left standing, the only thing I could see around me was a vague outline of Paula's features and her eyes glistening as they stared at me. I ripped the knife from my leg and stabbed it at her gut. With a wave of her hand, it slipped out of my grip and skittered across the concrete into the dark recesses around us.

I crawled away from her, trying to find an aspect of my power that wouldn't be futile against her. Had God granted me divine power like Sister Aggie's, I might've stood a chance, but Paula was right. I was trying to fight her with a fire that my mortal body could not withstand.

"Enough!" my shadow yelled, and I was lifted from behind and flung against a pillar. I hit hard against the cement column and stuck like glue. Hanging in place, my feet waggled beneath me, waiting for gravity to take hold again. "Let us be done with this!" He limped over to me and pressed his hand against my chest, the pressure so light that I had to look down to see if he was actually touching me. "Give me your allegiance! Be mine once again!"

"I won't kill my coven."

"Then kill your lover. He's a monster, anyway. The world will not miss him. You've seen it inside of him. The anger and violence still lives there, transformed into a tool for killing demons. He is nothing more than a shell."

Paula dragged Dane back over to me, shoving him close enough for me to touch. She retrieved the lost knife with only a reach of her hand. She placed it in my palm, closing my fingers around it.

My shadow leaned forward and whispered in my ear. "Do this for me, and I will spare the coven." I could feel his breath touching my ear. With his handsome features obscured, I could sense the serpentine guile. "I'll even bring Jessica back."

I looked at him, questioning his honesty. He smiled, pressing his hand behind me, our bodies nearly touching, as close to kissing as we could be without doing so. "Am I lying?" he asked.

I knew he wasn't. I wondered now if that strange power I'd always had was the devil inside of me, knowing the truth of others. Knowing when they were betraying their minds.

I looked at Dane and wondered if he would understand the sacrifice. I could see the fury in his eyes. This was the second time my loyalty was failing him in such a short time. I wanted there to be another answer. I wanted there to be a way out. Something that didn't involve me having to hurt someone.

Dane narrowed his eyes at me, and I raised the knife over my head. "Wait," he said, stilling my hand. "There's another way."

Paula yanked on his hair, bending his head back and opening his neck for my attack. "Kill him!" she bellowed.

Dane looked down at me past his cheekbones. "Look at his leg," he seethed. I blinked at him, disappointed by his so-called solution. Dane's eyes darted toward my shadow and I looked down at his leg. It was bleeding. He was injured. More specifically, he was bleeding from the same spot I was on my leg. "You are a part of him," Dane continued. "His pain is your pain, and your pain is his. They can fight your human half until you are near dead, but they can never kill you because that would be killing him, too."

Paula screamed and clawed at Dane's face. "Shut up!"

"Don't listen to him," the serpent hissed. "He'll say anything to save himself. You know what you have to do. You have to save your coven."

"They can't kill them either," Dane continued, and Paula grabbed onto his neck, strangling his words. "Re... mem... ber," Dane choked out.

"There are plenty of other ways to kill your coven." Paula turned and looked at me. "There are also plenty of ways to hurt them. It wouldn't be the first time we've taken over a convent. Oh, the things we can do to them. It would be far worse than death."

"Surrender yourself to me, Hennie," the serpent demanded.

I looked down at his hand barely pressed up against my chest. "You still can't quite touch me, can you? Can't touch your own shadow. You can chase it all goddamn day and never get it back."

"I don't want my shadow back, Hennie. I want to absorb it. I want you back inside of me. Forever!"

My soul buried inside of the most heinous creature ever to exist... forever.

"Never!" I stabbed the knife into my own shoulder. The serpent cupped his fresh wound. I dropped to the ground, released from his hold.

Paula shoved Dane away and grabbed me. She threw me across the room, against a hard brick wall.

I slumped onto the floor in more pain than I was ready to acknowledge. I sputtered and coughed, trying to force air back into my deflated lungs. Dust swirled around me as I disrupted the twenty years of filth that had formed around the furnace and the water heater next to me.

I couldn't even begin to formulate my next move. I was a pawn playing chess against a king, a queen, and a knight. My greatest power was useless. I wanted to keep my humanity, but at what cost? How much torture could I endure? How much could I watch?

Through the dim light, I noticed something red out of the corner of my eye. In a sea of gray and black, the scarlet bundle tucked between the wall and the water softener stood out like a beacon to me.

I reached over and pushed away the oil rag that was hiding the identity of the object. My fingers slipped around the smooth cold metal and I smiled. Ruby *did* have a backup.

I raised the revolver and admired the lustrous silver barrel. I had never been a gun girl. I had never enjoyed the feel of a deadly weapon in my hand, but this one... This one felt like it was designed, assembled, and polished just for me.

When I finally lifted my hypnotized gaze from it, I saw Paula stopped in her tracks a few feet away from me. She put on a smug smile, but the concern in her eyes was too much to be drowned out by false bravado. "You don't really think you can hurt any of us with that, do you?"

"I can hurt one of you with it." I placed the muzzle of the gun against my temple.

The beast roared in the distance, demanding my head on a platter, but of course that was the one thing they couldn't have. They needed me alive. They needed me to give myself to my shadow, or rather, return myself to the source of my existence.

"Hennie, don't do this." The serpent approached me and kneeled down beside me, just out of reach. His features looked more like a man again. "You're playing a game with powers you don't understand."

"I understand just fine. You want me back and I don't want to come back."

"No." He shook his head. "For fuck's sake, I have been trying to push you away from me for an eternity. I don't *want* you back. I *need* you back." He tipped his head and frowned at me. "Do you hear me, Hennie? Do you hear a lie in my words? I need you. If you destroy us, then you are destroying the last part of me that is connected to God. Is that what you want?"

"I want you to leave me alone."

"There is no middle ground here! If you die before you reconnect to me, I die. The only thing left of me is my body and my rage with no mind to guide them. I know you don't see how there is a balance in our Trinity, but I assure you, destroying me would be no different from releasing your murderous lover of the guilt you gave him. There must be balance. I must have you back and I am done asking!" He reached for me, but instead of his hands gripping me, I felt a cool aphrodisiac of power flooding my body, tugging me back toward the source. He was lassoing me back to him through our mutual power.

He said that everything I had been doing up to that point was only bringing me closer to him, and he was right. The endless power I took from him linked us. He was connected to me—the real me inside of my corporeal form. And try as I might, I couldn't give up the power he had shown me just to stay inside of it. The magical cocaine rush was running dry, and only a trickle remained. My drug-addled mind was going to follow those breadcrumbs anywhere, including right back to the man I had fled hell to get away from.

I knew what he was telling me was the truth. Somehow he needed me, but I couldn't believe that there wasn't a middle ground. The very core of me was a soul; borrowed or stolen, it contained a free will that demanded more than what I was being offered. I still had a choice, and my choice was the same as any mortal being... self-preservation.

I had to save myself.

So, I pulled the trigger.

CHAPTER 54

T HE HAMMER CLICKED.

A bright light filled the room and for a moment, I was certain death had arrived to carry me away. To where, I know not, but it had to be better than hell. I hoped it was better than hell.

As my eyes acclimated to the blinding light, I saw everyone frozen in place. My serpentine shadow was still in front of me, wide-eyed and panic-stricken. Paula was rushing toward me, eyes feral and hands outstretched like talons. Dane was on all fours, his face frozen in anguish, eyes closed tightly, as if he couldn't bear to watch my brains splatter on the basement wall.

A flicker of movement drew my eyes back toward Paula. The light danced behind her as a robed figure approached. The decidedly feminine silhouette weaved around Paula and kneeled down next to me on the opposite side of the serpent.

I stared at the red fringe coming out of her wimple and the smile on her face. It was beautiful and yet seemed so out of place. "Rachel?" I gasped. "What's happening?"

She shushed me gently.

"What did they do to you?"

She shushed me again and also lifted her finger to press against my lips.

"I was supposed to die, not you," I mumbled through her finger.

She rolled her eyes. "Will you shut up, so I can explain?"

"Seriously, you're even going to be mean to me in the afterlife?"

She chuckled at me. "We aren't dead, stupid. Time is frozen."

"Why the bright light, then?" I asked.

"What light?" She glanced around, but didn't see the blinding light that was causing my eyes to water.

"How are you doing this?"

"Something has happened, Hennie." Rachel's broadest smile returned. "Something I never thought possible. God is speaking to me."

My mouth gaped. "That's wonderful." I frowned. "How mad is He?"

Rachel laughed again and nodded. "Pretty mad, but mostly at him." She nodded to my shadow on the other side. I glanced over at him, this time noting the oblong pupils in his eyes. Being so close to his statuesque form was beyond creepy. "Things are going to change for us, Hennie. All of us. Starting right now."

"What sort of changes?"

"For one, I'm going to take over the coven. Apparently, I'm a late-in-the-game pitcher. Whatever that means."

I smiled at her. "Congratulations. I couldn't think of a better choice. What about them?" I motioned to the triad.

Rachel's smile died down into a thin line. "You've put Him in a difficult position, Hennie."

"I have?"

"He won't allow you to kill His son."

"But he's the devil."

"I know." Rachel looked back at Paula. "God won't forget the pain he has caused us. There will be retribution for it."

"I'm providing retribution right now." I nodded to the gun that, for some reason, I still had pinned to my temple. I realized I wasn't able to move it. My arm was immobile, like the others.

"Killing him is not the answer. It's much too complicated to explain now, but you have to understand, the devil has his purpose in this world. He always has. And he always will."

My brow dipped at the way she said *always*. An eternity of service to the world, not unlike his father. God watched over His flock, while the devil did what? Picked off the weak and weary? Or was he just the fence—a semi-corporeal, immortal boundary intended to keep the sheep from straying too far from home? And I was a part of him.

I glanced over at my shadow. "I have to go back to him, don't I?"

Rachel took a breath. "Eventually. However, there is a way to secure yourself to this body. It won't free you—that connection, unfortunately, can never be severed, but it will prevent him from trying to force you back to him. There are some caveats, though."

"Anything," I agreed without bothering to listen to the fine print. "What do I have to do?"

"It's already done." Rachel smirked at my confused look. "He is giving you permission to be here... on earth, for as long as this body lives."

I didn't feel any different, but I believed her. "He'll leave me alone now?"

Rachel's eyes flickered over mine. "Not exactly. He still needs you. You are part of him. Much like Paula acts as his physical presence on earth, you will be another facet. You will need to serve him."

"But I want to be good. I don't want to be evil."

"Yes, and that is what he needs. Without you, he's just a wrathful, violent child throwing a fit. I can't promise you will enjoy your servitude, but remember, he is as much your slave as you are his." Rachel stood up.

"Wait." I grabbed her leg with my mobile hand. "What will I have to do? How is this going to work?"

Rachel shook her head. "I honestly don't know. This has never happened before. You are an enigma to all of us, including God."

"That doesn't sound good."

Rachel's mouth tipped up again. I couldn't remember ever seeing her this happy or at peace. "I know you'll be up to the challenge. Just believe in yourself. And trust in God."

"Can the devil ever trust God?"

"God is the only one any of us can trust." Rachel took a breath and her head bowed slightly. "I won't remember this conversation when we speak again." Her eyes flickered over mine, moisture forming on the rim of her lower lid. "I'm sorry I can't be by your side when you're going to need me the most, but remember, I do love you." She turned and walked away.

"Rachel." I grappled at her parting robe. "Wait! What does that mean?" Her dark silhouette absorbed into the light, disappearing entirely. "Come back!"

CHAPTER 55

C LICK.

I felt the trigger move and the hammer impact, but nothing happened. I drew back the gun and flipped it open, checking for bullets inside. The chambers were full. I was only beginning to remember my conversation with Rachel. It was like a dream, but instead of slipping away as I woke, it was revealed piece by piece. Completing my puzzle.

"What have you done?" The serpent drew back from me and stood up.

"No." Paula said behind him. "No!" she screamed. "Damn you!" she screamed to the heavens, albeit through a good deal of piping and flooring.

The beast roared in the shadows, but it soon turned to a grumbling growl. He backed away, disappearing as if he had never been there to begin with.

My shadow stared at me, nearly comatose as he backed away, shaking his head. "I will make you pay for this, Hennie." He looked defeated and almost sad. "I am still your master, whether you choose me or not."

"And I am yours," I said confidently. His eyes widened incrementally. Apparently, I wasn't supposed to know about that.

"Yes, you are." He nodded. "And I look forward to serving you, should you require it." Much like the beast, he dissipated into nothingness.

I looked at Paula for her thoughts on this recent development. I knew she wouldn't be happy about losing to me, but I could see she wouldn't leave without making her opinion on the topic very clear.

The pipes above her rattled as her rage built. The edges of the room erupted in fire—a fire that water would not smother. I tried to use my power to dampen it, but much as inside Jess's burning house, it only served to open my mind to images that broke my concentration.

"I hope you know I am going to make it my duty to kill every last one of your sisters," Paula shouted over the roar of the flames on either side of us.

I glanced back and saw my coven scattering to get out of the inferno. Rachel glanced back at me with concern, but much as she warned me she would, she left to escape up the stairs. "Good luck with that. Rachel isn't quite as passive as Aggie was."

"Neither am I."

A pipe burst over my head, showering me with water. I wiped away the blinding stream and found that Paula was gone.

I stood on my wounded leg and reached for my magic to heal it. The wave of power that came through was as strong as it had ever been, and there were no more drug metaphors to match the high it gave me.

Freshly healed and woozy, I made my way through the basement to escape, but steam was billowing around me, masking my exit path. Everywhere I looked was a foggy firelight.

I pushed on until I reached a wall of fire. I moved back again and found another. I was surrounded by fire I couldn't put out with magic or water.

I coughed and hacked on the smoke that was replacing the fog. I made my circle once again, checking for an opening in the fire, but there was nothing.

I heard the cracking of wood, and I cringed. The building was about to collapse.

"Hennie!" Dane's voice shouted from above. I moved to it and saw him hanging his arm down through a hole in the floor above me.

I was so relieved I laughed. I jumped up to his outstretched hand. He grabbed hold of me and pulled me up through the jagged hole he had dug his way through with our emergency fire ax in the main floor hall.

"Thank you," I whispered and kissed him.

He paused a moment to enjoy the kiss, but as soon as I released him, he lifted me to my feet and pulled me along to the office, where we both slithered out the window.

CHAPTER 56

I SAT ON THE tail end of the ambulance wrapped in a smoke blanket while Dane got patched up by the paramedics. I stared out at the burning school, and relived all the memories that had come with it—some good, a lot of them bad.

I could see my fellow sisters huddled between a row of police cars, talking and pointing at the fire. I was glad that each and every one of them was alive.

I caught Rachel's glance over at me and I waved. She hadn't come to check on me, which surprised me. She was usually interested in my well-being—to the point of being annoying. She looked away, not willing to even lift her hand.

"I told you. I am not going to the hospital," Dane argued, with the paramedic treating him inside.

"Sir, your injuries are far deeper than you realize. You look like a bear mauled you. Some of these cuts go to the bone."

"Just stitch them up," Dane insisted.

The young medic huffed and shook his head. "I'll have to get more sutures. Wait here." I moved as he shuffled out of the back of the ambulance to pilfer supplies from another one.

Shortly after, Dane came out with his smoke blanket wrapped around his head. "I need to get out of here. Pretty soon, someone is going to recognize me."

"Oh, right." I nodded, remembering that he was a wanted felon. More wanted since he had escaped from his own execution. "Come on, I'll go with you. I can heal those cuts." I tugged his blanket.

"Hennie," Rachel said as she came up to me. "We need to talk."

"Oh, ah, sure." I looked at Dane. "Just go ahead. I'll find you."

Dane nodded and ran away before the paramedic could hunt him down.

I turned back to Rachel and smiled. "I'm so glad you're okay." I leaned over and hugged her. She flinched, but patted my back before stepping away from me. "You are okay, right?"

Rachel nodded. "I don't feel the presence inside of me any longer." She pinched the rosary around her neck.

"Good. And the others?" I nodded to the other sisters, who were taking a very keen interest in our conversation.

"They are fine too." Rachel opened her mouth to speak, but seemed to change focus. "And you're fine, I assume."

"Yes." I smiled. "Look, Rachel, if this is about earlier... I completely understand. You had to get yourself out of there. You did exactly what I wanted you to."

Rachel nodded. "Hennie, I didn't come over here to apologize for leaving you down there. I came over to let you know that... we are disbanding the coven."

"Oh." I looked back at the others. "I see." I took a breath. "After everything that has happened, it makes sense, but don't you think we should talk about it?"

"We have talked about it," Rachel said quietly and nodded to the girls. "There isn't going to be a convent anymore. Not in this form, anyway. We all think it's best that we go our separate ways."

I nodded. "If that's what you think is best."

"I do." Rachel nodded.

"Is this goodbye then?" I asked.

Rachel shrugged and shook her head. "I'm sure we'll see each other again. From time to time."

I nodded. "Okay." I smiled through my emerging tears. "Then I guess, goodbye... for now."

"Yes, goodbye for now." Rachel smiled back at me.

"I've got to go help Dane." I motioned vaguely in the direction he went.

"Oh, yeah sure. I'll let the girls know you said goodbye."

I glanced back at them and waved. No one waved back, but I got a nod from Meredith. Something, at least. Rachel turned to head back to them.

"Rachel," I called her back. She turned around to look at me. "Is this really how you want this conversation to go? You lying, and me pretending I don't know, even though we both know I do?"

Rachel took a breath and looked out onto the horizon where the sun was starting to pink the sky. "You're the devil's shadow, Hennie." She shrugged. "How can we still call ourselves good witches if we're using his power?"

I nodded and shrugged. "I don't have an answer to that."

"Neither do I." Rachel wiped away a tear. "I can't let you be a part of this coven anymore. It's not safe... for any of us. I'm sorry." She turned away and headed back over to her sisters.

I watched her leave, like so many people in my life had left. She wasn't dead, but it felt just as final. She was going on to lead the coven, and I was going on to do... what?

What servitude had I tangled myself into?

How much lower had I sunk by rejecting my place at the devil's feet?

Had I traded one shadowed existence for another?

The
Devil's
Shadow
FELICIA JEDLICKA

The Devil's Shadow

Book 2 of the Sister Witches

Kicked out of her coven and at the mercy of the devil, Hennie has been playing judge, jury, and executioner to the worst of the worst. When her flair for justice turns into an all-out bloodlust, it's time to call it quits, but giving up power is difficult.

While Hennie struggles to retain the last vestiges of her morality, an ancient anger awakens inside the body of an innocent girl. Since her power is useless, so she must recruit her former friend to help fight this evil.

Rachel's coven is stronger than ever. Their particular brand of power is just what Hennie needs to perform the exorcism to save this girl. However there is a cost for Rachel's cooperation.

In a rare moment of truce, Paula, Rachel, and Hennie are reunited for one common goal. They must exorcise a trespasser before its evil spreads like a plague over humanity.

Thank you so much for reading. I hope you
enjoyed the ride and if you aren't getting off here,
I encourage you to sign up for my newsletter
so I can return your generosity with new release
updates and special offers.

Sign-Up

You can also find me on Facebook or visit my
website. Keep reading!

Website

Facebook

About the Author

As a Nebraska native, and a small-town girl at that, I have very little to occupy my time beyond imagining a world outside of my own reality. By the grace of God and the seat of my pants, I have kept my waning attention span on the task of becoming an author.

So here I am, an indie author, peddling my words in cyberspace and enduring my comeuppances with an unwavering determination. I may not be a professional, and I certainly am not perfect, but if you've made it this far, you have to admit, this smartass yokel does spin quite a yarn.

From the self-inflicted sweatshop conditions of my unairconditioned childhood home, to the arthritis reaping positions of a sedentary lifestyle, I bring to you: my sarcasm, my oddity, and my heart. Take it with a grain of salt or a teaspoon of sugar, but take it for what it is: a story born of the mind, translated to paper, and gifted to you.

I thank you for your readership and even more for your support. Please recommend this book to your friends and family via any social media that you use. Word of mouth is still the best advertising and is greatly appreciated.

Most importantly, keep reading. I'll keep writing.